MY FLAWLESS LIFE

YVONNE WOON

MY

FLAWLESS

LIFE

KATHERINE TEGEN BOOKS
An Imprint of HarperCollins Publishers

Katherine Tegen Books is an imprint of HarperCollins Publishers.

My Flawless Life
Copyright © 2023 by Yvonne Woon
All rights reserved. Printed in the United States of America.
No part of this book may be used or reproduced in any manner
whatsoever without written permission except in the case of brief
quotations embodied in critical articles and reviews. For information
address HarperCollins Children's Books, a division of HarperCollins
Publishers, 195 Broadway, New York, NY 10007.
www.epicreads.com
ISBN 978-0-06-300869-4
Typography by Molly Fehr
23 24 25 26 27 LBC 5 4 3 2 1
First Edition

For my dad

1

Picture, if you'll indulge me, a portrait gallery.

It's a jewel-toned room wallpapered to look seamless, as though there are no windows or doors, no entrances or exits. The subjects clasp their hands stiffly at their waists, emanating a quiet power. Power that was framed and nailed into the walls. Power that trapped you, that seemed dead but was very much alive, that you could pass every day, not knowing it was there, watching you, altering the direction of your feet as you walked.

If you asked me to describe St. Francis School in a single image, this is the one I would choose. Not because it depicts a place steeped in old money or a sycophantic worshipping of the past, though both were true of St. Francis, but because it was a trick.

The thing about portraits is that they're an illusion. The subject puts on their best outfit, their finest face. The painter makes their shoulders squarer, their cheeks rosier, their fabrics richer. You believe what you're seeing is true, but it's a distortion.

Look closer. Maybe you'll spot a telling detail: a fly on the still life, a wrinkle in the skin, an errant brushstroke that makes the eye glint.

Are you paying attention?

I was standing in the portrait gallery at St. Francis when the message came in.

The room that evening was humming with people. We were there for the fall alumni gala, which was billed as a night for students to network with alumni about colleges, but it was really a fundraising event for the school. Every event in the Washington, DC, area is, at heart, a fundraiser, you just have to figure out who has the money and who's asking for it. In the hierarchy of fancy parties, alumni galas, even at a school like St. Francis, weren't high on the list of places to be seen at, but my family and I had long stopped being invited to public events, so the ones at St. Francis were all I had left.

"What do you think he did to get his money?" Adam said beside me, nodding to one of the portraits. "Oil? Railroads?"

"Newspaper magnate," I said.

"How do you know?"

"The newspaper on the floor by his chair," I said. "The

2

black smudges on his thumb and forefinger. Everything in art is a symbol."

He feigned skepticism, but I could tell he knew I was right.

Adam Goldman was one of my few remaining friends, if you could even call him that. We didn't spend time together outside of school; in fact, we rarely spent time together *in* school because he didn't like to be seen with me. I pretended I didn't care, that I wasn't bothered by the way all my former friends avoided me as if what had happened to me was contagious. Though Adam wasn't part of their group, he orbited them—the popular and powerful at St. Francis, which I once was a part of. Sometimes I resented that he had access to them when I didn't, though I was glad for his company, even if it was only in moments like these, when everyone else's attention was directed elsewhere.

"Okay, enough about the dead. How about him?" Adam nodded to a man who looked like he was in his thirties and was talking to Jessica from the volleyball team. The sticker on his shirt read *Mark, Dartmouth*.

"I say banker," Adam said.

"His clothes aren't nice enough."

"Corporate lawyer," he countered.

"He looks too friendly." I studied him. "Like he's trying to sell her something. I'd guess advertising."

Adam and I were similar in that we made it our business to know things. We traveled on the periphery, observing others, figuring out their secrets, though I liked to believe that I was much better at it than he was.

"What about her?" Adam asked, nodding to a woman talking to Rahul from AP Calculus. Her tag read *Sarah, Columbia.*

I considered her clean white suit, the way she crossed her arms and nodded her head. "Head of a nonprofit."

"Interesting," Adam murmured. "I would have guessed CEO."

"CEOs wear black. Charity heads wear white."

Adam looked unconvinced. "Is that true?"

"Probably not, but it sounds right, doesn't it?"

Adam adjusted his glasses, a tic of his. He styled himself as a gentleman of sophistication and culture. I thought he looked like a newspaper man from the 1950s—a mixture of dapper and bookish. Most of our classmates found him pretentious and out of touch with contemporary culture, which he took as homophobia and hatred of anything remotely feminine. "Men still aren't allowed to like beautiful things," he'd said, which was one of the traits I appreciated most about him—his dedication to beauty and how he took great pains to surround himself with it.

"Okay, what about her?" Adam said, nodding to a young woman standing next to an older man. "Third wife or daughter?"

I rolled my eyes. "Come on. Daughter."

"How do you know?"

"They look alike."

Adam squinted at her through his glasses. I was one of the only people at school who knew that he didn't actually need glasses and that the ones he wore were a prop with no prescription. Still, I indulged him and waited.

"You're right," he said.

That's when my phone vibrated. It was from a number I didn't recognize.

>I have a job for you.

Odd. I had gotten messages like it before, but normally they were phrased as requests.

<Who is this? I wrote back.

>No one important.

Also odd.

<I don't take cases from people I don't know.

>You'll take this one.

I tried to suppress my curiosity. It was probably just someone messing with me.

"Give me a second," I said to Adam.

"Another desperate soul with a problem that needs fixing?"

"You were once a desperate soul," I reminded him.

"I wasn't desperate," he countered.

"That's not how I remember it."

Adam pushed up his glasses. "I guess it's time for me to

network. If *Sarah* from *Columbia* is a CEO, you owe me one unit of information."

"And if she's not?"

"Then you can add it to my tab."

I watched Adam put on a pleasant face and approach her. They talked for a moment, and when she turned to get an hors d'oeuvre from the table, he mouthed to me, *You're too good at this.*

I shrugged and turned back to my phone. A mystery person who claimed they had a job for me that I wouldn't refuse.

<Why do you think that? I wrote back.

>Because it's about your best friend.

I felt my chest constrict.

<I don't have a best friend.

>But you did.

I could see her across the room: Luce Herrera, a golden silhouette standing in front of one of the portraits, her face framed as though she were mounted on the wall. She was there with her friends, the five of them conspiratorial as they whispered among themselves, their faces partially lit by the picture lights like they were works of art.

She must have felt my gaze because she looked up. For a fleeting moment, her eyes met mine. I had once known her face better than I'd known my own, but now it was unreadable, a mask of itself.

I quickly looked away. After a moment, another message came in.

>Don't be so conspicuous. She doesn't know.

I froze, suddenly aware that I was being watched.

<Who is this? I demanded.

>Oh, don't look so scared.

I scanned the room, taking a mental inventory of who was there. Everyone in our class usually went to the alumni mixer, and so many of them were on their phones that it seemed impossible to single anyone out.

<What do you want?

>I want you to follow Luce.

<I'm not a detective.

>But you are a fixer. And Luce is working on something that she needs help fixing.

<What do you mean?

>That's your job. Figure it out.

I paused, torn between curiosity and suspicion.

<I told you, I don't take jobs from people I don't know.

>But you do know me.

Our school was small enough that if my mystery sender was in this room, I had to know him. Or her. But how well did I know this person? Did we pass each other occasionally on campus, or had we once been friends?

<I don't know your name.

>You can call me Three.

Why Three? As if reading my mind, a new message appeared.

>**You'll find out why when you get to the end.**

I stared at the phone, bewildered. Before I could respond, another message came in.

>**I'll pay you $5,000.**

I considered myself someone who offered a high-end service to high-end clients, and charged accordingly, but even I was surprised at a sum so large for a single job.

<**Why doesn't Luce just hire me herself?** I asked.

Enough time had elapsed that I had started to think Three wasn't going to respond. Then a final message appeared on my screen.

>**When you finish the job, you'll know.**

I stared at the message, considering how to respond, when I saw a man extricate himself from conversation and find a drink. I'd been watching him all night and didn't know if I'd have another opportunity. I stuffed my phone into my bag. Before approaching him, I peeled off my name tag and put on a new one.

"Hi," I said, smiling.

He looked me up and down, then smiled, clearly pleased. "Hi."

He was on the younger side, generically good-looking, if not a bit square. If I had to guess, I'd say he worked in finance. His alumni sticker read *Brandon, University of Pennsylvania*.

"Do I know you?" he said, swirling his drink.

"I don't think so," I said. It was a lie. Though we'd never met before, I was certain he knew who I was; he just couldn't place me. It wasn't the first time it had happened.

He glanced at my name tag, which read *Heather, Senior.* It wasn't my real name. "Are you sure? You look familiar."

"I get that a lot. I guess I have a common face."

He smiled, amused. "I wouldn't say that." It appeared that my answer had quelled his curiosity. "So, Heather, what do you see yourself doing after you graduate from St. Francis?"

He was probably ten years older than I was, though that didn't stop him from flirting with me. I studied him with distaste. I could have told him the truth: that I had no interest in bantering with a mildly lascivious man and was only talking to him because I had been hired to, but instead, I told him what he wanted to hear.

"I'd like to major in economics and go into finance," I said. "The plan is to eventually get an MBA. I've heard UPenn has a great program."

A surprised grin spread across his face. I'd gotten it right. "It does."

We chatted a little bit more. I asked him questions about his job and feigned interest when he talked about wealth management and diversification. When I couldn't take it anymore, I scrawled my fake name on a napkin and asked him for his card, which he eagerly gave me after writing his personal email address on the back.

A caterer walked by with a tray of hors d'oeuvres, and while Brandon helped himself to a mini quiche, I took the opportunity to excuse myself, weaving through the crowd until I was out of his line of vision. There, I crumpled the fake name tag and put it in the trash. Then I texted my client, Heather.

<All set. Can you meet in the hall bathroom in five minutes?

>Sure, she wrote back.

I slipped my phone into my bag and made my way to the door.

There were fancy names for my job—disaster consultant, crisis manager—but I preferred *fixer*, which was what most of my classmates would call me if you could find anyone who would admit to hiring me.

Kids at St. Francis didn't need help getting internships or building their résumés; they had their parents for that. What I fixed were the more delicate issues that they couldn't ask their parents to repair. I restored reputations, I suffocated rumors. I kept secrets from spilling, and if they'd already spilled, I cleaned them up. In short, I solved problems, and I was great at it.

The bathroom was empty. I checked my appearance in the mirror. People used to say I dressed like Audrey Hepburn—prim and sleek in crisp white shirts and tailored trench coats that made me feel like I was walking through a vintage black-and-white photo of Washington, DC. I still had most of my old designer clothes and wore them even though I had nowhere to go. Up close, they were showing signs of wear, but I couldn't afford new ones, so I had to make do with what I had.

I wiped a smudge from beneath my eye. I'd gone a little heavy on my eyeliner that night, but I didn't hate it. It made me look tough, like someone who flicked other people's opinions about her into a tray like ash.

The door opened.

Heather Harmond didn't look like an heiress. She didn't appear glamorous or wealthy, and if you didn't know her last name, you'd never guess that her great-grandfather started one of the biggest weapons manufacturing companies in the country. Heather was neither confident nor powerful like her father, nor conventionally beautiful like her mother. She was quiet and awkward, with only a few friends, and walked around school hunched, as though she was coiling into herself, hoping that everyone would leave her alone to her hobbies.

"Hey," I said, catching her eye in the mirror over the sinks.

"Hey," she said.

I took out a stack of business cards from my pocket. On top was Brandon from UPenn, along with four others I'd coaxed out of alumni under the pretense of being Heather.

"Contact them whenever. They're expecting to hear from you."

Heather looked sheepish as she took them from me and thumbed through the cards, reading their names and titles.

"I only needed four," she said.

"I know, but I threw in an extra just in case."

Though Heather didn't have to network in the conventional sense—she had a trust fund and definitely never needed to work, let alone go to college—her parents were the kind of people who wanted their offspring to prove to them that they could "make it on their own," which they defined by a series of arbitrary expectations that they enforced without warning in an attempt to try to mold her into the kind of daughter they thought they should've had. All of this Heather had relayed to me two weeks prior, when she'd contacted me to ask if there was any way I could do it for her. Much to her parents' distaste, she suffered from anxiety and was willing to pay me a sizable sum to get a handful of business cards to show her parents.

I sympathized with her. Though being rich was nothing to pity, being bullied and belittled by your family members was unpleasant at best, and having a trust fund didn't make it go away.

"Do you think they'll notice that it wasn't me if I ever meet with them in person?" Heather asked.

"No way. They've already forgotten my face. I picked

these men specifically for this reason. They're the kind of people who think girls are interchangeable."

Heather looked unconvinced, but we both knew it didn't really matter if I was right. "I probably won't meet them in person anyway," she said. "My parents want me to collect business cards so they have proof that I'm not as big of a failure as they think I am. Whether or not I follow up is beside the point. Everyone knows I'm getting into Princeton no matter what I do."

"Do you even want to go there?" I asked.

"It's inevitable. My name is on two of the buildings."

"Are they good buildings, at least?"

Heather grimaced. "A gym and an athletic facility."

"What is it with rich people and sports buildings?"

"It's the only part of college that alumni can still participate in," Heather said. "A library would have been nice, though."

"At least it's not a dorm," I offered. "Filthy, sagging futons. Hookups. Vomit."

"Or a dining hall," Heather said. "No one's excited to go to a dining hall." She looked down at the business cards, then met my gaze in the mirror. "How do you talk to people like that? You make it look so easy."

"My dad always said that there are infinite ways to get someone to like you, but only three are foolproof: make them laugh, compliment them, or ask them questions."

The mention of my dad made her go quiet. Of course. Sometimes it slipped my mind.

"Also, it's easier when you're pretending to be someone else," I said.

"I think you're just good at what you do," she said, and took out her phone. A moment later my phone vibrated, alerting me that I'd received a payment.

"Thanks," I said.

"I should be the one thanking you," she said, and slipped the cards into her pocket. "This will keep my dad off my back for at least a few weeks."

"May he name a science building in your honor."

Heather gave me the beginning of a smile before opening the door and disappearing down the hall.

I waited a moment, then returned to the crowd in the gallery, snagging a canapé from a tray before I ducked outside. It was drizzling, the mist blurring the campus streetlamps into dim yellow orbs. St. Francis looked like an old convent, its stone buildings designed to inspire both awe and supplication.

Alone, I read the cryptic messages again.

Luce. Three. When you finish the job, you'll know.

I should have known. I should have written back and rejected the job. I should have stayed away. The canapé was dry, but I finished it anyway. So many jobs were banal. Nothing more than minor distractions. I didn't mind doing them, but when they were done, I felt just as empty as I had before.

I want you to follow Luce.

What do you do when someone offers you a chance to get closer to the life you once had? Do you take it?

The road blinked in and out of focus through the wipers as I drove home.

My actual name was Hana Yang Lerner. I was seventeen years old and a senior at St. Francis, one of the most elite private schools in the country. I had long black hair from my mom and a handsome, mare-like face from my dad. Freckles scattered the bridge of my nose. A sign of trust-worthiness.

The media liked to use euphemisms when talking about me. I was *blossoming into a beautiful young woman*, they used to say, which meant I was old enough to receive the male gaze. I was *exotic*, they'd say, which was code for mixed-race. I had *almond-shaped eyes*, which was code for part-Chinese.

I'd spent my entire life in Alexandria, Virginia, a pictur-esque suburb of Washington, DC, where every house had an American flag flying out front and was decorated with tasteful seasonal décor. It was like living in a greeting card. Serene, still—a carefully crafted image to convince visitors that nothing bad ever happened there.

Everyone worked in DC, and in politics, or at least adjacent to it. My parents did once, too, so I suppose you could call me a political creature. At one point in time, people thought I had a bright future. No one thought that anymore.

My house wasn't actually a house, but a dated town house a few miles away from the home I grew up in. We'd moved there just a year and a half ago, in a frenzied rush that still made me physically ill when I thought about it. As a result, I hated the town house. Technically there wasn't anything egregiously wrong with it—it was just a generic rental with generic furniture and generic décor, on a generic street where all of the townhomes looked alike, but that was exactly the problem. It felt temporary, like it wasn't ours, and every time I stared at the beige walls or the beige carpeting or the beige couches, I was reminded of the life we'd lost.

The downstairs light was on when I got home. Predictably, my dad was still up watching the news, pretending not to be waiting for me.

"Can you believe this?" he said, gesturing at the screen. Ruby, our Cavalier, was asleep on the couch beside him.

I had no idea what he was talking about but humored him anyway. "I can't believe it."

The news always exasperated him. He still hadn't gotten used to being an onlooker. "You know, you don't have to stay up every time I go out."

"I wasn't, and of course I do," my dad said, before turning off the TV and following me into the kitchen. Though it was a joke, it also wasn't. He studied me. "So how was your night?"

I hated how worried he looked when I went out on my own. "Fine," I murmured, peering into the fridge. "How was date night?"

He glanced at the ceiling. My mom was in the room directly above us, reading in bed. "Fine."

Twice a month, my parents went out under the pretense of a date, but I knew that they were actually going to couples' therapy. This was how things happened in our house—in secret. Everything was about keeping up appearances, and they were good at it.

Take, for example, my father, Skip Lerner, former and longtime Democratic senator of Virginia, once loved by all, the darling of the media with his charmingly wholesome face and boyish flop of hair. If you'd slept through the last two years, you wouldn't guess that he'd been forced to resign after what I liked to call our Catastrophic Event, or what other people referred to simply as *the crash*, which sent our lives into a spiral; that behind his grin he was treading water, gasping for air, trying to grab hold of a rope that was drifting away.

And then there was my mom, the beautiful and elegant Francine Yang, former philanthropist who still carried herself as if she sat on the board of multiple charities, who spent weekend nights trying on her expensive clothes as though she had somewhere important to go, and who arranged and rearranged the décor in our town house so that it looked like we had money and influence so that she could distract herself from the fact that most of our belongings had been auctioned off.

"Where'd you go?" I ventured. It wasn't that I enjoyed making my dad lie; I just wanted to see how far he'd take it.

"Oh, just that little Italian place near the waterfront." He said it so casually that I almost believed it. He'd always been a good liar. "Was the catering bad?" he asked, watching me make a cheese plate from odds and ends I found in the fridge.

I shrugged. "You know. The food at those things always looks better than it is."

He murmured in agreement and stole an olive from my plate. I waited for him to say good night and retreat upstairs, but instead he settled into the chair next to me.

"You know, most kids your age eat frozen pizza at this hour," he said.

"Did you see the state of the fridge? There isn't much to choose from."

From the outside we looked wealthy, but we were deeply in debt. Desperate debt, the kind that paid for imported charcuterie and chardonnay instead of groceries and milk, for a town house that we could barely afford to furnish, and two aging luxury cars that we couldn't afford to service. The kind of debt you took on because you were chained to an image of yourself that you couldn't let go.

My father smiled and squeezed my shoulder. "If I'd known you were going to be hungry, I would have ordered something for you."

Though I knew they hadn't gone out to eat, he said it so convincingly that I almost believed him.

"Okay," I countered. "Next date night, I want carbonara."

"The veal is much better."

"You can't eat veal," I said in disbelief. "It's politically incorrect."

"I'm not a politician anymore. I don't have to be correct."

He stole the last olive from my plate, flicked it off the back of his finger, and caught it in his mouth—one of his more impressive party tricks. It was what he did when he wanted to make me laugh.

"I wanted that," I protested. Still, I couldn't help but smile.

He feigned innocence and eyed the last slice of manchego on my plate.

"Don't even think about it."

He nodded to my phone. "I think someone's calling you."

I turned to look, and before I realized it was a ruse, he grabbed the cheese and retreated to the stairs with a smirk.

"Hey!" I shouted.

"Shh," he whispered with a conspiratorial grin. "You'll wake your mother."

I threw a dried apricot at him, which he dodged, letting it hit the wall behind him.

"Teenagers and their phones," he said. "It's too easy."

"Go to bed," I said.

"You go to bed."

"You owe me an olive and a wedge of cheese."

"Veal it is."

People always asked me if I was angry at my father for what he'd done. They asked it expecting a nuanced and complicated answer, but the real one was simple. It was impossible to be mad at him.

There wouldn't be any veal, but I didn't care. That was the problem with charismatic people. Even when you knew they were lying, you couldn't help but want to believe.

2

Remember Forever.

That was my first memory of Luce Herrera. She'd written the words on the back of her hand in Sharpie. I could see them from where I was sitting, a few seats back, along with her chipped polish and the silver cuff at the top of her ear.

It was the first day of ninth grade, and there'd been talk of a new girl who'd moved from a private school an hour away, where she was rumored to have been expelled, though no one knew why. Her dad was the new history teacher.

I remembered how she'd tucked a paperback into her textbook and read it, pretending not to notice that everyone was looking at her. How she'd glanced back at me while I told my friends about my summer vacation, and then, to my surprise, rolled her eyes. How the room had muffled around me and my chest had turned red.

I was still popular then, still a person that everyone listened to, that everyone wanted to be seen with. It shouldn't have bothered me. It didn't, I told myself as I sat through class, trying to focus on what the teacher was saying, but my attention kept drifting to her paperback, to her black nail polish, to the words she'd written on the back of her hand.

What did they mean? I hated that I wanted to know. It was such a crass grab for attention. And yet. I stared at the back of her neck, where a thin gold chain disappeared beneath her collar. A secret.

When class was over, I packed up my bag and followed her into the hallway.

"Hey," I said, my voice sharp to get her attention.

She turned, more confident than I'd expected her to be. On another face, her oversized features and heavy eyeliner might be considered crude, but on hers they fit perfectly. She had a luster to her that made me unable to look away. I faltered. "Why did you roll your eyes at me?"

She studied me, half-amused, half-curious. "Because I knew you were bragging."

"I was talking privately with my friends."

She rolled her eyes again. "Okay."

"Maybe you shouldn't be eavesdropping on other people's conversation."

"Oh, come on, you were practically begging for everyone in the room to look at you."

"And you weren't?" I asked. "Barely hiding your book so that everyone knew you weren't paying attention. Writing random words on your hand, just waiting for someone to ask you what they mean."

She raised an eyebrow. "Does that mean you want to know?"

I wasn't sure if I hated her or if I hated that she saw through me. Or maybe I didn't hate that at all; maybe it felt refreshing. "Of course I do."

A look of surprise passed over her face. She tilted her head, a dare. "Guess."

"Song lyric."

"No."

"Line from a book."

"Getting closer."

"Angsty poetry."

"Farther."

"Revenge note."

She let out a laugh, so sharp and satisfying that I almost forgot that I didn't like her. "No."

"Just tell me."

Down the hall, a door opened, and the new history teacher emerged. Her father.

"Gotta go," she said. "I guess you'll just have to live in suspense."

"That's rude," I called after her.

She held up her hands, as if there was nothing she could

do about it. "See you around, Hana," she said, though I'd never told her my name.

The next day I found her sitting in the same seat in class, reading a book. She didn't acknowledge me when I walked past her, but when I sat down with my friends, I noticed that the message from the day before had been replaced with a new one. *Library. 80.92 BL.*

It was for me. I scrawled it in my notebook.

When class was over, I told my friends I had to study, then went to the library, where I searched the shelves until I found a faded pink paperback, its spine creased. *Forever . . .* by Judy Blume.

I thought back to the words written on her hand—*Remember Forever*—and realized that they were just a reminder to return a library book.

I'd never read it. I wasn't much of a reader; to be honest, I barely read at all—a fact that I didn't publicize. But this book I brought home and read in one night.

The next Friday in class, I dropped a note on her desk when I walked by. *Hadsley Hall, boys' bathroom, 3:30.* There, she'd find two upperclassmen who had set up a store out of gym bags, selling rare candy and snacks you couldn't find in vending machines, along with energy drinks, vintage dirty magazines, and other contraband that varied week to week—"specials." My friends and I liked to stop by and get boxes of Pocky after class.

On Monday, she slipped a brown paper envelope on my

desk as she walked by. When I peeked inside, I blushed. It was a vintage *Playboy* magazine from the "store." The message on her hand read *Page 65*.

I waited until class was over to flip through it, trying to convince myself I wasn't interested in looking at the photos. Page 65 was the centerfold: a glossy brunette with arched eyebrows, her lips pursed in an O. Scrawled across her chest was a note: *It's Blitz! (crank the volume up)*. An album by the Yeah Yeah Yeahs, my phone told me. That night, I locked the door to my bedroom, put on headphones, and turned the volume up high. It was like listening to pure electricity, a jolt to the veins. I sank into my bed and flipped through *Playboy*, studying its soft shapes while the drumbeat emptied my brain.

The next message I left her was my address.

Her father dropped her off the following weekend. I watched through my bedroom window as their car pulled through the gates, and felt inexplicably nervous. Luce was cool in a way that no one else at St. Francis was. She knew about books and music that I had never heard of, and didn't seem to care about the wealth and power that everyone else used as currency. What if she hated my house and thought it was pompous? What if she thought my room was too childish, my bed too frilly, my shelf of collectible dolls that my mother had given me over the years worthy of an eye roll?

I straightened the books on my nightstand. I normally

didn't keep books there, but in a last-minute effort to look cultured, I'd taken a few from my dad's study and arranged them by my bed.

Before ringing the bell, Luce paused on the front walk and looked up at the house, her face betraying the slightest hint of panic. It made me feel better. Maybe she was nervous too.

"Nice place," Luce murmured when I opened the door.

Though my first impulse was to assume that she was being sarcastic, she seemed sincere. "Thanks," I said, then stood there awkwardly, unsure of what to do. When my friends came over, we raided the snack pantry and retreated to the family room, where we splayed ourselves over the couches and gossiped while we watched TV, but Luce didn't seem like someone who wanted to while away the afternoon watching minor celebrities bicker. "Do you want anything to eat or drink?" I asked. "We have soda, iced tea, sparkling water, chips, salsa, chocolate pretzels, cheese and crackers, dried mango—"

The words came out faster than I'd intended and revealed how nervous I felt. Luce studied me; she'd clearly noticed, and I felt my face grow hot. It wasn't like me to be this self-conscious, and I let out a breath. "Wow," I said. "I've never sounded more like my mom."

Luce laughed. "I wish my mom rattled off a list of snacks every time I entered the house."

"Oh, she doesn't for me," I said as I led her to the kitchen.

"It's just for guests. I only get: where have you been, why are you late, what are you wearing, why is your hair like that, why didn't you pick up your phone?"

"*The Greatest Hits*," Luce said. "With bonus tracks 'Have You Finished Your Homework' and 'Don't Forget to Set the Table.'"

"And remixes 'I'm Doing a Load of Laundry' and 'Do You Have Any Dishes in Your Room?'" I said.

"Do you ever get lost in here?" Luce asked.

"Here? As in my house? No. It's not *that* big, is it?"

Luce looked at me as if the answer was obvious. "It's huge," she said, picking up a clay sculpture sitting on the side table.

I froze. "I can't believe you touched that."

Luce put it down quickly. "Why? Is it really expensive or something?"

"It's an original 1912 sculpture by Fornay."

All the color drained from Luce's face. "Who's Fornay?"

"You've never heard of him?"

I waited a beat, watching her sit in her discomfort. "I'm kidding," I said. "It's supposed to be a dog. I made it when I was eight."

She picked up a pen and threw it at me. "You're a jerk."

"So are you."

Luce laughed. "I know." She examined the sculpture. "It really doesn't look like a dog."

"I never claimed to be an artist."

Our housekeeper, Genie, was vacuuming the living room, so after grabbing snacks, I led Luce up to my room and watched as she scanned it, taking in my rosette bedspread, my doll collection, the framed Georgia O'Keeffe print over my bed. Seeing it now from her eyes, I felt embarrassed by how girly everything looked, but to my relief, she smiled. "I always wanted one of those dolls when I was a kid," she said. "I remember looking at them through the store window with all their little accessories and trying to figure out which one most looked like me."

"Same," I said. "They have one now that looks Asian, but I don't have her. Back then, the closest was the Melanie doll, who had brown hair."

"Melanie was the closest to me, too!" Luce said.

We studied each other, our faces now connected by Melanie, who looked nothing like either of us.

"Melanie," Luce said. "The ambiguously Cuban/Chinese/pick-your-race doll."

We both grinned as her eyes drifted to the pile of books on my nightstand. "Marquez?" she said, clearly impressed.

I had to look again at the spines on my nightstand to realize she was talking about *Love in the Time of Cholera*, which I had included in the pile. I felt my chest grow hot. I nodded and hoped she wouldn't ask me any specifics.

"What do you think?" she asked.

"Oh, I um, I just started it, so I haven't really gotten into the story yet. But I like it so far. Why, have you read it?"

"Earlier this summer," she said. "I thought it was well written."

"Totally," I said, trying to sound like I knew what I was talking about.

"What do you think of Florentino so far?" Luce asked.

"I think he's . . . interesting." It was the blandest thing I could think of.

"Really? I thought he was kind of clingy at first."

I swallowed. She didn't seem to be letting the subject go. I had to come clean. "To tell you the truth, I haven't actually read any of it," I admitted. "I mean, I started it, but I couldn't get into it, so I put it down." It was a small lie to replace a larger one. I couldn't tell her that none of the books on the nightstand were mine and that I didn't read much at all other than magazines.

I waited for Luce to look at me with a mixture of pity and derision, but instead, she seemed relieved. "Same," she said. "You know when you have to read the same line over and over and you still can't remember what happened? That's what it felt like for me. I mean, I finished it, but it was an effort. I think maybe I'm just not in the right place for it now and I should try it again in a few years. Have you read *Love Story*, though?" she asked. "If you're looking for something romantic, that's a book that will make you cry."

"I love crying," I said, which made her laugh.

"Seriously, though, you should check it out."

"I will," I said, and I meant it.

Luce hopped on my bed and sank into the plush pile of pillows. "I've always wondered why people have so many decorative pillows on their bed, and now I know why. This is luxurious."

"They're mostly annoying, to be honest," I said, curling up on the other side.

"Where do you put them when you sleep?"

"I throw them all on the ground. It's kind of fun to do when you're upset."

Luce ran her hand down a velvet pillow. "So tell me the truth."

"About what?"

"St. Francis. The people. The teachers. What do I need to know?"

I settled into the reading pillow behind me. There was nothing I liked more than dispensing advice. "Everyone has a tutor, everyone has family connections, and everyone is eavesdropping on everyone else, so you have to be careful about what you say. Don't leave your textbooks out during exam season because they'll disappear and you won't be able to study. Always act like someone's taking photos of you that they'll post the next morning, because they are. Never eat the nachos in the dining hall, and never gossip over email or text, only in person so there's no evidence. Outside of that, it's like any other school."

Luce rotated her necklace. "So what have you heard about me?"

"Your dad's a teacher. You moved here from Holy Innocents. You were expelled."

I searched her face for a reaction, but she refused to give me one.

"Is it true?"

She sighed. "I didn't want to tell anyone. But yes, my dad is a teacher."

I rolled my eyes. "Not that."

"What do you think?"

I considered how she was trying to cultivate an image of not caring when she clearly cared very much. "I don't think you were expelled. I think you left for a really boring reason," I said. "Maybe your dad got the job and you didn't like your old school much anyway, so you switched. But the expulsion rumor took off and you didn't correct anyone because it intimidated people and you liked that."

I studied Luce, looking for a hint that I was right, but I couldn't read her.

"I don't blame you," I added. "I would have let the rumor take off too. It's a kind of armor."

"You're wrong," Luce said with a shrug. "I was expelled."

I went quiet, unsure if she was telling the truth. "For doing what?"

Luce hesitated. "I'm not allowed to say."

Allowed by whom? She pulled a stray hair from a pillow. It had to be bad if she couldn't talk about it, though it was hard to imagine her doing any of the things that immediately popped into mind.

"All I can tell you," she said, "is that it had to do with a boy. And not in the way that you think."

3

"Have you ever fantasized about having a superpower?"

That was the question Luce had asked me the last time I was inside her house. It was August, the week before sophomore year, and we were sprawled on her bed, eating popcorn and scrolling through videos on my phone while her parents cooked dinner downstairs.

"The power to generate more superpowers," I said without hesitation.

Luce threw a piece of popcorn at me. "That's cheating."

Her room had always been strangely appealing despite being slightly ugly. At its base layer, it was dowdy, as though it had been decorated by someone's great-aunt: faded floral quilt, crocheted curtains, ivory wallpaper with tacky little clusters of flowers that made it look like a wedding invitation from the '90s. Atop that, she'd plastered posters and photos, creating a glossy sheen that gave the room the same energy as someone wearing a vintage wedding dress with high-top sneakers.

"You didn't set any rules." I fished the popcorn from my lap and ate it.

"So you want to be God?"

"I've never thought of God as a superhero, but I guess he is."

"She," Luce corrected, then frowned. "They?"

"I thought you didn't believe in God."

"I don't. The ancient Egyptians were right. We should be worshipping cats. But anyway—okay, so you have the ability to generate new superpowers. What's the first one you give yourself?"

"To read other people's minds."

"You already have that superpower," Luce said.

"I do not."

"You have the uncanny ability to look at someone and know exactly who they are and what they want."

I appreciated the compliment, but knew it wasn't true. "I can't tell what you're thinking."

It was, in a way, the highest compliment I could give.

Luce must have felt it, because she went quiet. "Really?"

"I mean, sometimes I can tell. Like I know you're embarrassed when you start picking at your nail polish."

Luce blushed and stopped fidgeting with her nails.

"Or that you're listening even if you act like you aren't, when you rotate the ring in your ear."

"I always listen to you," Luce protested.

"It's fine. I know you don't really care about the political science program at Yale. I just appreciate that you pretend to listen."

Luce cringed. "Is it really that obvious?"

I shrugged. "But other than a few tells, you're a mystery."

Luce bit the side of her lip, her way of trying not to smile at a compliment. Another tell. "Okay, so what superpower do you think I'd choose?" she asked.

I'd been thinking about it since she'd asked me. "Shapeshifting."

Luce laughed. "Shape-shifting? Why do you think that?"

I wasn't exactly sure why. Though she'd remained the same since we'd become friends, I sensed that she was itching to change herself. In what way, I wasn't certain. "I don't know," I admitted. "If that's not it, then what would you pick?"

Luce had propped herself on an elbow. "I'd be rich."

"That's not a superpower."

"Of course it is," Luce said. "It's the only one that's real."

"So what you're saying is that I'm already a superhero?"

"You are," Luce said. "You've just chosen to use your powers for fashion."

"I'm going to take that as a compliment."

"You should," Luce said, her voice earnest. "You have an amazing wardrobe."

"Okay, so what would you do with this 'superpower' once you had it?"

"I'd rise up the social ranks. Become the despot of the school."

I rolled my eyes. "I'm serious. What would you actually do?"

Luce hesitated. "It isn't about what I'd do or buy. It's about how I'd feel."

"What do you mean?"

"It would make me feel more confident. Like I fit in."

Luce was the most confident person I knew, so her revelation was surprising. "But you're already so confident."

She looked at me like I had said something quaint. "You really can't read my thoughts, can you?"

"You know, in a way, we both want the same thing," I said.

"What do you mean?" Luce asked.

"Why do you think I want to read people's minds?"

"Honestly, I have no idea. Having to know every passing thought someone has about me? You couldn't pay me to have that power."

"I just want to be liked," I said. I'd never admitted it to anyone before. "I want to feel like I fit in."

"But you do fit in," Luce said, confused. "You're one of the most popular girls at school."

"I guess I'm always worried that it isn't really me they like, but my *comma, label*."

"What's a *comma, label?*"

"You know, Hana Yang Lerner, *comma, senator's daughter.*"

Luce studied me. "I always thought you were the most confident person I knew," she murmured.

Though we were sitting on opposite sides of the bed, it felt like we were almost touching. "I always thought that of you."

"Melanies for life," Luce said.

"For life," I agreed.

"You know what I'd do after I became the despot of the school?" Luce said with a conspiratorial grin. "I'd date Logan O'Hara."

Logan was the prize of St. Francis. The stroke of the rowing team and all-around model citizen, he had the energy of a beloved Olympic athlete who, after winning the gold medal, appeared on screen breathless and grinning, saying things like, "I couldn't have done this without my mom, who drove me to practice every morning; my teammates, who've always pushed me to do my best; my geriatric dog, Noodle, for waking me up at five a.m. every day to go outside and making sure I never missed early-morning practice; and microwave quesadillas, for always being there for me in a pinch."

He had the kind of face that made you want to be patriotic, that made you want to hate him, until he made you laugh and then you couldn't. His parents were powerful lobbyists, and he and I had been orbiting each other since we were kids, our parents traveling in the same circles, frequenting the same events. I knew what his room looked like, what his housekeeper's name was, what takeout restaurants his parents got most of their meals from.

"I thought you didn't like him," I said.

Though she'd tried to hide it, Luce had always been interested in Logan. She often asked me about his house, what his parents were like, what music he listened to.

"I don't," Luce said. "I just want to see what he's really like under that mask."

I knew what she meant. Despite all the time I'd spent with Logan, I felt that I still didn't *really* know him. He was too perfect, always saying the right thing, always flashing a smile at the right time. All things we do to conceal. I knew it well because I did it too. We were similar in that way.

"You know what they say," Luce said. "The nicer the house, the harder it is to find the trash."

"His literal trash is disguised as a cabinet," I said. "Very hard to locate."

"Have you ever glimpsed an underlying personality beneath all the teamwork and academic integrity?" Luce asked.

"He likes to draw," I offered. "He's pretty good. I've seen some of his sketches."

"Are they just of the American flag over and over again?" Luce asked.

"Barbecues and slabs of meat," I corrected.

"White bread and boxes of Entenmann's coffee cakes," Luce said.

"You know, you don't have to be rich to date him."

Luce looked at me as if I'd said something incredibly naive. "You do realize that I've been around him dozens of times and I don't think he's ever actually talked to me."

"That can't be true."

"Has he ever mentioned me?"

I hesitated. "If I could read his mind, I could tell you."

Luce rolled her eyes. "He likes rich people, and he likes blondes."

I shrugged. "Everyone like blondes."

"That's a kind of superpower too," Luce said.

That was two years ago. Luce and I had long since stopped being friends, and I'd assumed our lives would never intersect again. Yet there I was, sitting in my car outside of Luce's house with my dad's old DSLR camera, watching her shadow pass behind her curtains. If I could go back to that night in her room, I'd change my answer. The superpower I'd choose would be to control time. To travel back and change things, to travel forward and see if the decisions I was making were right. To make it slow down when I was happy and speed up when I was upset.

Luce's hair was blond now, and she and Logan had been dating for over eight months—a development that had seemed both surprising and entirely predictable if you knew Luce and her distinct ability to get what she wanted. That, I supposed, was her actual superpower.

I'd been staking out her house all week. Though I hadn't accepted Three's case yet, I couldn't put it out of my mind.

Luce is working on something that she needs help fixing.

It was probably a practical joke. Still, a little voice in the back of my head kept asking me: *What if it isn't?*

I considered what Three's message could mean. The most obvious interpretation was that Luce had gotten involved in something bad. She was in over her head and needed help. But what had she gotten involved in?

It could have been about her family. Although her parents were kind and minded their own business, they didn't have a lot of money, which had always bothered Luce. Maybe they were in a financial bind and Luce had done something to help them.

She had always been a straight-A student, so it probably wasn't about her performance, though she was entrepreneurial, and I could imagine a reality in which she started doing homework for her classmates to get money, which she could then use to help her parents get out of their mystery financial crisis.

Or maybe it was about her social life. From the outside, it looked perfect—she hung out with the most popular and powerful kids at school, thanks to her boyfriend, Logan, who catalyzed her social ascent—but I knew that those same friends had once looked down on her. What if they found out about her parents' financial situation, and what Luce was doing to help them, and were getting ready to report her to the school?

I felt the momentary high of turning a puzzle piece until it fit perfectly into its vacancy before I scoffed at myself. It sounded like the plot of a mediocre thriller. I sank deeper into my seat and felt more convinced than ever that I was wasting my time.

Before I'd decided on the stakeout, I'd casually asked Adam if he'd heard any rumors about Luce. Anything strange that she'd been up to? He hadn't. I didn't have access to her social life, which revolved around a friend group that had shunned me, so with no leads, the next best thing I could think to do was park my car in the shadow of her neighbor's magnolia tree and see if I could glimpse anything out of the ordinary.

So far, it had been a bust. She had no guests, no plans. The only activity I could see were the silhouettes of her and her parents occasionally passing in front of the curtains of her modest ranch house. I spent most of my time working on my assignments by the light of my phone and wondering if it really was just a prank. There were plenty of people at school who, out of boredom, might find it funny to rile me up by sending me texts about my ex–best friend.

I was about to stuff my notebook in my bag and turn on my car when the front door of the house opened and Luce stepped out.

I froze and watched as she slipped into her mom's old Volvo and drove past me down the street, her headlights grazing the top of my head as I ducked beneath the dashboard. When she reached the main road, I peeled away from the curb and followed her.

She drove north to a wealthy neighborhood in McLean and pulled up to a brick mansion with a crescent driveway and two decorative oil lamps flickering on either side of the front door. I'd never been to this house before and noted the address in my phone. 551 Hayworth Street. Luce parked out of view, and when she stepped outside into the night, she didn't approach the front door but instead crept into the shadows behind the decorative hedges and disappeared.

I slowed as I drove by, scanning the front lawn for her outline, but saw nothing. At the end of the block, I cut my lights, turned around, and parked in the shadow of an oak tree nearby, where I had a decent view of the front door. Across the street, a dog barked.

What was Luce doing, sneaking around a mansion at night? I gazed at the house, wondering who it belonged to.

I was squinting at the lawn, looking for Luce, when the front door opened and a rectangle of light stretched across the stone walk. A person appeared in the doorway. I fished the camera out of my bag and zoomed in to get a better look.

A boy's silhouette filled the frame. His back was facing me while he talked to someone inside. Though I couldn't see his face, I knew who he was immediately and steadied my hand, waiting for him to turn.

Even at a distance, Logan O'Hara looked beautiful: a Roman sculpture cast from bronze. He was dressed like he was trying to make a good impression—tan pants and a crisp oxford that fit him perfectly, its creases catching the light. He exchanged words with a person inside whose face I couldn't make out, then paused.

Behind him, another boy stood in the doorway of the house. At first glance, I thought I was seeing things. The second boy looked almost exactly like Logan: The same mahogany hair, the same outfit. He stood with the same posture, and when he walked, he moved with the same deliberation. Even their faces looked similar. I might have guessed they were twins had I not known that Logan was an only child.

I blinked, bewildered. Then, *click*, took a photo. *Click*. Another.

Logan turned to his double and murmured something to him that I wished I could hear. Then he trotted down the steps and disappeared into the darkness. I heard a car door slam, an engine shudder to life. A pair of headlights illuminated the driveway. Across the lawn, I caught a glimpse of

Luce's face behind the hedges, furrowed with focus as she watched Logan's car pull down the crescent drive.

Back in the doorway, Logan's look-alike had already receded into the house. All I could make out was a glimpse of an arm, then a shadow, long and distorted, stretching across the grass until the front door closed and the lawn went dark.

I didn't understand. What had I seen? Two Logans: one real, one fake. An inverted truth, a dream. Had I even seen what I thought I had? I looked up at the mansion, which glowed from the inside. A silhouette passed in front of the window on the first floor, its secrets protected by curtains.

The only reason I had seen any of it was because of Luce, who had remained out of sight the entire time. She was clearly watching Logan without him knowing. But why? As his girlfriend, Luce had access to him in ways that no one else at school did. She spent time in his house, his room, his car. She had to know his phone password and could have read a text thread or email that tipped her off to something secret, something that he didn't want anyone to know. But what?

The most obvious answer was that he was dating someone else, but that didn't seem to be the case, given his look-alike. I tried to think of alternate possibilities. Why would someone meet their look-alike? Maybe they were related, and the look-alike was a long-lost twin that no one knew about. It seemed both plausible and impossible, a plot out of a soap opera.

I searched the yard for a shadow moving along the hedges when the lawn sprinklers turned on, making me nearly jump out of my skin. Down the road, Luce's car shivered to life; she had already crept past me. I didn't have time to follow her. Before I could fumble with my keys, she sped down the street and was gone. I dropped them in my lap and stared at the halo of mist over the lawn, still stunned. It was late. I should go home.

In the distance, a dog barked again. I wondered what it was barking at when someone rapped on my window.

4

A face appeared on the other side of the glass. I felt electrified, as though time had stopped.

I picked up my keys and started to turn on the car when I heard my name.

"Hana?" a boy said, his voice muffled.

I blinked. His face began to take a familiar shape.

"James?"

James Li was the last person I'd expected to find outside of a strange mansion in McLean. I cracked the window. "What are you doing here?"

"I came to ask you that," he said.

A light switched on in an upstairs bedroom of the mansion. We both turned. "Don't just stand there out in the open," I whispered, and nodded to the passenger seat of my car. "Get in."

On the long list of people that I didn't want to be sitting

alone with in a car, James Li was at the top. Not because I didn't like him—I did, very much, or at least I used to—but because he had an uncanny ability to see the truth.

We'd been childhood friends—our mothers had met by chance at a fundraiser when we were little and had bonded over being the only two Chinese women in the room. As a result, James and I had spent most of the early part of our lives being bored in varying locales—his house, my house, convention centers, banquet halls, hotel lobbies. Some of my best memories were with him, sitting beneath a white-clothed table with a heaping plate of catered desserts, watching feet shuffle around us while we read mini mysteries to each other and tried to solve them.

Things were different at St. Francis, though. We'd never traveled in the same social circles. I'd been popular and outgoing, the person everyone had wanted to be friends with, while James had preferred the company of a few close confidants and books, and had a healthy disdain for parties, small talk, and sporting events—all things that life at St. Francis revolved around.

My then-friends had only started to notice him in ninth grade when he'd showed up after summer break four inches taller, with a face that had somehow sharpened, as though all of his features had come into focus.

"He's actually pretty cute," they'd said, which had felt confusing and bizarre. For a moment, I hadn't realized they were talking about James—my James. The one who ate all the cereal from our pantry and drank all of the good seltzer flavors, leaving me only the lemons. The one who always asked me too many questions and said the one thing he knew he wasn't supposed to say, because why not? Watching my friends ogle him, I'd felt like I was rediscovering him, looking at him for the first time.

That was in the BCE era. Before everyone had started to distance themselves from my family. Before I'd overheard our mothers arguing in the kitchen, which marked the slow, then incredibly quick disintegration of their friendship, then ours. Before I'd called him an impostor and shut him out.

Now I studied him. He did look good, I realized. Tall and precise as an arrow, with a boyish face that made him look like someone who felt things deeply. Though he dressed decently, he didn't seem to care much about what his hair was doing or what he wore, and though he hadn't intended to look cool, the overall effect was one of confident aloofness. But more appealing was the way he carried himself. He didn't care about impressing people who were more powerful or popular than he was; he was more interested in ideas—articles, books, movies—and because so few people merited his attention, it was easy to imagine how thrilling it would feel to have his gaze turned to you.

"So what do you have to do with all of this?" James asked me. His voice sounded like the opening notes of a song that I hadn't heard in ages. It was the first time we'd spoken in two years.

"You go first," I said.

"So we're doing this again."

"What's *this*?"

"Circling around the truth."

I'd been avoiding looking directly at him for the past two years, but now I met his eye. We'd spent so much time together when we were young that for most of our lives, it had felt like we were each other's shadows.

"You're the investigator," I said. "Why don't you guess?"

James was the editor in chief of the *Kestrel*, the school newspaper, and had, since we were kids, wanted to become a journalist.

"The mansion. Logan O'Hara. The almost-Logan. Luce Herrera. And now you," he murmured, considering me. "Well, I saw you pull up after Luce, and judging from the camera and the unfinished homework, I'd bet that you were staking out her house and followed her here. My question is why."

I'd forgotten how good he was at this. Had I known that he was going to show up out of nowhere and hop into my car, I might have hidden my things. He had, however, given me one crucial piece of information—that he had already been at the mansion when Luce and I had pulled up, which meant he hadn't followed either of us there. He'd come on his own.

"Maybe it's for a case," he continued. "A case involving Luce Herrera. Now that's a subject that Hana Yang Lerner would not be able to turn down." He looked at me. "Am I right?"

I tried to keep my face unreadable. "Of course not."

"You're a good liar," James said. "You can convince most people. But you can't convince me."

Though I refused to concede that he was right, I could tell he knew that he was.

"Okay, my turn." I sized up the details: the spiral notepad sticking out of his coat pocket; his outfit, which was all black, the choice of someone who wanted to remain out of sight; the location of his car, which he'd parked out of view on the other side of the driveway. "You were staking out Logan and he led you here. I'd guess you were following him for a story you're working on, and now you're realizing that it's much more complicated than you initially assumed, and you're panicking because you hate being confused. You were relieved to find me here because you know I'm better at figuring things out than you are, but you're too proud to ask me for help, so you've decided to act like you know more than I do, with the hope that I'll tell you what I know."

James winced. "I'm glad you never joined the school paper."

"Because I would have taken your job?"

"Because you're difficult to work with and would erode the friendly atmosphere."

I felt my throat tighten. I should have expected his bluntness, considering we were both taking jabs at each other, but it didn't make it hurt any less. Though I wanted to believe that he wasn't right, I knew deep down that he was. Despite my lack of social standing, I still had a high opinion of myself. What James couldn't understand was that I had to. It was my armor. I didn't want to see what I looked like without it.

"Then why are you sitting in my car, trying to work with me?" I asked.

"Because you told me to get in," James said. "And I didn't come here looking for you. You happened to be here and are the only other person who witnessed what I just saw. So I don't have many other options."

"Well, unlike you, I don't need any help."

James looked unconvinced. I wasn't either. What I didn't want to admit was that I liked this—the sparring, the banter, the challenge of talking to someone who was almost as good at what I did as I was. It felt comfortable, like I was reliving a memory.

"Just ask," James said. "I know you want to."

I feigned ignorance. "Ask what?"

James gave me an impatient look. "Fine. You don't want to share notes. I'm not going to beg." He was reaching for the door handle as if to leave when I stopped him.

"Okay," I said. "What's your story about?"

Late one Thursday afternoon, when most of the school had already gone home, Ethan, a junior reporter on the school newspaper, walked into the boys' locker room looking for a lost pair of earbuds, when he heard a voice in the last stall of the bathroom.

"I-I'm sorry," a boy said, stammering.

It sounded like Chris Pilker-Johns, a freshman and recruit to the rowing team who had been sitting out of practice recently due to a hamstring injury.

Ethan froze so as not to be heard.

"Tell that to him," another boy said from the same stall. This one sounded like Logan O'Hara.

Ethan bent down and inspected their shoes. Their orientation suggested that Chris was standing with his back against the wall, and Logan was in front of him, pushing him into the cinderblock.

"I will," Chris said, his voice frantic. "Okay. I will."

"Now repeat after me," Logan said. "You didn't see anything."

"I didn't see anything."

"Good. If I find out you told anyone, I'll ruin you."

Ethan slipped out of the locker room. Later that day, he told James what he'd heard. They believed that the bathroom conversation was about hazing rituals imposed by the rowing team—a notable subject because the team had a remarkably wholesome image. They were the model citizens of school, who rose before dawn to exercise, volunteered in their free time, and prided themselves on their integrity. James had always been wary of the rowing team, and this tip, he believed, was the first crack in their veneer. He'd been watching the most powerful members of the team, but his eye had been trained on Logan, the unofficial captain. James had been scoping out a crew party with the hope of proving his hypothesis correct when Logan left early and drove thirty minutes away to the mansion in McLean.

"So how did you get here?" James asked me from the passenger seat of my car.

The prickly part of my brain, the part that had learned that any information I shared could be used against me, told me that I shouldn't divulge the details of my case. But why? It wasn't even my case yet, and if I was being honest, I wanted help.

"An anonymous client texted me," I said, then corrected myself. "*Potential* client. They told me that Luce is working on something that she needs help fixing and offered me five thousand dollars to look into it. They called themselves Three."

James looked bewildered. "Three? Why?"

"They said I'd find out at the end of the job. All I know is that they go to St. Francis, I know them in real life, and they're rich enough to afford paying me ten times my normal rate."

"That doesn't really narrow it down," James said.

"I know."

"I'm starting to think this has nothing to do with hazing on the crew team," James murmured.

"No," I said. "I don't think so."

"Let's line the facts in a row," James said. "Logan threatens Chris in the bathroom, making him say that he didn't see anything. Then an anonymous person hires you to help Luce fix something she's 'working on.' You follow her to a mansion, where she's spying on Logan, and see him meet with a look-alike."

"And now here we are," I said.

"Here we are," James repeated, then studied me. "This is what you do. So what do you think is going on?"

I was used to people asking for my advice, but only because I was the one person willing to help. This felt different, like a peer asking me for my expert opinion, and it felt good. "I think that Logan has a secret. A secret that both Chris and Luce discovered. Or are in the process of discovering. And we just got a glimpse of it too."

James's gaze drifted to the mansion. "The crew star, meeting with a look-alike in a strange mansion at night. Why?"

For the first time in a long while, I had no idea. All I felt certain of was that this was what Three had been referring to. This was what Luce was "working on."

"And your anonymous client?" James asked, his mind running parallel to mine. "How do you think they fit in?"

I thought back to the messages from Three. It seemed there was only one way for me to find out. I had to figure out what Luce knew, which meant unearthing Logan's secret.

I turned to James and recited the last message Three sent me. "When I finish the job, I'll know."

5

The best thing to do when you can't sleep, other than take diazepam, which was what my mother was partial to, is to put on the most sedate nature documentary you can find and watch it in the dark on the living room couch while you eat graham crackers dipped in warm milk.

I'd been having trouble sleeping for the past two years, but that night it was Logan and his look-alike who were keeping me up. Every time I closed my eyes, I saw the odd gaze of Logan's almost-twin, his face a ripple of the original. Had I not taken photos of them, I might have convinced myself that my eyes had betrayed me, that it had been a trick of the light and the distance. What had Luce discovered? What had I seen?

"Where are we tonight?" my dad said from the hallway, startling me. "Ah, the sub-Sahara."

I felt my chest deflate. "You just shortened my life by a year."

"Without me, you wouldn't have been born," my dad countered, "so technically, I've only ever extended your life."

I rolled my eyes.

He studied me, holding his smile a little too long. That's how I knew that despite the joking, he was concerned. "So what's keeping you up?" he asked.

"You know, you don't have to worry about me so much. Zack stays up late all the time and you don't hover over him."

"I hover over Zack," my dad said. "In this household, we practice fair and impartial hovering. But Zack's a little more straightforward. When he's up, it's because he's busy blowing up cyborgs on his computer screen. You're harder to read."

It was impossible to not be charmed by my dad, to not want to trust him. A part of me wanted to tell him what was bothering me. Instead, I shrugged. "Just the soul-crushing pressure of navigating modern teenage life in the age of perfection inflation and digital permanence."

My father frowned. "I see."

"And you?"

"The same."

I laughed.

He glanced at the screen. "Well, I'll leave you to it, then."

Before he turned to go, I called out to him. "Dad? Do you ever miss our old life?"

I'm not sure why I asked it, since I already knew the answer.

"Every day."

Nothing appeared out of the ordinary at school the next day or the day after that. I watched, still stunned, as my classmates chatted with their friends and played Frisbee on the quad, completely unaware that Logan O'Hara had a look-alike that he was meeting with in a strange mansion.

All the while, I studied him. In the dining hall, sitting amid his friends like he was holding court. On the second floor of Hadsley Hall, whispering to his friend Keith as they walked past each other, their palms touching in a smooth handshake. In the back of AP English, murmuring to Luce while his fingertips grazed her wrist. To an outsider, they might have looked like a happy couple.

Though I wanted to take the case, I was scared of it—not of what I'd seen at the mansion, but of how the entire fix appealed to a deep desire to repair my relationship with Luce. I knew I couldn't get our friendship back, but the idea of having a reason to get closer to her, even if it meant watching her in secret, was too tempting, and it troubled me that Three knew this about me. In that way, the case felt like a trick, a crisp twenty-dollar bill left in the middle of the sidewalk while everyone else walked by. Surely something would go wrong if I reached out and grabbed it.

So I waited, hoping I would find a reason to decline, but the more I watched Logan and Luce, the more their secrets ate away at me. James felt the same; I could see it in how his attention in class strayed from the lecture and found its way across the room to Logan or Luce or me.

We hadn't spoken since that night in the car, where we'd left things on awkward and uncertain terms. I wasn't on the school paper and he wasn't a fixer; though we'd ended up at the same place that night, we had different goals. Mine was to figure out what was going on, fix it, and keep it secret, whereas his was to broadcast it to as many people as he could. I wasn't about to help him solve the mystery so he could go write about it in the school paper, and he wasn't about to help me solve it so I could get paid to keep it under lock and key. So we'd parted ways with the unspoken understanding that we'd go it alone from there. Best of luck. Have a good life.

So why did my gaze keep drifting to him during class? Why did I find myself noticing the way he clenched his jaw while he took notes, or the way he tilted his head while he was listening? Why could I not stop thinking about how it felt to sit next to him in the dark, to hear him say my name? My car had felt like a portal that night, existing outside the complications of the past or present. Even though I'd told myself I liked to work alone, I couldn't help but want to find my way back there.

I must have been staring, because James looked up, his eyes meeting mine. Quickly, I looked past him to the clock on the wall, which I pretended to be engrossed in reading. When he turned back to the board, I did the same and trained my gaze on it for the rest of the period.

After class, I packed up my things and hurried out the door. The school library was usually empty in the late afternoon when everyone else was busy with sports or extracurriculars. I sat at my usual table, which looked out over the quad, and opened my computer.

I should have been starting my AP History paper, but I couldn't focus on it when the question of what Luce had discovered about Logan loomed in my mind. So instead, I opened the browser and was typing the word *doppelganger* into the search bar when my phone vibrated.

>**Have you made a decision yet?**

It was Three. I clutched my phone, unsure of how to respond. Three had to be referring to whether or not I was going to take the case. When faced with the question, I felt paralyzed.

>**I'm surprised by your hesitation**, Three wrote. **I thought you'd be excited.**

I was considering what to write back when a voice startled me.

"'The doppelganger is a sign of wickedness,'" James read from my computer.

"You scared me," I said.

"Sorry."

"You should walk a little louder or something," I said. "Stop being so respectful of library etiquette."

"Noted for next time," James said. "So you're taking the case?"

"What? No. I mean, I don't know. Why do you say that?"

James nodded at my computer. "You're doing research. Have you made any headway?" He asked it like he was testing me, like he had also been doing research and wanted to see if he'd discovered more than I had.

"Lots, thanks," I said.

He squinted at my screen. "I read that link too. Did you know that dictators used to find people who looked similar to them, then surgically alter their faces to make them look identical so that they could go to events in their place? That way, if there was an assassination attempt, the doppelganger would be killed, not the dictator."

"Fascinating," I murmured, then lowered my voice. "So you think Logan might be the target of an assassination?"

James shook his head, not wanting to admit that I had almost, maybe, sort of made him laugh.

"Did you follow me here?" I asked.

James gave me his very serious reporter look. "Yes. I was staking you out."

"Very funny."

He clutched his backpack. I assumed he was going to set it down by the chair next to mine, but instead he took a seat a few tables away from me.

"What are you doing?" I asked in a hushed whisper, even though we were the only ones in the room.

"Sitting."

What I really meant was why was he going to a different table, but surely he knew that. And anyway, why did I care where he sat? I'd come here on my own. I had turned back to my computer when I heard a pencil tapping against a desk.

"Would you mind?" I asked.

"Sorry," James said, and tucked it behind his ear. "Just a habit."

He opened his laptop, and I had returned to my screen when I was interrupted by another sound.

"Are you purposely typing loudly?" I whispered.

"This is how I type."

"It sounds like you're writing an angry comment."

"You know I don't engage with comment sections. But sure. I'll try to be a little softer."

"Thanks," I said, but instead of resuming my research, I hesitated. "What exactly are you typing, then?" I ventured.

James gave me an amused look. "I thought you were worried about me following you here."

"I was."

"But now you want to know what I'm writing?"

"You could be hacking into my computer right now," I said. "Transferring funds. Stealing my identity. Buying a plane ticket to a foreign country."

"If I were going to do that, I'd probably choose someone a little richer," James said.

"Fair," I mumbled.

"So you want to know if I've made more headway than you have," he observed.

"I didn't say that," I countered.

"You're saying it without saying it."

"Well, have you?" I asked.

James let out the beginning of a laugh. "Will you think I followed you here if I sit at your table?"

"Yes, but I think that anyway."

Though he rolled his eyes, I could tell he was holding back a smile. He closed his laptop and sat beside me, and for the first time in a while, I felt the fist in my chest relax.

As it turned out, he'd made about as much headway as I had.

The basic mystery of the case was simple: Luce had uncovered a secret about Logan. Three wanted to hire me to figure out what Luce knew so that I could help her fix it, whatever that meant. So what had Luce discovered?

We'd caught a glimpse of it when we'd seen Logan meet with his look-alike at the mansion. So the first logical step was to look up the house.

It was easy enough: all I had to do was search the public tax records. James had done it too. Separately, we'd both discovered that the owner of the mansion at 551 Hayworth Street was a woman named Marion Goodjoy. An internet search revealed that she was eighty-eight years old, came from a family that made its money from logging, and had, in the past, donated to multiple charities, mostly involving Alzheimer's research. In photos of her online, she had the frail yet frigid look of a wealthy person who treated waiters poorly. According to her husband's obituary, she was long since widowed and they'd had no children. Neither of us knew anyone who knew her, and she seemed to have no connection at all to Logan, making it unclear why he would be at her house, let alone with his look-alike. So for our purposes, Marion Goodjoy was a dead end.

The next logical step was to talk to Chris Pilker-Johns, whom Logan had threatened in the bathroom, ostensibly because he'd uncovered the same secret as Luce had. I hadn't talked to him yet, though I'd been toying with ideas on how to approach him. James, on the other hand, had already tried.

"He wouldn't talk," James said, a bit sheepish. "He was too scared."

"What did you ask him?"

"I told him that I'd gotten a tip about a private conversation he'd had with Logan. Then I asked if there was anything he wanted to tell me about it."

I winced. "Why did you ask him like that?"

"Because it was the truth," James said.

"Did you offer him anything?"

"A chance to speak truth to power," James said.

I rolled my eyes. "Something he wants. A favor. I help you, you help me."

"Journalists don't work like that. It's not ethical."

"Why would Chris tell you anything when you're offering him nothing and talking to you means Logan will ruin his life?"

"So you think free concert tickets or an invite to an elite party is going to convince him to talk?"

"Is that what you think I do?" I said with a laugh. "Give me some credit. I'm a lot more creative than that. Why don't you let me try to talk to him?"

"Definitely not," James said. "He's my contact. Not yours. I'm not about to go talk to Luce, am I?"

I begrudgingly accepted that he had a point.

"I'll try him again," James said. "See if I can get him to trust me. Chris is an insecure freshman trying to find his place at school. If I can assure him that no one will trace the information back to him, he'll talk. No favors needed."

I sighed. "So we'll never find out what he saw."

James clenched his jaw the way he used to when he knew I was right but didn't want to admit it. "Okay, but seriously," he said. "Logan, the mansion, the look-alike. What do you think is going on?"

The most obvious explanation was that they were twins. "Maybe Logan's parents separated them at birth because one was sick and they prized health and excellence," I said, thinking out loud. "They gave the weak twin up for adoption. Then, his adoptive parents passed away and the twin was given to their family friend, Marion Goodjoy, a barren heiress. Somehow Logan and his twin discovered each other and finally met in Marion Goodjoy's mansion, which is what we stumbled upon."

I bit my lip. It already sounded unbelievable.

"So why would they be dressed the same?" James asked.

"They weren't wearing the exact same outfit. And anyway, everyone around here dresses like that—it's the classic prep-boy uniform."

"And if he was just meeting his twin, why would Logan be so upset that Chris found out?"

"Because it looks bad for his family?" I offered.

"It's possible," James said.

"Okay, what if Logan's dad has a secret second family?" I said. "It's not an uncommon story, especially in DC. Maybe his dad had an affair, fathered a child, paid his mistress to keep the child hidden. And this doppelganger isn't his twin but his younger brother. Logan found out by taking one of those ancestry tests and arranged to meet his brother at a third-party location. Maybe Marion is his neighbor. Or maybe she's a family friend."

"If they have different mothers, they probably wouldn't look exactly alike," James said.

"It was dark and we were looking at them from a distance," I said. "Maybe they don't look as identical as we think."

"Maybe," James murmured, though I knew from his tone he was skeptical.

It was typical of him to pick apart my theories without offering any reasonable ones of his own. It was what he did when we were kids, solving minute mysteries under the hors d'oeuvres table.

I should have been irritated with him. I was, I supposed, but I liked it. What a small thrill to have someone to be irritated with, to have someone to talk to about a case. I eyed his hand, which was inches away from mine, and remembered all of the times I'd doodled words and pictures on it with a pen. I'd always thought of his hands like river stones, smooth and comfortable when held in the palm.

"What?" he said, looking at me strangely.

I clammed up and feigned ignorance. "What?"

"You're looking at me in this really weird way."

"Am I?"

Had I really been fantasizing about holding James's hand? This was getting out of control. I had to go. I glanced at my phone. "Well, it's been a fun brainstorming session, but I should go. My history paper isn't going to write it-self."

"Okay," he said, clearly surprised by my abrupt depar-ture.

"So are you going to take the job?" he asked as I packed up my things.

Though I kept telling myself I was on the fence, I knew what I was going to do. "I don't know. Are you going to drop the article or go all Woodward and Bernstein?"

James let out a laugh that transported me back to the couch in my old living room, the music blaring, our home-work abandoned on the coffee table, a shared bowl of popcorn wedged between us as we read each other famous conspiracy theories from the internet.

"To do that, I'd need a partner," he said. "Woodward couldn't have covered Watergate without Bernstein."

"Huh," I teased. "I wonder where you'd find one of those."

As I turned to the door, James called out to me. "Hey, is your phone number the same?"

I felt a strange sensation that I could only identify as nervousness. "Yeah."

"Great. When I solve the case, I'll call you to give you the answers."

"I guess that means I won't be hearing from you for a while."

I walked out the door before he could see me grinning.

The path was dappled with the afternoon sun as I walked to my car, trying to convince myself that maybe it would be fine to work on a case with someone else. Just this once.

In the distance, I heard music and saw Logan sitting in the open trunk of his SUV with Luce and their friends, his jacket draped over her shoulders, a symbol of ownership.

I watched them from the path. The parking lot was the unofficial seat of power at school, a place where the rich and popular could see and be seen, their gleaming chariots pulsing with music, their bodies outlined in a seam of golden light as they gazed out over the campus, surveying their domain.

Luce had learned to play the part. She leaned against the side of his car, her blond hair just beginning to show its roots, her legs dangling against the bumper as she sucked a lollipop. Logan was telling a story that must have been fascinating, because everyone was rapt, listening. To anyone else, it might have looked like Luce was, too. She nodded her head at the right time, acted surprised when everyone else did. But in the moments in between, when she thought no one was looking, her face hardened and her gaze grew distant, troubled.

Everyone laughed, and after a brief delay, Luce joined them, her tongue a shock of raspberry blue.

I turned away and texted Three.

<I looked into what you asked me.

Three took a moment to respond.

>And?

<I'll take it.

I stole one last glance at Luce. As if she could sense a change in the atmosphere, her eyes met mine. I held them for a beat, wondering what she would do. She gave me a defiant look, then turned to Logan and pulled him into a kiss.

6

I told myself I wasn't going to talk to Chris Pilker-Johns. I really did. But then I got to thinking about how James would never be able to get information from him, but maybe I could, and if I did, I might be able to solve the case right then and there. Chris had discovered the same secret that Luce had, or at least that's what our going theory was. All I had to do was ask.

Of course, it wasn't that easy. I had to think of something to offer him in exchange for information, which meant I needed to figure out what made him tick, which was tricky because he was a freshman, and someone whom I would never have otherwise trained my focus on.

"Do you know anything about him?" I asked Adam at school the next week.

We were standing on the edge of the quad at the end of free period, looking at a group of freshmen play Frisbee.

"I don't even know which one he is," Adam said.

I nodded to an acne-prone boy who was snatching one of his friends' sunglasses and laughing. Chris was long and gangly like a puppy, with oversized features that made him look like he had yet to grow into his face.

"Truly don't think I've ever given him a second glance," Adam said.

"His parents are lawyers. He's on the crew team but hasn't been practicing because of an injury. He seems generally well-liked but not the most popular kid in his class."

Adam squinted at him. "Doesn't like to be at the edge of the group, is always pushing toward the center," he observed. "Likes to use jokes and props to gain the attention of others. He looks socially ambitious, like he's trying to prove himself." Adam turned to me. "How do you rate my assessment?"

"Ten out of ten," I said.

"Why are you suddenly interested in a random freshman?"

"I need to get some information from him," I said, trying to sound casual. "Part of a case."

Adam wasn't buying my nonchalance. "The same case you looked so freaked out by on the night of the alumni gala?"

"No," I said, lying. "And stop assessing me. I can see your gears turning, and I don't like it."

"It's your medicine," Adam said. "You should learn to tolerate the taste every so often. So what do you think this Chris knows that you want to extract so badly?"

I considered not telling him, but doing so would make it even more likely that I'd discover nothing, so I lowered my voice. "Something about Logan and a rumor I heard about a conversation they had in the locker room. You haven't heard anything about that, have you?"

"No," Adam said, his interest piqued. "Why are you even asking me about Chris when you already know the perfect person to talk to?"

"Who?"

Adam looked at me like it was obvious. "Your brother."

It was just before dinnertime when I got home from school, which was by design, because however unpleasant school was socially, home was worse.

The scene I happened in on looked like this: my father standing on a chair, fanning the smoke detector with a manila folder; my mother scraping a tarry substance that I assumed was once food from a baking dish into the trash; and my brother, Zack, standing by the open window, which my mother must have asked him to crack, playing a game on his phone.

Judging from the sheepish look on my father's face, I guessed that he had forgotten to set the timer on the oven and was preparing himself for an unpleasant evening.

"Can you set the table?" my mother said to me. The

edge to her voice told me I was right. Ruby circled her ankles, begging for a scrap.

Also notable was my mother's outfit. It was one of her Professional ensembles—a tailored pantsuit that she used to wear when she was meeting with someone important, something she rarely did anymore. My mom had a whole range of categorizable outfits. Press Conference Attire and Media Interview Outfits. Gala Gowns, which shouldn't be confused with Fundraising Gowns. Morning Show Outfits, and her classic I'm Like You ensembles of mom jeans and untucked button-downs, which she wore when trying to look approachable to people who might otherwise find her foreign or severe. She wasn't foreign, of course; she was born in Virginia to Chinese immigrants. She could, however, be severe, if by *severe* one meant that she was a keen observer of others and was guarded with her interior life.

Now she mainly wore what I thought of as her Recovering from Social Tailspin Outfits: baggy pants and loose shirts, often ones she'd worn the night before and slept in, and, of course, robes.

If I had to guess, I'd say that she'd met with another potential client for the event management business that she'd been trying to get off the ground since the Catastrophic Event. Given her mood, I'd guess that she hadn't gotten the job.

I watched her cut open a bag of frozen vegetables and dump them into a bowl and considered what to say. We hadn't been on great terms, and I'd been trying to avoid conflict by staying out of her way.

"So how was everyone's day?" I ventured as I got a stack of plates from the cabinet.

"Fine," my father said.

"Fine," my brother said.

A silence hung over the room as we waited for my mother to answer. "Fine," she said, then busied herself with arranging things on the table so she didn't have to engage. "You've been out a lot," she said to me. "You've been coming home late."

I could see her gathering information: my clothes, my shoes, my hair, the heft of my backpack—what did they tell her about how I'd spent my day, about where I'd been?

"Tutoring," I explained.

My brother raised an eyebrow, but I ignored it.

My parents didn't know about my side job. My dad might find my fixing endearing, but my mother would be appalled. Instead, I told them I was tutoring underclassmen, which explained the money and gave me a reason to leave the house when I needed to. Zack knew some version of the truth—he was a freshman at St. Francis, so he'd heard whispers about the services I offered—but he rarely looked up from his phone, let alone shared information with my parents.

"It's all in the calendar," I continued.

My parents, though seemingly lax about my comings

and goings, tracked my whereabouts on a shared online calendar. We'd used it when my dad was a senator; we'd had more plans then. It was a way for us to know where everyone was at any given time. Now they used it to track my and my brother's plans, though my brother rarely went anywhere, so it was really just for me.

"Why do people need tutoring this early in the school year?" my mom asked.

"College essay editing. Help with papers. If you fall behind now, you'll be screwed by the time midterms come around."

She gave me a circumspect look but reluctantly accepted my answer.

We ate. The food was limp and unappetizing; of the many talents my parents possessed, cooking wasn't one of them. A bowl was passed around. The sound of chewing, a knife scratching a plate. No one spoke; we hardly looked at each other. Through the open window, voices drifted in from the family next door. They were chatting, laughing. My mother wiped her mouth with her napkin. She was listening; we all were. The fan over our oven whirred, sucking up all the air in the room.

After dinner, I retreated upstairs and caught my brother before he disappeared into his room.

"Hey," I said. "What do you know about Chris Pilker-Johns?"

Zack gave me a suspicious look. "Why? Are you going to 'tutor' him?"

"Maybe. What's he like?"

"Kind of pompous. Acts like he's more important than he is. Always exaggerates stories to make himself seem cool."

"Say I wanted to get information out of him. What do you think I'd have to offer?"

"Getting him a fake ID and an invite to some upper-classmen parties would probably do the trick," Zack said, the disdain clear in his tone.

I couldn't believe it. James had been right about offering him a party invitation.

Zack looked impatient. "Are you done?"

I nodded, and he closed the door. Behind it, I could hear his computer chair creak as he sat in it. "I'm back," he said into his gaming headphones as I walked down the hall to my room. I had to get to sleep. I had plans in the morning.

The next day, I woke up early and drove to the riverfront. It was still dark out. The fog was thick over the Potomac. Cars were scattered in the parking lot above the docks. I parked in the corner beneath a tree to be less conspicuous and stepped outside.

The rowing team practiced at the Head of the River, where docks bobbed beneath a rolling park dotted with picnic tables, which were all empty save for one, where a boy sat, looking out on the river. I hadn't been sure if he'd be there and felt relieved to find that my instincts had been right: even when injured, Chris would still come to crew practice in solidarity with his team. It was the perfect time to talk to him because all of his teammates were on the water.

Dew clung to the grass as I walked toward him, when a voice interrupted me.

"Hana?"

My breath seized. It was James.

"What are you doing here?" I demanded.

"Really, I should be asking you that, don't you think?" James said. "Because it looks an awful lot like you're about to go talk to Chris when we explicitly agreed that I was going to talk to him."

I'd been caught. "I'm just here to check out practice. See if anything looks unusual."

"Oh, come on," James said.

"We're investigating Logan," I said. "It's totally normal to want to see him in his element, which is crew."

"And are you noticing anything?" James said, gesturing to a boat gliding through the water in the distance.

"Not yet," I said. "But maybe I will."

"So you came here by yourself? You didn't think to tell me."

"You're here too. You didn't tell me."

"Chris is my source for an article that I'm researching. I don't have to tell you that I'm going to talk to him."

"You can't call him a source if he hasn't told you anything."

"I can't believe it," James said. "You were really coming down here to undermine me."

"I'm not trying to undermine you. I just don't trust your process."

"And I don't trust your process," James said.

"Great. So here we are. Two people who don't trust each other."

"What are you even going to offer him?" James asked.

"None of your business."

"So you have no idea."

"I have some idea."

"What is it?"

I hesitated. I didn't want to tell him.

"You're kidding," James said, studying me. "In exchange for telling you Logan's secret, you were going to offer him a party invite."

"Not just any party invite—Tiffany's party, which all the underclassmen want to be seen at. And I was going to get him a fake ID." Though I was rarely invited to parties anymore, Tiffany's were an exception. A year prior, I'd made a rumor about her visiting a plastic surgeon over the summer go away, and as a bonus, she'd offered me a standing invite to all of her parties. Adding one more person wouldn't be hard.

James didn't look impressed. "Okay, you're staying here and I'm going down to talk to Chris. I'll fill you in on what I find out when I get back."

"Fine," I muttered.

While James trudged down the hill to the picnic table, I found my way to a large rock jutting out of the lawn. Everyone called it Coin Rock because it had a small brass historical marker nailed into it that looked like a penny. From there, I had a perfect view of the river, where I could see Logan setting the stroke. The oars of his teammates followed his pace. They sliced through the water, their backs turned as he led them into the fog, an act of trust. I watched as it closed around them like breath in the cold.

When James returned, he looked confused. He nodded to his car. "Get in."

"What happened?" I asked.

"I was more honest this time," James said, turning the heat on. It smelled burnt like toast. "I told him I knew he was threatened by Logan. He looked freaked out and eventually admitted that he had been threatened but wouldn't tell me why. I asked if it had anything to do with Logan's family, hoping his reaction would let us know if our theory about Logan and his look-alike being brothers was true. But Chris only looked confused, then said no. Which means that whatever this doppelganger secret is that Chris and Luce have discovered—it isn't about twins or secret families."

"So Logan's look-alike isn't related to him?" I asked.

"I don't think so."

"Did you get anything else?"

"When I pressed him on what Logan was threatening him about, all he would say was that it had to do with one of Logan's friends and that if I don't drop it, he'd tell Logan I was asking questions."

"One of his friends?" I repeated. "Is his look-alike a friend of his?"

"I don't know. He seemed pretty panicked that I was there and kept glancing at the water. I think that's the only reason he told me anything. To get rid of me before the boat docked and Logan saw us talking."

"Do you think he was lying?" I asked.

"He seemed pretty earnest."

I wasn't convinced. Though James was good at discerning lie from truth, everyone made mistakes.

"So Chris discovers something about Logan and one of his friends. Logan finds out and threatens him in the bathroom, warning him not to tell anyone or he'll ruin his life. Then we see Logan at an old woman's mansion, meeting with a look-alike. How does it all fit together?"

James looked just as puzzled as I felt.

Through the fog, I could just make out the edge of a boat, skimming through the dark water, but as soon as I started to make out its shape, it disappeared again into the mist. Above it, the night dissolved into dawn.

7

"*So this is it, the* seat of power," Luce said to me.

It was a little over two years ago, the spring of our freshman year, and we were walking through Logan's house to the game room in the basement, where we were celebrating the end of midterms.

"It's just a house," I said, already embarrassed by her mocking disdain masked as anthropological interest in the upper-class lives of my friends, which I worried also extended to me.

Luce let out a laugh. "Just a house? It feels like we're inside a design catalog."

Logan's house had always felt deserted. It was huge and excessively air-conditioned, with furniture that looked like it had just been taken out of its packaging. In all the times I'd been there, I'd never seen anyone in the pool other than the occasional vacuum that snaked around the deep end. His parents, though around, were rarely visible. I only saw traces of them—a glass abandoned on the counter, a sweater draped over a chair, a pair of glasses resting on a magazine. Instead, the house was populated with people they hired to tend to it, who snuck around us, trying to stay out of sight.

It was Luce's first time at one of our get-togethers. She'd never been invited, and though she'd often asked me to bring her, I'd always deflected by saying that it wasn't very fun. The truth was that Luce, though interested in my friends, also seemed to resent them, and they in turn resented her, and the thought of forcing them together for the sake of Luce's curiosity sounded unpleasant at best.

Everyone was already there when we arrived. It was a small party, just Ruth, Marianne, Keith, Logan, and me—the original St. Francis lifers, who'd been there since elementary school. Luce took a seat on the sectional next to Ruth and Marianne, who didn't look pleased to see her.

They were talking about our English teacher, Ms. Slater, who was new that year and who had tricked us all into thinking she was our friend because she was young and hip in an aging-punk-rocker kind of way, and then shocked us with brutal grading.

"All the new teachers are pretty merciless," Ruth said, eyeing Luce. It was a clear dig at Luce's dad, Mr. Herrera, who was the new AP History teacher.

If Marianne was our group's rosy-cheeked Renaissance muse, then Ruth was a brutalist painting. Severe yet visually pleasing in its stark minimalism. Not for everyone, but revered nonetheless.

"Maybe you're not as smart as you think you are," Luce said with a shrug, and grabbed a handful of popcorn from the bowl on the table.

At the end of the couch, Logan and Keith turned to us, amused with Luce's retort.

"Merciless," Keith said of Luce. "Just like her dad."

Keith was Logan's best friend and a mash-up of paradoxes—a perennial jock and crew star who surprised us when he tried out for Shakespeare's *Macbeth*, that year's school theatrical production, and got cast as the lead. Now he sank back into the couch cushions and resumed reading curled-up pages of the play.

While Ruth simmered, Logan got up, retrieved two sodas from a glass mini fridge, and handed them to me and Luce without us having to ask.

Luce looked surprised. She always expected the worst of people.

"Don't mind Ruth," Logan said to Luce. "She's an acquired taste."

"Chopped liver," Keith said.

"Marmite," Marianne chimed in.

"Bitter melon," I said.

Ruth frowned. "I like all of those foods. Well, the first

two, at least. I've never tried bitter melon." She turned to Logan. "I thought you were on my side."

"I'm trying to be a good host," Logan said, and sat across from Keith, where a worn paperback of *Macbeth* lay on the cushion. He picked it up. "Okay," he said with a dramatic flourish. "Art thou ready to practice thine lines?"

Even Ruth managed a laugh. With Logan reading the part of Lady Macbeth, they began to rehearse one of Keith's scenes.

"I still can't believe you're acting now," Marianne said to Keith. "It's so cute."

Keith only shrugged. "I like movies. I always thought it would be cool to act in one. This is the closest thing."

"Art thou calling Macbeth cute?" Logan asked.

"Seems like someone is getting a little too into it," said Ruth. "Maybe you should start acting too, Logan."

"My dad would flip," Logan said. "And anyway, I don't have time."

"Cursed be thine father and waning be thine moons," Keith corrected.

"Keith found time," Marianne said.

Keith nodded. "Mine moons art plentiful."

"Keith doesn't have my dad," Logan said.

"Cursed be not mine father," Keith said.

"What, acting doesn't fit your image?" Luce asked Logan.

"Definitely not," Logan said. "I mentioned once that I

wanted to take some art classes in college, and he basically said that it would be a waste of time."

The room went quiet. We all knew about his parents and their high expectations.

"If you're interested in it, it wouldn't be a waste of time," Luce said.

"Tell him that," Logan murmured.

"Maybe Macbeth should be cute," Keith said. "Maybe that's the way I make the interpretation mine."

"I know we're supposed to like Shakespeare, but I honestly can't figure out what he means half the time," I said.

"Same," said Marianne.

"You just have to feel the words," Keith said. "This whole play is about people hiding their intentions and backstabbing each other for political gain."

"We wouldn't know anything about that," Ruth said sarcastically.

"Seriously, some of this stuff cuts pretty deep," Keith said. "Listen to this: 'False face must hide what the false heart doth know.' If that doesn't apply to every person at St. Francis, I don't know what does."

"Are you saying we're all fake?" I asked.

"I'm saying you're already performing Shakespeare," Keith said. "You just don't realize it."

"So we're all actors, then?" I asked. "Putting on a nice face. Saying the right things. Pretending everything is fine."

"Playing the part our parents assigned us," Logan said.

His eyes drifted to mine, and a tacit understanding passed between us.

The thing about Logan and me was that everyone around us had agreed that it was inevitable that we end up together. In theory it made sense, and though we'd played along because we were both people pleasers, I knew he wasn't interested in me like that, and I wasn't in him. I'd considered it, of course—it was impossible not to when everyone around you was suggesting it, but when I was alone with him, I couldn't help but feel like I was looking at the worst parts of myself: the carefully crafted image, the smile and false cheerfulness, which seemed to strain in moments when no one was looking. I could never really know him because he was hiding himself, the same way that I was. I wondered what role he would play if he could choose. What role I would play.

"So what are we in, a tragedy or a comedy?" Logan asked.

"Are you laughing?" Keith asked.

"No."

"Then there's your answer."

The humor had left the room, and we sat, hushed, no one sure what to say next.

"So are you friends with all the theater kids now?" Marianne asked, breaking the silence.

"Not really," Keith said. "They're all a little suspicious of me. I have been talking to Adam, though. He's actually pretty funny."

"Ugh, Adam," Ruth said. "Always wanting people to look at him."

"I didn't know he was in the play," I said.

"He isn't," Keith said. "They convinced him to do the marketing—posters and playbills, stuff like that—so he's around sometimes during rehearsals."

"I find him cringeworthy," Ruth said.

"He can be a little much," Marianne said.

"The way he always name-drops people his parents know," Logan said. "As if he's the only one at school with connections."

"And how he sucks up to the teachers," Ruth groaned. "I can't stand it."

I didn't know Adam well, nor did he inspire an immediate reaction in me the way he seemed to in others, but I could see what they were all talking about. He had a quiet desperation to be seen that was uncomfortable to witness.

"Yeah," Keith said, uncharacteristically quiet.

"But everyone at school name-drops," Luce countered. "And everyone sucks up to the teachers; you just don't like that he's good at it." The room went silent. "I think Adam's funny," she continued. "At least he's doing his own thing. He's not boring, which you can't say about most of the other people at school."

I blinked, stunned at Luce's insult. Marianne and Ruth clearly felt the same. I tried to figure out what I could say to keep the peace when I noticed Logan lingering on Luce, chastened. Was he embarrassed?

"Right, so should we do the thing?" I said, trying to change the subject.

Keith closed his book. "Yeah. Anon or whatever."

Ruth looked like she was going to say something to Luce but decided against it.

A bowl containing pens and slips of paper sat on the coffee table. I handed it to Keith, and while he passed it around, I caught Luce's eye and silently demanded to know what in the world she thought she was doing. She only shrugged.

"You know the drill," Keith said. "Write down the worst thing you've done this month. Don't hold back."

It was a game we played. We wrote the worst thing we'd done in recent memory and put it in a jar. Then we chose a slip at random and took it home. It was both a release of pressure, the only time in our lives that we could have any relief from the perfection demanded of us in our everyday lives, and an exercise in trust. A way of chaining ourselves to each other with our worst deeds.

I wondered if Luce would roll her eyes at it, but instead she took a piece of paper and began to write. I did the same. When everyone was finished, we each chose one.

I folded it into my pocket without reading it, as was the rule, and resumed conversation. All the while, I felt it there in my jeans, someone else's secret. It was a solace, knowing that I wasn't the only one who had tried and failed again at perfection. I didn't know then that it was the last time I'd go to a party at Logan's house.

On the ride home, I unfolded it. Usually, I could guess the author, either by their handwriting or the confession itself, but this time, I wasn't sure. It looked like Keith's handwriting, but it could have been Logan's, too. I read it again, wondering what it meant.

I haven't been honest about who I am.

I thought about that slip of paper as I drove through the winding streets of a town thirty minutes outside of Alexandria. Though that last party at Logan's house had been over two years ago, the confession had stuck with me. It could have applied to any of us.

"Where are you?" James's voice pulled me out of my thoughts and back into the car.

"Drifting, I guess," I said.

It was a rainy autumn night, and we were following my phone's navigation back to the mansion in McClean. The roads were slick with matted leaves, and the pattering on the windshield made everything blur into an impressionist painting.

James's house had been on the way, so I'd picked him up. Though I'd known I was going there, I hadn't considered what it would feel like to pull into the driveway, to see him open the door and saunter over to my car. I'd always loved

James's house. Amid a sprawl of ornate monstrosities, his was an unpretentious blue house on a square of grass with an apple tree out front. It reminded me of him—practical, familiar. I was glad that it hadn't changed.

"I have a mystery for you," James said, the way he used to when we were kids, huddling under a ballroom table, the tablecloth muffling the sounds of adults around us. "A crew star and his look-alike meet at an elderly heiress's mansion at night. The crew star and his look-alike are not related. What are they doing?"

It felt more like a game to think of it as a mystery from a book. "Some kind of con," I said. "They want the heiress's fortune, so they're tricking her somehow. Maybe she has dementia and they've taken over her house and have forced her to live in the attic."

"Very *Jane Eyre*," James said.

I was embarrassed to admit that I hadn't read *Jane Eyre*.

"The problem is that the crew star is already rich," I said. "He doesn't need a fortune. He doesn't need anything."

My phone navigation told me to turn right.

"He has to need something," James said. "Or *want* is a better word. Rich people do wildly despicable things all the time to get what they want. So what does the crew star want?"

I thought back to the party at Logan's house and the way he'd talked about how his father wouldn't approve of him acting or drawing.

"To please his parents," I said, when, through the blades of the windshield wipers, I saw a person standing in the middle of the street.

I slammed on the brakes. The car squealed as it skidded through the rain. James shouted. My head jerked forward. Out of the corner of my eye, I saw James lurch, his head thudding against the window. I closed my eyes and willed the car to stop until finally, all went still.

"What was that?" James asked between breaths.

I took a quick inventory of myself, then him. James was rubbing his forehead but seemed otherwise okay. I squinted through the wipers to the road, but it was empty.

"I—I thought I saw someone," I said.

I was too stunned to move. A wave of nausea passed over me. I felt like I was going to be sick. "Did I?"

The logical thing to do was to get out and check, but I couldn't. I was too scared of what I might find.

"Did you hit someone, you mean?" James asked. "No. There was no one there."

"Are you sure?"

James hopped out of the car to check. I tried to gauge his expression through the rain mottling the window, but I couldn't.

"There's no one there," James said after hurrying back inside. "It must have been that." He pointed to a bronze statue in the middle of a roundabout. "Some Confederate general."

I sank into my seat and let out a sigh of relief. "Sorry, it was hard to see in the rain."

James studied me with concern. "Of course."

"Are you okay?" I asked him.

"Yeah. Are you?"

I nodded, but I wasn't actually sure that I was.

Behind us, a driver laid on his horn.

"Okay, okay," I murmured, and pulled down the road, steadying my hands on the steering wheel so that they would stop shaking.

We drove the rest of the way in silence, listening to the patter of the rain and the swish of the wipers until the steady voice of the navigation system announced, "You have reached your destination."

8

Two years ago, in a life that now seemed as distant as a dream, I saw something strange outside my window.

I was in my bedroom, trying to write an essay about John Milton but too distracted by my thoughts to work, when I noticed movement through the curtains. I pulled them back to see a police car driving past the front walk.

After a series of car break-ins one summer, everyone had pooled their money to pay for overtime officers to patrol the streets, so it wasn't uncommon to see a police car rolling past our house. Still, I had an odd feeling about it. I let the curtain drop and turned back to my computer.

Then, out of the corner of my eye, another police car. Or was it the same one? I peeked out of the curtains again. The street was empty; nothing was moving. Then, through the canopy of trees, I thought I saw a flash of blue paint, a glint of metal.

Across the street, I spied our neighbor Susan staring at our house from her living room window. What was she looking at?

I ventured downstairs. My parents weren't home, and my brother was at a friend's. The house was quiet except for Genie, who was vacuuming, leaving clean streaks of carpet in her wake. I felt sick to my stomach as I crept over them to the front door. I didn't look out the bay windows. Something about the way Susan had looked at our house, as though she was seeing something new and grotesque about it, told me that I should keep my face hidden. Instead, I leaned toward the pane of frosted glass that framed the door and tried to see a muddled version of what was outside, when a shadow passed over it and someone banged on the front door.

I froze. Normally, I would have answered, but an unnatural stillness had settled around the house.

I held my breath and backed away from the door.

Through the pane I could see the glint of an officer's uniform. He rang the doorbell. Its chime echoed down the hallway, though if Genie heard it over the roar of the vacuum, she didn't let on.

I ran upstairs and called my dad on his cell phone. When he didn't pick up, I called my mom, but hers went to voice mail too. According to our family calendar, they were both in meetings; neither would answer for the next hour. I could call their assistants, but say what? A police officer was here and I was too scared to answer?

I stood in my bedroom, unsure of what to do. I wanted to look out the window and see what was going on but didn't want anyone to know I was there. Maybe I was overreacting. Maybe there was suspicious activity in the neighborhood and they were here to do a routine check. Maybe they had already left.

The doorbell chimed again, asserting their presence.

I tried Luce. No answer. Then texted her.

<Hey, are you there?

Usually, she wrote back almost immediately, but that day, she was silent.

It was an unseasonably hot Friday in late September, the first month of tenth grade. Earlier that week, my friend Cecily had invited me and few of our other friends to her pool. I hadn't been planning on going; after getting close with Luce, I'd started to find their company petty and unpleasant and had grown distant from them.

Now I stuffed my swimsuit in a bag and crept downstairs.

There was a path behind our house that wound around a neighbor's side yard and out into the street beyond. I dusted off my bike, walked it through the bushes, and pedaled out into the thick Virginia heat.

Cecily's house was ten minutes away by car, double that

by bike. We called it a house, but really it was something completely different. A mansion, maybe, or an estate, but even those didn't feel accurate. The best word to describe it was *compound*, which was fitting, since Cecily's parents were government contractors. No one was exactly sure what they did, only that they made a lot of money and were rarely home.

Marianne, Ruth, and Sloan were sitting poolside when I arrived.

"Hana," Cecily said, emerging from beneath a sun canopy with a glass of iced tea. "You came."

I forced a smile and tried to look carefree. "I finished my paper earlier than expected and didn't want to miss it."

Cecily spritzed herself with tanning spray and nodded to the doors. "There are drinks inside. Help yourself."

After changing into my swimsuit in the bathroom and splashing my face with water, I sat in the empty seat next to Marianne. She was splayed in a lounge chair in red sunglasses, her bikini straps slipped off to prevent tan lines. A glossy magazine languished in her lap, unread, while she, Ruth, and Sloan gossiped about who'd gotten dumped over the summer, who'd gained weight and who'd lost it, and who'd done secret summer school.

"No Luce?" Ruth observed, lowering her sunglasses.

"Not today," I said.

Ruth exchanged a look with Marianne, then said, "Shame."

I was too on edge to socialize, so I sipped my iced tea and stared at the swan float drifting around Cecily's magnificent pool, the water bluer than the sky and so still that it looked like glass reflecting the clouds.

I'd hoped that if I left, the police officers would go away, our neighbor Susan would resume her daytime TV habit, and I'd ride my bike into our driveway with little fanfare and find my mother inside, emptying takeout into serving bowls for dinner. It would be like nothing had ever happened. A reset.

"Would you ever do it?" Ruth asked me.

My heart lurched. "Do what?"

Ruth looked at me funny. "Go under the knife."

I let out a breath of relief. They were talking about Cara Hutchinson and how she'd supposedly gotten a nose job.

"No way," I said, trying to steady my voice.

Ruth frowned. "Easy for you to say. You were born with impeccable skin and no unwanted hair anywhere on your body. You could have food poisoning for three days and still look like you walked off a photoshoot for an all-natural makeup campaign."

Normally, I would have relished the compliment, but that day I was too anxious to enjoy it.

"I'd like to change my nose," Sloan said. "It's too big."

I'd always thought Sloan's nose was nice.

"My mom said she'd pay for laser hair removal," said Cecily.

"You should do it," Ruth said. "Morgan got her unibrow done and said it wasn't that painful."

"She also gets Botox," Sloan said. "She claims it's for her migraines."

"Is that why she makes that weird face when she's surprised?" Cecily asked.

"It probably is for her migraines," I said. "It's not like anyone has wrinkles at our age."

They all seemed to ignore me. "Speaking of hair, supposedly after she heard Luke say she was furry, Nina started bleaching her arm hair," Ruth said.

"Brutal," Cecily said. "But she does have hairy arms."

I secretly hated conversations like these. Though the point was to make yourself feel better by mocking others, it only made me more self-conscious. Was everyone thinking the same things about me?

While they debated the pros and cons of waxing, I checked my phone. Still no response from Luce or my parents.

"Are you okay?" Marianne asked me while the others continued the conversation. "You don't seem like your normal talkative self."

"I'm fine," I said, and gave her a thin smile. "Just stuff with my mom." It was a perennial excuse, one that didn't require any further explanation because everyone clashed with their mother.

"You need to add water," Marianne said, getting up from her chair. "It cheers everyone up." Before I could blink, she dove into the pool, her blond tresses undulating through the water as she surfaced.

"Come on," she said, coaxing me with her finger. "Empty your brain for a minute."

Maybe she was right. I managed a smile and plunged into the water behind her, enjoying the shock of cold on my skin. Marianne had already lifted herself onto a swan float and was wringing out her hair. I swam a few strokes, then flipped on my back and let myself float. The voices of my friends were muffled through the water, both present and distant. I drifted, admiring the clouds as they passed above me, and for a moment, it felt like everything was going to be okay.

I don't know how long I was there. A while. Then a shadow stretched over me, blocking the light. A voice, urgent. Then my name.

I emerged to find Cecily's housekeeper standing by the edge of the pool. "Miss Hana," she said. "There's someone here for you."

Everyone had stopped talking. Though there were no sirens, no shouting, the atmosphere had changed, as though it was now under pressure. I glanced around, bewildered, but no one offered an explanation.

Everyone's eyes were on me as I hopped out of the pool,

grabbed a towel, and followed Cecily's housekeeper inside, my wet footsteps evaporating in the heat as though I had never been there at all.

My mom's assistant, Claudia, was waiting for me in the kitchen, typing quickly into her phone. When she saw me, her face dropped.

"What's going on?" I asked.

Claudia was pretty and efficient, with a perky ponytail that bobbed as she walked and an answer for any question. But now, for the first time since I'd known her, she looked like she didn't know what to say. She tucked her phone in her bag. "Let's just get you home."

The drive back was a blur. I remember the gates closing behind us as we pulled out of Cecily's driveway. I remember asking Claudia again what was going on and her hesitating before managing to say, "It's your dad."

My dad? I was confused. My heart dropped. "Is he okay? Is he hurt?"

"No, it's nothing like that."

Time stretched out, making the short ride home feel like an eternity. We pulled down my street and saw all of the familiar houses that I'd grown up next to exactly where they should be, their American flags flapping in the wind. That's when I saw the reporters.

They swarmed the street in front of my house, making it almost impossible for us to turn into the driveway. They were in vans, in cars; they crowded us, pressing their cameras and microphones against the windows of the car as we waited for the gate, which we normally never kept closed, to open.

I shrank back, startled by their ferocity, by their muffled voices shouting questions as they tried to peer through the tint.

I must have looked scared, because Claudia reached over and touched my hand. "It's going to be okay."

My bathing suit had soaked through my T-shirt and shorts, making my skin prickle in the air-conditioning and my hands shake. I tucked them under my thighs to keep warm and nodded, grateful for her lie.

We found my mom pacing the kitchen in front of the TV, talking frantically into her cell phone while Ruby circled her legs, barking. Another cell phone rang and rang on the counter. Claudia rushed to pick it up, and I was left to piece things together from snippets of their conversations.

"I don't know where he was that night," my mother said.

"Genie said they asked to see the garage," Claudia said.

"Can we get access to this purported video?" my mother said.

"They're both here. We haven't told them yet," Claudia said.

"The reporters are saying he could be charged with manslaughter if she dies," my mother said.

I was huddled over Ruby, trying to calm her down, when I heard my dad's name on the television.

The screen showed a video of him being escorted down the steps of the Senate office building by police officers. I watched as reporters swarmed him, their cameras flashing like gunfire. He winced at the sudden assault and shielded his face with his arm.

According to the anchor, four days prior, a local woman had been hit by a car and was in critical condition. The driver had left the scene, and the case had gone unsolved until video footage was discovered of a black Land Rover fleeing the scene. My father.

He was being arrested, though it wasn't clear what they were going to charge him with. He had yet to make a formal statement.

I felt suddenly light-headed and steadied myself on the arm of the couch.

"Turn that off," my mother said, cupping the receiver of the phone.

I took my time getting the remote. I wanted to turn it off but couldn't stop watching. The camera cut back to the sidewalk, where my father was telling the reporters that he had no comment at this time. He sounded nervous, which made me scared. I watched one of the police officers place his hand on my father's head, guiding him into the back seat.

Now, my mother mouthed.

Ruby yapped at my feet. I turned it off, but it didn't

matter; the image of my father's face, blank and scared, was already seared into my memory.

It couldn't be true. And yet all the evidence was there. According to my mother's side of the phone conversation, they had impounded his Land Rover, which we rarely drove and had been parked in the garage for days with a crushed headlight and a sickening indentation on the side. And there on the screen was the blurry yet damning video footage from the security camera of a nearby house showing his car swerve then collide with a grainy figure on the edge of the screen. If you didn't know, you might be able to convince yourself it was a street sign. Or a mailbox. Or a statue.

It couldn't be. They'd gotten it wrong. Except they hadn't.

9

I tried to compose myself as we pulled up to Marion Good-joy's mansion, which looked exactly as it had the night we'd seen Logan there: hedges trimmed, oil lamps flickering, curtains pulled.

Even though my father's crash was two years ago, I still thought of it constantly. Flashes of memory appeared when I least expected them to, catching me off guard. All it took was the click of a camera, the glint of an officer's badge, the distant wail of a siren to thrust me back into the past. Or, like today, an illusion cast by a statue in a roundabout.

I still felt shaken by it. Since my dad's crash, I'd been a nervous driver, worried I'd repeat his mistake. I was, after all, driving my father's Land Rover, the dent still in the side, the headlight fixed cheaply so that it shone a dim yellow because we couldn't afford a proper job after all of the lawsuits. I gripped the steering wheel, trying to will my hands to stop trembling.

James didn't say anything, but I was sure he had some idea of what I was thinking about.

It was just a trick of the darkness, I told myself as I parked where I had two weeks before and turned off the engine. Nothing to dwell on.

We'd returned to the mansion out of desperation. We didn't have any leads on the case—Chris was a dead end, we'd researched ourselves in circles, and I'd staked out Luce's house more nights than I cared to count and had discovered nothing.

"It's funny that someone who made their money from logging lives in a brick house," James said.

"It hadn't occurred to me, but yeah."

A light was on upstairs. I wondered if it was her bedroom.

We weren't sure what we expected to see. We were still trying to figure out Logan's secret, and through it, what Three had hired me to help Luce fix. We were hoping to get another glimpse of Logan's look-alike, though we didn't know if he lived there. I eyed the neighboring houses, manicured and still. The only signs of life were the dim glow of a few distant windows.

"Who do you think lives in that one?" James asked, nodding to a castle-like mansion perched atop a long driveway.

"A reclusive widow whose husband died under mysterious circumstances," I said. "She only comes out on the evening of the third Friday of every month, when she opens the door and puts a single empty dinner plate on the front stoop, which she collects in the morning. No one knows why."

"A dinner plate," James said, intrigued.

It was a game we used to play when we were kids and bored at fundraising events with our parents. We'd started playing it with discarded business cards, which we'd collected from tables. We'd read each other the names and invent mysteries about the eccentric rich people they belonged to.

"What about that one?" I asked, nodding to a Tudor looming behind a halo of sprinklers watering a vast, velvety lawn. Two luxury sports cars were parked in the driveway.

"High-powered corporate couple with matching haircuts who spend most of the week flying around the country separately for work," James said. "They own apartments in New York and LA, love going on juice cleanses, and spend their evenings watching the news on their exercise bikes."

"They own a lot of stocks," I added.

James grinned. "Okay, that one," he said, motioning to a columned colonial mansion framed by spiral topiaries.

"Plastic surgeon and his third wife, who owns an online exercise empire," I said. "She secretly gets procedures done by him. They own three little dogs who pee all over the house."

"What kind of weird rich person do you think you'd be?" James asked.

"I don't know if you remember, but I was already rich once," I said.

"Yeah, but you had to be on your best behavior because everyone was looking at you. What if no one was looking and you could do whatever you wanted?"

I was embarrassed to admit that I'd never considered a life other than the one I'd had. When I was living it, I'd assumed life would always continue that way, and when it was gone, the only life I could imagine was the one I'd lost. So instead, I said the first idea that popped into my mind. "I'd install hidden doors and passageways all over my house. Behind bookshelves, camouflaged in the wall-paper."

"Classic," James said. "Where would they lead to?"

"An office where I kept confidential files. Another one that had an electric organ that I'd play when I had guests staying with me, to really freak them out."

"An organ?" James asked. "Why?"

I shrugged. "My parents forced me to learn the piano, but I always thought the organ would be cooler. If I'm ever rich again, I'll get one."

"You do realize there's a device called a keyboard, which can sound like an electric organ and isn't that expensive?"

"Not the same," I said. "Also one passageway would have to lead to a tunnel that led outside, in case I needed to escape."

"But it's your house. Why would you need to escape?"

James would never understand that no matter how financially secure I was, I would always feel like I was one mistake away from losing it all. I shrugged. "Just in case. What kind of eccentric would you be?"

I waited for him to say something annoyingly righteous, like he'd give all his money away and live in a spare house, eating only ramen while he investigated the sins of the upper class, but he surprised me. "I'd buy the house behind yours. We could build connecting tunnels. That way you'd have somewhere to escape to."

Somehow, without me realizing it, the tenor of our conversation had changed from teasing to sincere, and though I had many talents, sincerity wasn't one of them. "Classic James," I murmured. "Can't think of your own eccentric lifestyle, so you're borrowing mine."

"What, so you'd prefer it if I bought a twenty-four-hour news network and made it honest? Or donated all my money to charity and lived like an ascetic?"

"Those are definitely more on brand."

"You realize I could do those things while living in the house behind yours."

"I guess you could." Sitting there with him felt like

putting on a well-loved sweatshirt—so easy to slip back into, to remember why it had always been your favorite. "It's not much of an escape hatch if everyone knows where I'm going, since we'd clearly be friends."

"Then we'll just have to pretend like we don't know each other. It would be a secret friendship, only done through hidden doors and tunnels."

Though he'd meant it to sound fun, it didn't feel very different from my life right now. Even my fantasies about the future involved me being alone.

"Why do you like to do this?" James asked as if reading my mind.

"Do what?"

"Fixing. Forcing yourself to be around all the people that tore you down. Doesn't it just unearth the past?"

When I first started fixing, I liked being in proximity to my old life. My ex-friends were the only life I knew, and interacting with them felt familiar. But I quickly learned that I would never be invited back into their fold, nor did I want to be. They'd already shunned me; it would never be the same. What I truly wanted was to reverse time, to have all the pieces of my old life put themselves back together. Fixing other people's problems could never do that, but it was a distraction. Focusing on other people's problems, learning that I wasn't the only one who was suffering, turned out to be a comfort, like a secret written on a slip of paper and tucked into my pocket. If I poured myself into someone's life, if I fixed their problems, I could, for a few moments, forget that mine existed.

I was about to respond when a pair of headlights caught my attention.

"Wait," I said, putting a hand on his arm. "Look."

A car was pulling into the driveway of the mansion. Though the windows were closed, I could hear music pressing against the glass. I took a picture of its license plate just before it vanished into the detached garage on the side of the house.

We waited until a man emerged from the darkness. It was hard to see what he looked like, though I could tell from his stocky stature that it wasn't our doppelganger. Judging from the music, his laid-back posture, and the way that he sauntered across the pavement, I guessed that he was young. He was looking at his phone, and from its glare I could make out a protruding brow and a neck as thick as a linebacker's. He was wearing a polo shirt with sunglasses hanging off the collar. I watched the glowing rectangle of his phone sway, suspended in the night, as he walked to the side door and stepped inside. A light flipped on inside, then another. We watched him walk through the house like that, a trail of lights turning on, then off. *Follow me*, they seemed to say.

It took days to find the name of the man in the polo shirt. First, I'd brokered a trade with one of our classmates,

Analisa Jimenez—in exchange for a small favor, I would get her an advanced copy of the forthcoming album of her favorite pop singer, Nico Smith. Nico Smith's manager was a family friend of another classmate, Paulina Williams, who had agreed to help me if I got her tickets to a sold-out art show that Adam's neighbor had curated, which meant I had to text Adam, and so on and so forth.

When Analisa agreed, I sent her the license plate of the man's car and asked her to run it. Analisa's father was one of the most famous defense attorneys on the East Coast and subscribed to a database that could run plate numbers. She sent it to her father's assistant, who retrieved the owner's name and address.

His name was Ian Goodjoy, and according to his address, he lived in the brick mansion. He ran a nonprofit called A Brighter Future, which funded early literacy programs. In the professional headshots of him online, he appeared to be in his late twenties and had the look of an aging frat boy who had stuffed himself into a suit. He was Marion Goodjoy's grandnephew.

A Brighter Future. Why did it sound so familiar?

According to his bio, Ian Goodjoy had gone to St. Francis, then Princeton, after which he decided to move back to Virginia and found his nonprofit because his passion was education. Fine. Normal. Boring.

I clicked through its website, looking for anything that seemed amiss, but it seemed like a generic, unremarkable organization. I didn't recognize anyone on the board or staff. I'd never been to the address listed or seen anyone pictured in the photos.

"So we have a guy living with an elderly relative, running an education nonprofit," James said. "So what?"

We were sitting on the quad during lunch period, trying to piece together all the scraps of information we'd found.

"Why do I know this place?" I murmured. Had my mom worked with them before? Had we gone to one of their fundraising events?

"The fact that he went to St. Francis seems notable," James continued.

Or maybe one of my classmates had volunteered there for our school's Community Service Day?

"But what does it have to do with Logan or his look-alike?" James asked.

I wasn't sure. "Three hires me to figure out what Luce is working on. I learn that Luce has been uncovering a secret of Logan's, which involves him meeting with a look-alike in a mansion. We later learn that a man named Ian Goodjoy lives there. Ian runs a nonprofit called A Brighter Future."

"Maybe they're volunteering?" James offered.

"Why would they want to keep that a secret?" I said.

James shook his head. "I don't know."

I picked at my sandwich. Across the quad, the dining hall door opened, and Adam stepped outside with his friend Caitlin. Just after they parted ways, my phone vibrated.

>So, how's it going?

It was Three. Beside me, James was still talking about the case.

"Hey," I said, interrupting him. "Look at this."

Just as he read the message, a new one came in.

>I see you've enlisted a friend. I didn't authorize that, but I suppose I can tolerate it.

I froze and scanned the campus. Dozens of people were scattered around the quad, most of them with their phones out. Three could have been any of them, including Adam, who was walking down the path, looking at his phone. It couldn't be him, could it? Or maybe Three was inside, looking at us through a window.

"What should I write?" I asked James.

"Anything. Doesn't matter. Just keep them talking."

<It was an accident, I typed back. Parallel cases that converged.

>Now that there are two of you, have you made any progress?

It was normal for clients to check in about the progress of their cases, but Three wasn't a normal client, and I didn't want to divulge any information until I had a sense of what their intentions were.

<I have some leads. Why, are you in a rush?

>That difficult? I knew I'd given you a hard one, but figured you'd be a little further along by now.

The way Three talked about the case made me wonder

if they already knew what Luce was up to and had hired me as a test.

<If you already know what Luce is working on, then why don't you just tell me what it is so I can fix it?

>You seem upset. Is it because you're confused?

<I'm not upset.

>But you are confused. And you don't like feeling confused. Would you like me to help you feel better?

<What do you mean?

>Since it's looking like you're not going to get there on your own, I'd like to offer you a hint. It's a shame because they always said you had a bright future.

Part of me wanted to reject Three's hint just to prove that I could solve it on my own, but when I glanced at James, he looked at me like I was out of my mind. "Take it," he said.

<Okay, I wrote. What is it?

>I already gave it to you.

How could Three have already given me a hint? We'd barely exchanged any substantive information.

>Do you understand? Three asked. Or have I finally given you a case you can't fix?

I reread Three's messages, trying to decode them, when two words stood out to me.

"Bright future," James said.

"Like Ian's nonprofit," I whispered. "A Brighter Future."

Logan's secret had something to do with that place.

"What if it's a front?" James said. "What if they don't really do what they say they do?"

"A front for what, though—?" I began to say, when a new message came in.

>Oh wait, Three said. Silly me. You already had a case you couldn't fix. The big one. The most important one.

I wasn't sure what Three was talking about. I'd never been given a case I couldn't fix.

>You know what I'm talking about, don't you? Three asked.

I didn't, but something about Three's tone worried me. It felt like a riddle. One that I wouldn't like the answer to.

>Oh come on, really? Three said. Better put your phone away. You might not want your partner to read this.

My throat grew dry. Was I getting nervous?

>No? Okay.

James gave me a questioning look, but I ignored it. I could feel his breath on my shoulder as we waited for the next text to come in.

>You. You're the case you haven't been able to fix.

I gripped my phone. James's voice sounded suddenly distant, muffled. "What is that supposed to mean?" he asked.

I didn't know. It was true and it was a lie.

>But don't worry, Three said. We'll fix that, too, by the end.

10

I had no idea what Three was talking about. At least that's
what I told James. The texts didn't mean anything; they
were just cryptic comments meant to rile me up.

Except I worried they weren't. Three was right—the
one thing I'd desperately wanted to fix was my own life.
Sure, Three could have guessed as much, but what did
they mean when they said, *We'll fix that, too, by the end?*

I thought about Three's riddle as I walked down the
halls and sat through class. When I got home, I ate dinner
quickly, then excused myself to my room, where I opened
my computer. The only way I would figure out what Three
meant was if I got to the end of the case, which meant I
needed to untangle Logan's secret, the thing that Luce was
working on.

According to Three's hint, Logan and his look-alike had
something to do with Ian Goodjoy's nonprofit, A Brighter

Future. But what? It was possible it was a front, though for what, we weren't sure. Everything about it online looked normal, unremarkable. I typed its name into my browser and scanned its results, trying to find some previously over-looked detail that might unlock the case, when my phone vibrated. It was Adam.

>If you were deciding between two brands of coffee, one with a logo of a goat, and another with a logo of a mountain, which would you choose?
<I don't drink coffee, I wrote.
>I know. It's a hypothetical.
<The goat sounds kind of childish, so I'm inclined to choose the mountain, but I'd remember the goat more, so maybe that's the best logo.
>That's what I'm thinking, Adam wrote. Memorable over classy.
<Are you working for Starbucks now? Because if you are, I want free smoothies.
>No, but I'll note that for the future. I'm trying to build my branding portfolio for summer internship applications.

I let out a long exhale. I should have been looking at summer internships or working on my college applications or even just making some headway on my homework, but I couldn't bring myself to. Three was right. I once had a bright future. Now it didn't seem that way anymore, so why bother trying?

<That's great, I wrote back.

There was a long pause. Finally Adam replied.

>Are you okay? You seem different. No banter. No witticisms.

<I'm stuck on a case. I can't figure it out.

>Do you need an extra opinion? I'm always here for you.

I let out a laugh. Adam was always coming up with new ways to try to get me to tell him about my cases. Normally, I deflected, but that night, I hesitated. Adam's parents were heavily connected in the nonprofit world. I might as well ask.

<I can't tell you, but I can give you a hint.

>I love hints.

<Have you ever heard of a nonprofit called A Brighter Future?

> . . . that's not a hint. It's a question.

<Hints can come in many forms. So have you?

It took him a moment to respond.

>I have.

<And?

>I thought you were supposed to know everything, he wrote finally.

<I do know everything. This is a test.

>Why are you suddenly interested in charity?

<I've always been heavily involved in giving back to my community.

I could picture Adam rolling his eyes.

>It can't just be about volunteering. You wouldn't need me for that.

<Just tell me.

>What fix would involve a boring education nonprofit? Or maybe it's an auxiliary fix to the main fix. An Inception of fixes.

Adam knew me too well.

>Okay fine, he wrote. I don't know much about it other than what you probably found online. But I do know someone who does.

<Who?

When he didn't write back, I sent him three more messages.

<Is it someone at school?

<Our year?

<Do I know them?

>Yes, yes, and yes. Hold on. I just need to relish this moment in which I know something that you don't.

I sank into the pillows and waited for him to respond.

>How about this, he said. I'll give you a hint in return.

I was tired of hints. I had too many of them, and none seemed to lead anywhere. I grumbled as I feigned enthusiasm.

<I love hints.

A brief pause, followed by a message.

>She never stays in one place.

I stayed up late, thinking about Adam's clue, trying to figure out what it meant. Then, on the edge of sleep, when the remnants of the day refracted back to me as if distorted through a prism, it came to me. I felt a tug in my chest. A thread beginning to unravel.

She never stays in one place.

I thought of Adam's clue later that week as we pulled up to a crass white mansion that looked like a casino modeled after the Pantheon.

"You're kidding, right?" James asked as I cruised past the house looking for a parking spot. The street was already packed with cars.

Dumb little topiaries carved into spirals framed the front walk. A luxury real estate sign was out front. COMING SOON, it said.

"You want to solve this mystery, right?" I asked.

James looked up at the house with distaste.

"Then we have to talk to Tiffany."

Tiffany DeLuca was the answer to Adam's riddle and the reason why A Brighter Future had sounded so familiar to me—because she used to volunteer there.

Adam's clue, *She never stays in one place*, referred to her family. Tiffany was our classmate and the daughter of a contractor who built some of the most grotesque mansions in the DMV area. They were constantly moving around, living in one monstrosity before selling it while they built the next one. Every time they got ready to sell the house they were living in, Tiffany threw a moving-out party, where she invited everyone in our class who mattered. And me, thanks to the fix I'd done for her the summer before, when I'd made a rumor about her visiting a plastic surgeon's office disappear.

For the past few years, Tiffany had dated a boy two years older than us named Dev Prashad. He'd gone to St. Francis, then taken a break from Georgetown, which was a rich person's way of saying that he'd dropped out, and had gotten a job at a nonprofit started by a fellow St. Francis alum. A Brighter Future. I vaguely recalled Tiffany volunteering there for our community service requirement.

She and Dev had since broken up, and Tiffany had been known to bad-mouth him. I hadn't seen him on A Brighter Future's website, which meant he must have quit.

"If anyone can help us understand what A Brighter Future might have to do with Logan and his look-alike, it's Tiffany," I said.

The door was unlocked and music thudded from deep inside. We followed it to a family room packed with people who had been forced inside because of the rain. The lights were dim and music blared over a built-in speaker system. It felt sticky and humid; everyone's breath was fogging up the windows.

We pushed through the crowd, looking for Tiffany. I hadn't been to one of Tiffany's parties since before the

Catastrophic Event, and for a moment, everything felt normal, as if no one noticed or cared about my presence, when, over the din, someone shouted, "Run Red Skip."

The room grew quiet as though a shadow had been cast over the party. Everyone was looking at me strangely, as if waiting for me to respond. My face grew hot. I didn't know who had said it. It didn't matter—it could have been anyone.

It was what the newspapers had called my dad after the news had broken, after a photo of him looking agitated and red in the face while being escorted by police officers had been printed on the front page. Run Red Skip, the senator who hit a woman and left her for dead. I hadn't heard it in a while, yet the familiar feeling of shame came rushing back.

"Who said that?" James asked from beside me. His voice cut through the tension in the air, making it deflate. No one answered.

"That's what I thought," James said to the room.

Slowly, people turned back to their conversations, and the party resumed.

I backed toward the door. Tiffany wasn't there anyway, so there was no need for me to linger.

"Hey, are you okay?" James asked, catching up.

"I'm fine," I said, too embarrassed to look him in the eye.

"They're just looking for someone to bully so that they feel better about themselves. You know that, right?"

"Yeah. Sure."

"I'm serious," he said. "You're not your dad and you're not responsible for what he did."

I felt a knot form in my stomach.

James nodded to the stairway. "Come on. Let's do what we came here to do, then get out of here."

All of the rooms upstairs were empty except for one. The light was on and the door was open just a crack. Through it, I could see Tiffany curled on the bed with a handful of her friends while her new boyfriend, Chet, divided blue powder into lines on a school binder.

"Wait in the room across the hall," I said to James.

"What? Why?"

"People share information with me because they know I'll keep it a secret," I said. "Tiffany's not going to tell me anything if I'm with the editor of the school newspaper."

James looked like he was going to protest, but then stopped himself. He knew I was right. "Fine."

I watched him slip into the guest room, then turned to Tiffany's door and knocked lightly. Everyone looked up. It took a moment for Tiffany to recognize me. She was drunk.

"Hana Yang Lerner," she said, a grin spreading across her face. "I was beginning to think you didn't party."

With her seal of approval, everyone else in the room relaxed and went back to their conversations.

Tiffany had the compact look of a gymnast, with a cascade of curly brown hair and a spray-on tan that made her look like she'd spent the weekend at a resort. In the hierarchy of wealthy people at St. Francis, Tiffany was at the bottom. Although everyone loved her parties, they mocked her family behind her back for having poor taste and lacking a pedigree education. They had hustle money, which was different from family money or corporate money or surgeon and lawyer money. We'd never been close, but I'd always felt an affinity for her because we were both looked down on by the same people.

"I don't, really," I said.

She eyed me with curiosity before leaning over the binder and snorting a line of what I assumed, given its color, was Adderall.

When she was done, she wiped her nose and motioned to the tray. An offering.

"I'm good," I said. "I was wondering if you could show me where the bathroom is."

"Down the hall, first door on the left."

"I couldn't find it. Could you show me?" I said it deliberately to make sure she understood.

We locked eyes. Her eyelid twitched. She rubbed her nose. "Sure."

"So what do you want?" Tiffany asked once we were in the hallway.

"I was wondering if you could tell me about A Brighter Future."

Her face glitched in recognition. It was subtle; had I not

been paying attention, I might have missed it. She held her smile, though it now seemed hollow. "What?" she asked, tilting her head.

"A Brighter Future," I repeated. "The nonprofit. Dev used to work there?"

"Oh, right. Of course."

Did she seem overly cheerful? As though hiding an internal panic?

"What do you want to know?" she asked.

"You volunteered there, once, right? I was wondering if you knew anything about what they do." I paused. "What they *really* do."

I wasn't sure what to ask about or what I expected to hear. All I knew was that I wanted to get her talking.

"What do you mean?" she asked.

"I don't think they're just a nonprofit," I said. "I think they're doing something behind the scenes and I'm trying to figure out what."

"I don't know anything about that," she said. "I was only there for three days and all I did was file."

She avoided my gaze when she said it. Was she lying?

"But you dated Dev, who used to work there. You must have heard about it from him."

Tiffany coiled a strand of hair around her finger. "Why do you want to know? Is it for a case?"

"I can't talk about my cases." It was my way of saying yes.

I waited, hoping she would warm to me. "I told you. I

don't know," she said, then gave me a pointed look. "And if I did, I couldn't talk about it anyway."

My heart raced. She knew something. While I tried to figure out what to say that would get her to talk, she reached over my shoulder and pushed open the door behind me. Her hair smelled of coconut shampoo. "The bathroom's here." It was her way of signaling that the conversation was over.

"What would it take for you to tell me?" I said, my voice low.

"I can't tell you what I don't know." Her eyes hardened as she met my gaze. "And if I were you, I would focus on not knowing anything either. For your own sake."

It was a warning. Whatever she knew had to be bad.

"What if I can't let it go?" I asked as she turned and walked down the hall.

Tiffany hesitated. "Like I said, all I did was volunteer there for a few days," she said, her words slow and deliberate. "And all they had me do was file."

My breath caught in my throat. Of course. It was a tip, one that should have occurred to me sooner.

I watched her heels sink into the hallway carpet as she disappeared into her bedroom, then hurried to the guest room, where James was hiding.

"She wouldn't talk," I said, my voice excited. "She told me I should leave it alone, which means whatever it is that A Brighter Future is doing must be bad."

James gave me a confused look. "So you got no information, and yet you sound happy?"

"I didn't get zero information," I said. "She gave me a tip."

"Which is?"

"Whatever it is we need to know is in their file cabinets," I said.

"And how do we get to the file cabinets?" James asked.

"We volunteer there."

11

On *Monday at lunch, James* and I met in the parking lot, where we huddled in my car and dialed the phone number listed on A Brighter Future's website.

On the second ring, a woman answered. She sounded friendly, unassuming. Her name was Linda. I told her that my friend and I were students at St. Francis and had a passion for education. Were they accepting new volunteers? Of course, she said. We could come in the following weekend.

After I hung up, I turned to James.

"It's set," I said. "The only thing we have to do now is wait."

But I hated waiting and I hated not knowing. My excitement over Tiffany's tip at the party had worn off, and although we had a lead, I couldn't stop thinking about what Three had said to me.

You. You're the case you haven't been able to fix. But don't worry. We'll fix that, too, by the end.

I didn't understand. My life had nothing to do with this case, so how would it help me fix it?

I was getting closer to an answer, I could feel it, and maybe that was the problem—part of me was impatient to get there and find out what Three meant, but part of me was terrified. What if I got to the end and didn't like what I found?

I tried to distract myself by focusing on what I could do. I still wanted to try to get Tiffany to talk. There she was, walking through the halls at school, holding a piece of information that might unlock the case. If I could get her to tell me what was really going on at A Brighter Future, I might understand why Logan was meeting with his look-alike in the founder's mansion, which was what Luce was chasing.

All I had to do was figure out what to offer her.

In the meantime, I tried asking my mother—she had, after all, once worked in philanthropy—but she hadn't heard of A Brighter Future, nor did she recognize anyone on its staff.

"Why are you interested in this place?" she asked me.

We were standing in the kitchen after dinner while my mom scraped the remains of our frozen meals into the trash.

"I was thinking of volunteering there," I said.

St. Francis required all students to complete twenty hours of community service per year. They claimed it was to teach us to give back to the community, but the real reason they made us do it was to pad our college applications.

"For your community service requirement?" she asked. "You're not chatting in the park again this year?"

She was referring to the parks cleanup project, which was where most people at St. Francis did their community service because it was outside and felt more like taking a walk with friends than doing work.

I ignored her comment and shrugged. "This place sounds cool."

"Really?" She gave me a suspicious look, unable to believe that I could be interested in giving back to the community. What made me feel worse was that she was right.

I retreated to my room, where I opened my laptop, only to aimlessly stare at the browser until the words blurred. The thing I wanted then, more than anything, was to call Luce. But I couldn't.

"Hey, Hana Bear. Something bothering you?"

I startled.

My dad was standing in the doorway of my bedroom, his hands stuffed into the pockets of his pants.

I couldn't tell him about Three or the case, though

part of me desperately wanted to. Instead, I fixed my face. "Everything's fine," I said, feigning ignorance. "Why do you ask?"

My dad's expression shifted to gentle concern. "You know you can talk to me. People used to say I was a good listener. I can't make any promises now, but I can tell you that I'll try my best to live up to my former self."

I let out a quiet laugh.

"Seriously, though, what's on your mind?"

I thought about Luce, about Three's last message to me, and finally, about my mom and the way she looked at me, like I was incapable of good. "Am I a bad person?"

His face softened. "Of course not."

"But I'm not a good person."

"I've known you since you were a baby, and you've always been good," he said. "Though, maybe the way to think about it is that no one is all good or all bad. We're just people, doing the right things most of the time, doing the wrong things some of the time, making mistakes, and doing our best."

It didn't make me feel better, but I liked hearing his voice nonetheless and wanted him to keep talking.

"What do you miss about our old life?" I asked him.

He leaned against my dresser. "I'll tell you what I don't miss. I don't miss the commute. Or the nonstop phone calls and emails. Or the endless onslaught of fundraisers."

"So many fundraisers," I said.

"Everything's a fundraiser," he said. "I miss the people. The way it feels to shake a stranger's hand and connect with them in a way that makes their face light up. I miss our house and going for walks in our neighborhood and having Melinda and Dave and James over for dinner. I miss turning into our driveway after a long day at work and seeing the house lit up from the inside."

If I closed my eyes, I could almost imagine myself in my old room, watching his headlights stretch across the ceiling.

"I miss those things too," I said.

"Maybe one day you'll miss this." He gestured at my barren walls.

I laughed. "There's no way."

"It's not that bad, is it?"

"It's not the *place* I dislike. It's the *After*."

The smile faded from his face, and his gaze shifted to the carpet, a habit of his when something saddened him. "I know," he said. "Well, it's getting late. You should get some sleep."

Though I wasn't going to bed yet, I nodded for his benefit and listened to his slippers pat down the hall. After his door clicked shut, I turned back to my computer when I heard the hallway floor creak.

My brother, Zack, was peering into my room.

"Were you just talking to someone?" he asked.

He was bleary-eyed from gaming. I wondered if my dad and I had been talking loudly.

"No," I said. "Just a video."

I don't know why I lied. I supposed I wanted to keep my late-night conversations with my dad for myself.

"Did it bother you?" I asked.

"No, just going to the bathroom and thought I heard something."

"Okay, well, good night," I said.

"Good night."

I held my breath and listened to him return to his room. My mother was taking a shower. My brother most likely had his headphones on. My dad was probably watching TV. No one would notice if I snuck downstairs and out the front door.

I was just going for a drive to clear my head. That's what I told myself when I pulled out of our street and meandered to the outskirts of town, where I eventually found myself in the parking lot of a humble church. There was nothing notable about it. It looked plain, unremarkable. I had driven by it before; I supposed my subconscious had led me here on purpose.

The main building was dark, but I could see a light on in the lower level. A classroom.

If my father were there, he'd probably make me go inside. I could almost hear him saying, amid my protests, that I'd arrived there for a reason and had to find out why.

I wasn't religious, and outside of going on holidays with my parents, I rarely went to church, nor did I have any interest in starting.

It's just a church, I could hear my father say. You can go in.

But I couldn't.

I stared at the glow from the classroom. It had a strange magnetism to it, as though it were trying to pull me inside.

That's when the car pulled into the lot. I recognized it immediately and froze.

Luce stepped outside. *Click*, she locked her car, then hugged her chest in the chill of the night. She was still in her clothes from school. Her blond hair was tied in a loose braid. She glanced over her shoulder as though checking to see if anyone was looking, then walked toward the church door. I held my breath and watched her disappear inside.

It felt like a dream. I sank back in my seat, shocked and bewildered. Had it really been Luce? Maybe it was a trick of the light, and she was just another girl with dyed blond hair, wearing combat boots and a button-down. Yet there was her car with its little scented tree dangling over the rearview mirror.

There's a reason why you came here, I could hear my father say. Go in and find out.

I couldn't. I was too shaken. I had to leave.

I don't remember driving home, only that I found myself in bed, staring at the familiar pattern the streetlights left on my ceiling. I didn't text James to tell him what I had seen. Something about my excursion felt wrong, as if it had occurred in another dimension, an alternate life. I wanted to forget it had happened. Had I really seen Luce there? Had it really been a coincidence?

I fell asleep clutching my phone, feeling the phantom vibration of Luce texting me at long last, telling me that she forgave me.

12

In order to understand what happened between me and Luce, you have to go back to the penultimate week of ninth grade, before the Catastrophic Event, before everything had fallen apart. This was how it started.

It was the day before exams, and I was fine, completely fine. At least that's what I told Luce while I sank into my desk chair, face puffy, eyes red, staring at the ceiling through my fingers as I tried to comprehend how screwed I was.

I needed to stay up. I had to finish my essay and memorize my flashcards. I had to catch up on my reading and review my notes. I had to practice my conjugations and write an outline and follow up on my internship application. I had to write thank-you letters. I had to print my résumé. I had to practice my interview questions. What were my greatest strengths? My weaknesses? Why did I want the internship? What would I say was my passion?

Luce was on speakerphone in my lap. Flashcards littered the carpet around me.

"You don't sound fine," she said. "Just let me come over. My dad can drop me off."

"I can't. I don't have time."

"It's just a test," Luce said.

"It's worth forty percent of the final grade. If I don't ace it, my grade will plummet, my GPA will drop, I'll lose my class ranking, I won't get into Yale, and—"

"And what?" Luce said as my voice trailed off. "Finish the thought."

I swallowed. I didn't want to say it out loud.

"And you'll have to go to a 'lesser' school," Luce said. "Is that really so bad?"

"You don't understand," I said, feeling my face get hot. Why was I getting so mad? "I have to go to Yale. My parents expect it. I expect it. Everyone expects it."

"I get it. You were wearing little Yale shirts when you were a baby. Your parents planted the seed early because they wanted it for you. They watered it and it grew. It became a marker of success, and eventually you and your parents and everyone you knew assumed it was an integral part of your personality. Your destiny, even. It became such a defining characteristic that you don't know who you would be without it. Am I right?"

My breathing slowed. She was right, though I didn't want to admit it.

"Do you want to know why I left my old school?" Luce asked.

Of course I did. It had always bugged me, the fact that I didn't know.

"So you already know that my dad taught European History there."

"Yeah."

"After exams, one of his rich students asked to meet him for office hours, but off campus, at a café nearby. A strange request, but my dad agreed because he was dedicated to his students and assumed that maybe this person wanted to talk in a more casual environment. But when he showed up, the student tried to bribe him with an envelope stuffed with cash for a higher grade. My dad refused, and the student's parents, who were powerful members of the school's board, retaliated and got him laid off, claiming he wasn't meeting teaching standards. I had a full ride because my dad was a teacher, but without him there, we had to start paying, and we couldn't afford it. So when he got the job at St. Francis, I transferred. We're lucky he even got it, honestly. It was only because the dean at my old school loved my dad and put in a good word at St. Francis."

I went quiet. I'd been expecting something more run-of-the-mill, like Luce getting caught vandalizing school property or posting something incendiary about the school online. "I didn't know," I said.

"Nick Rawlings." Luce said the name like it was sour. "That was the student's name. He was three grades older than I was. Do you know what he's doing now?"

Her tone made me afraid to ask. "What?"

"He goes to Yale."

Her comment struck a nerve. "What are you trying to say? That everyone who goes to Yale bribed their way in?"

"I'm saying the meritocracy is a sham and you're making yourself miserable trying to get a prize that isn't worth it."

"That was one person. It's not like it happens all the time." Why was I getting so defensive?

"Oh, come on, you grew up with these people. You can't possibly believe that."

I wondered why our conversation was making me so angry, when I realized. "Do you think I'm like them?"

There was a long silence. "Of course not." Luce had tried to sound convincing, but I could hear her voice waver.

"Why did it take you so long to answer then?"

Luce hesitated as if trying to figure out how to say it gently. "Because you aren't and you are. I know you work hard. I see you trying way too intensely in class and studying too early for all your tests and putting in extra hours in your clubs. That's part of what I love about you. You try to earn what you have. But your dad is Skip Lerner. We all know you're getting into whatever college you want."

The flashcards in my lap suddenly seemed ridiculous. I

wanted to be mad at her. I wanted to tell her that she was wrong, that she didn't know what it was like to be me—to be constantly picked apart by the media, to be under pressure at all times—but she'd already heard all of that. How could I be mad at the only person who was ever honest with me? It wasn't her fault that it was the truth.

"It doesn't mean you don't deserve it," she said, as if reading my mind. I could already hear the apology in her voice. "Because you do. Just that things come easier for people like you."

"I know," I whispered.

"You know, I still think about what I would do to him if I could go back in time," Luce said.

"What do you mean?"

"I never confronted him. I was too scared of retaliation."

"So what would you do? If you could go back."

Luce took a long time to respond. When she did, her voice was cold. "I'd ruin him."

I'd never have guessed that I'd still be thinking about what Luce had said that night, but there I was, over two years later, sitting in class, watching her lean over her desk while she took notes and wondering if she felt the same way toward Logan that she did toward the student who had gotten her father fired.

I'd been stunned when Logan and Luce had started

dating, partly because I was jealous—not of her dating Logan, but of her entering my friend group after they'd ousted me—and partly because I'd always thought she quietly resented him. Now I wondered if I'd been right.

I turned back to my notes and tried to solve the problem on the board, when my phone vibrated with a text.

>I need your help.

It was from a classmate, Amber Garlin. In fact, she normally sat a few desks away, but that day she was absent.

<With what? I wrote back.

>I'd rather talk about it in person. Can you meet?

<Sure. When?

>Can you do tonight?

That evening when I got home, I found Zack in the kitchen, microwaving a plate of frozen bagel bites for dinner. Our parents were out—another "date night"—so we were on our own.

"Where are you going?" he asked. He had the slack-jawed look of someone who had just emerged from staring at a screen in a dark room for hours.

"Tutoring."

He narrowed his eyes. "Right."

"Do you have plans?"

The microwave beeped. "2066. Nuclear wasteland dystopia."

I considered my brother, whom I saw every day but

rarely interacted with anymore outside of our daily pleasantries. When we were little, we were so close. "My job tonight is on Fairview."

Zack looked up at me, interested. "Which house?"

"Half a mile down. The gates with ivy on them."

"The Fredericksons?"

I shook my head. "The one on top of the hill. The Garlins."

"Huh." I could tell Zack was mildly curious about what I was going to their house for, but he wouldn't ask. He was good at minding his own business.

"Have you been back?" I asked. "To Fairview. I purposely avoid it."

"Accidentally. I was in Mike's car a few weeks ago and his mom drove us down it."

"And?"

Zack only shrugged. "The new owners made some changes. You'll see."

13

The trick to keeping your composure when dozens of cameras and lights are pointing in your face is to pick a spot in the distance, just above eye level, and focus on it.

On the day of the press conference, my father wore a sky-blue tie and a navy suit. His PR team told him it made him look likable. A little American flag pin was fastened to his lapel.

The room was crowded with people. I saw them from offstage, a pack of wolves ready to rip us apart. Before we walked out onto the podium, my mother inspected us. "Remember, don't look at the ground," she said to my brother, then turned to me and lowered her voice. "Fix your face," she said. "Don't show them how you feel." Then she closed her eyes, willed herself calm, and stepped into the blare of the evening news.

The reporters grew quiet as we walked to the lectern.

My mother and I stood on either side of my father, with Zack next to me, like our public relations team told us to. Being surrounded by women helps, they said. We weren't supposed to speak. We were there as symbols, to show that he had family who loved him. Three American flags.

My mother had always pitied the political wives on TV who stood next to their husbands while they apologized for sending lewd photographs to women on the internet or harassing their interns and coworkers or just generally abusing their power. Now her face tensed as she forced a smile.

"I'm here, with the support of my family, to apologize and announce my resignation," my father said into the microphone. He was already sweating. I couldn't watch.

Earlier that morning, I'd splattered makeup on my dress, and though I'd washed it off as best I could, you could still see the faint outline of it by the seam on my waist. I wondered if it was visible on TV, when Zack nudged me, a reminder to keep my face raised.

The reporters held out their microphones, their eyes wide, ravenous. I hated how happy they looked to have a scandal to talk about. I scanned the room, looking for something in the distance to focus on, when I saw a moth flutter around the back wall. It must have gotten trapped inside, though it was hard to imagine how it had gotten so deep into the building. It would die in this room. No one helped moths. This was what they did: they flew blindly toward the light and made their own prison. I watched it flit against the wall, still hopeful it would find a way out. It didn't know it was doomed.

After the press conference, I wasn't the daughter of a senator anymore. My father was negotiating a plea bargain; we were being sued. The official story of what happened that night was that my father, potentially tipsy, had gone for a drive by himself, swerved off the road on a curve, and had struck a pedestrian. A woman, slightly older than my father. Her name was Mary. According to the video footage, he hadn't even gotten out of the car to check on her. Instead, he'd paused, then jerked the car into reverse and sped away.

We were told we were lucky. The victim had survived but not without serious injury. She would most likely walk again, but it would take time, and the road to recovery was going to be long and expensive. The lawyers warned us that we should start preparing ourselves. "For what?" my mother asked. "Losing everything," they said.

We had no power; we could offer no favors. We wouldn't be invited to fancy parties; we might even have to move out of our house. There was a stain upon our family. People looked at us as though we had black marks on our foreheads. If my father was bad, the rest of us must be bad too.

Luce and I had already had our falling-out, so I'd returned to my old friends, who, with some reluctance, were sympathetic, at first.

"They'll broker a deal," Ruth said.

"The news always makes things seem worse than they are," Marianne agreed.

Logan nodded. "Stuff like this happens all the time in DC. People will forget once the next scandal comes around."

"All sorts of scumbags are still floating around DC," Keith added.

His choice of words didn't make me feel better, but I was glad they were willing to accept me back into their fold. Except they didn't, really. They only wanted me to tell them what had happened from the inside. Once it became clear that I didn't have any secrets to share, their interest waned.

We did end up losing our house and had to sell all of our things to pay the lawyers and the settlement money. I couldn't afford to go to restaurants and coffee shops with my friends like I used to, so they stopped inviting me. I often found them whispering, then going quiet when I approached them in the dining hall. They looked less than excited when I sat with them in class. Hangouts happened less frequently, which I initially chalked up to midterms approaching, until I discovered they'd been making plans without me.

Without the insulation of my friends, I was set adrift. People murmured when I walked down the halls. Crowds parted as though my bad luck was contagious. Though people would talk to me in private, they didn't want to be seen with me in public. It was around that time that Luce started to hang out with Logan. They'd apparently grown close after being paired together as reading partners in Spanish, and the shock of seeing her in my seat at lunch with my former friends, of catching them whispering to each other under the stairwell before class, of spotting Luce sliding into the passenger seat of his car, was enough to knock the air out of my chest. It felt like a betrayal. Not because I wanted Logan—I didn't—but because she'd chosen him, and them, after they'd discarded me.

On the day before we moved, I found my mother sitting in her robe among the boxes of detritus that weren't valuable enough to be sold off, looking through an old photo album of Zack and me as kids. She rarely cried, so finding her like that frightened me.

"Mom?" I ventured.

She looked startled to see me. The rims of her eyes were red. She had been crying.

I wanted her to tell me that we'd find another house, that home wasn't a physical place but wherever your family was. But she didn't say any of that; she only turned back to the photograph in her lap. It was of the four of us years ago, posing in front of the house on the big rock under the tree, grinning in the sunlight.

"We'll be okay," I said, though it was really a question.

She didn't say anything for a long time, and I wondered if she had heard me. Finally, she spoke. "I'm not sure."

Fairview was our old street, the one I'd grown up on. I knew it by heart: each gated driveway and landscaped lawn, each American flag undulating in the breeze.

Our house was a yellow colonial, the shade of the sun. It had five bedrooms, four baths, and a wise old tree out front with a wooden swing that had been there when we'd moved in. My parents had said that of all the amenities, the swing had been what had charmed them. It was a sign of a loved house, a place that already felt like home.

I drove down the street slowly, the road unfolding in front of me like a memory. I hadn't been here since we'd moved; I'd gone out of my way to avoid it. I could still picture the reporters on the day we left, how their vans littered the sides of the street, how they swarmed our car and pushed their gear against the windows, trying to see inside, making it nearly impossible to move. I could still see the look on my mother's face as she stared out at them, horrified, ashamed, realizing that this was our life now.

I slowed as I neared it, fighting the urge to pull into the driveway. Though if I hadn't had the muscle memory, I might not have recognized it. The new owners had painted it an austere white with black doors and shutters. I idled in front and peered through the gate. The downstairs windows were dark with blinds and the flowers out front had been replaced with trim green hedges. The light in my childhood bedroom was on, and through the window I could see that the new owners had changed the wallpaper from the vintage marigold print that had always adorned my walls to a childish pink. A shadow passed across it. Though I knew the new owners had nothing to do with us leaving, I couldn't help but view them as usurpers. I waited for her to reveal her face, this girl who had taken over my room, but she didn't come to the window, and I wondered if she knew who I was, and if she sometimes thought of me, too.

Half a mile down the road was a gate ensconced in creeping ivy. I buzzed, and when it opened, I drove up to a shingled mansion that resembled the main building of a country club.

Amber was waiting for me in the doorway, wearing a plush coat over a slip dress that looked like fancy pajamas. A little bichon yapped at her ankles.

She gestured for me to park out of the way by the side of the house, and when I did, she came over to the car and opened the passenger door. Syrupy perfume filled the air as she slipped inside. She glanced up at her house nervously.

"I only have ten minutes," she said.

Amber Garlin was heiress to the Jenkins Soap conglomerate, which was started by her maternal grandmother and now offered pharmaceuticals, baby food, and topical ointments. Though I hadn't been in her house in years, the last time I'd been there, I'd remembered it smelling of roses.

Amber was neither popular nor unpopular. She felt more like a famous actress who made occasional cameo appearances in high school when she was bored. A true trust fund eccentric and probably the richest person at St. Francis, she carried herself like she was the vixen of a 1940s noir film and spent most of her time in the art room or the theater, talking about classic films.

"Let's not waste any time, then," I said. "What can I do for you?"

"I need you to get my name off the list."

"What list?"

Amber looked impatient. "Pete's list. The one he's going to give to the dean."

Though I prided myself on picking up on things quickly, this time, I didn't know what she was talking about. "Wait, hold on. What?"

"You haven't heard yet? Pete was caught."

"Pete Lasky?" It was a dumb question; there was no other Pete.

Pete Lasky was a senior who ran an underground business called Your Mother's Medicine Cabinet, colloquially referred to as YMMC, where he sold prescription pills and other illicit substances.

"They're saying the dean is going to expel him unless he gives them a list of everyone he's sold to," Amber said.

It must have just happened, otherwise I would have heard about it. "And you bought from him."

"Just once," she said, though I could tell by how quickly she said it that she was lying. Not that it mattered. Plenty of people bought from Pete; I wasn't one to judge. I wondered what Amber's preferred substance was, when the realization dawned on me. *Plenty of people bought from Pete.*

Of course. It was the perfect fix.

"Can you get my name off?" Amber asked.

"Sure," I said, but my mind was already elsewhere.

"How long will it take?" she asked. "Can you be sure no one else will find out?"

It was a run-of-the-mill fix—easy, though I didn't tell Amber that. I told her I could get it done within three days, and assured her I'd be discreet. No one, including her parents, would find out.

Though she looked skeptical, she agreed, and when our ten minutes were up, she retreated back to the house. When the door shut behind her, I took out my phone and texted James.

<I know how to get Tiffany to talk.

14

Pete Lasky currently drove a used orange sports car, which he whizzed around campus in, flying over the speed bumps just for the thrill of it. He was a haphazardly lucky person—despite his sloppiness, everything always seemed to go his way. He perpetually looked like he'd just rolled out of bed, and was often found telling cringeworthy jokes or bragging about some expensive contraption he'd rejiggered to ferry his trash to the garbage can so he didn't have to get up from the couch, or to scoop and launch dog poop into his neighbor's yard, which he never seemed to get in trouble for.

Like Tiffany DeLuca, Pete had hustle money, which his parents made by running a massive car dealership whose irritating jingles had permanently lodged themselves in my brain. As a child, Pete was even featured in their print advertising, where he was pictured as a mischievous toddler in the front seat of a luxury SUV, with the caption, *Great for the whole family. Lasky Cars Last-ky!*

It was dark when we pulled up to his house, where his orange car was parked behind a host of similar midrange lookalikes. All the cars he drove were borrowed from his parents' used fleet, and he switched from one color or model to another when it suited him.

"Why do we even need to get Tiffany to talk?" James asked. "She already told you at her party, in fewer words, to look in the filing cabinet on our volunteer day."

"Yeah, but what are we supposed to look for? It'll be easier if I can get her to tell us what she knows. And I need to see Pete anyway about another case, so I'm hoping it'll be two birds, one stone."

James glanced at the house. "What are you going to offer him?"

After I'd told him about my idea, he'd asked if I wanted company, and though I didn't need help, I'd surprised myself by saying, "Sure."

"I have some ideas," I said, and stepped outside, leaving James in the passenger seat. "I'll be back in a bit."

Earlier that day, I'd texted Pete to ask if I could come by, to which he'd immediately written back, saying yes. Now he opened the front door looking surprisingly put together in a dress code outfit of a button-down and khakis.

Strange, I thought, considering he hadn't been at school that day.

His hair, normally wild and overgrown, was combed back. He ran a hand through it as though he was nervous, then gestured inside. "Welcome to my humble abode."

Though I'd known Pete for years, I'd never been to his home. He had always been popular-adjacent—invited to the parties and hangouts, where he often played the role of the prankster, but never a member of the core.

His house felt like an expanded version of an Outback Steakhouse—dimly lit, with wooden walls and décor that made it look like a hybrid lodge–sports bar. He led me through the living room, where his mom and sister were watching football, past an office, where his dad was on the phone, also watching football on a smaller television, to a game room in the back, where he motioned to a couch in front of an elaborate gaming setup.

"Hana Yang Lerner," he said. "One might say that it's never good news when you're the one texting, but I disagree. I like when someone shakes things up."

"Is that what I do?"

"In your own way," he said, and disappeared behind the bar, where he fiddled with what I assumed were glasses for drinks.

"I like to think that I make things disappear," I said.

"To the outside world, maybe, but not to the people on the inside. I like a good backroom deal."

"So how are you holding up?" I asked, in an attempt to warm him to my side.

"Oh, you know, I've been better. But also worse. Can't complain, really."

Only Pete, when faced with expulsion, would say that he couldn't complain.

He emerged with two cans of soda and what looked like a plate of cheese and fruit that he had arranged in a child's rendition of a fancy cheeseboard. "Are you hungry?"

He looked so pleased with his work that I felt bad saying no. "Sure," I said, and took an olive.

"So you heard what happened," he said.

After my meeting with Amber, I'd asked around and had pieced together bits of information as the news had spread.

"The broad strokes. Is it true that they aren't involving the police?"

"So far, yeah. It only brings bad press to the school."

"And that they offered you a deal if you inform?"

A look of embarrassment passed over his face upon hearing my word choice. *Inform.* I'd chosen it intentionally. "News travels quickly," he said.

"So it's true that you keep a list?"

"Of course I keep a list. How else would I keep track of my business?"

It was a fair question. "Honestly, I'm surprised they offered you a deal. How did you swing it?"

"I have my ways." Pete drummed the armrest of the couch, seemingly eager to change the subject. "You know, I've always respected you," he said, apropos of nothing.

"Thanks," I said slowly. "And I've always respected you." It wasn't true, but it wasn't untrue either. To be honest, I'd never given him a lot of thought.

"We're similar, you and I," he continued.

"Are we?"

"We're both businesspeople. We both work in the underground economy. We both know how to read people."

"That's one way to put it."

"We're integral to the functioning of the school. Without us behind the scenes, the school would descend into chaos."

It seemed a bit of a stretch, especially on his part, but I let it go. "You think so?"

"Without the chemical enhancements I sell, no one at St. Francis would even come close to finishing all their homework and extracurriculars and internship applications and volunteer responsibilities. People would crumble under the crushing pressure of capitalistic society and the parents that demand our participation in it. They'd have psychological breakdowns and be at each other's throats. Who knows what would occur? And your work—well, it's obvious that if everyone's dirty laundry was just lying around, we'd be living in a much less civilized world than we are now."

He meant it as a compliment, though I wasn't sure to what end, nor was I convinced that either of us were integral to St. Francis. To the veneer of a polished student body, sure. To its actual well-being? Unclear.

"So they caught you with prescriptions," I said, eager to get to business. "And then threatened expulsion? Or what's the damage?"

"Prescriptions in excess," he corrected. "And they backed down from expulsion once it became clear that I would fight it. Instead, they're threatening academic probation unless I give them a list of everyone involved. Then they'll offer two weeks of unofficial suspension instead."

"What's *unofficial suspension?*"

"It doesn't go on my permanent record and I don't have to report it to colleges. I just can't come to school for two weeks and have to perform forty additional hours of community service."

It was an incredible deal considering his offense. I was surprised they'd offered it to him and wondered how he'd gotten it. Though his family surely paid full tuition, I doubted they had a lot of sway with the school or its board.

"So are you going to do it?" I asked.

"Give them a list? If I were your client, wouldn't you tell me to?"

"I would," I admitted.

"So let's see. You're here because someone hired you to ask me to get their name off my list."

I tilted my head to indicate he was right.

"But who?" Pete said, enjoying the challenge of guessing. "It has to be someone who's rich enough to afford your services instead of trying to broker a deal with me themselves."

I could see him mentally scanning the list of people he was going to rat out. "Boy or girl?"

"Girl."

"Upper or downer?"

"Her personality or her preference?"

"Preference."

Amber seemed like the kind of person who'd do both. Uppers at parties, downers to relax. "Both."

Pete looked intrigued. "For work or pleasure?"

There was no way Amber was taking uppers to study. "Pleasure, definitely."

Pete thought about it for a moment before a grin spread across his face. "Amber Garlin."

I nodded and was about to start negotiations when he cut me off.

"Sorry," he said. "But I can't take her off the list."

His finality surprised me. "Why not?"

"Don't want to. She's a real pain, you know. Always complaining that my pills are expired or that I emptied the capsules and filled them with baking soda. It's always the rich ones that nickel-and-dime you. You should watch out. Make sure she pays you what she owes."

"There's got to be something I can offer you in exchange for removing Amber's name," I said.

Pete exhaled but didn't say no, which meant there was room for negotiation.

"I could set you up with a good lawyer. I have connections."

"Unfortunately for you, someone with better connections has already set me up with a lawyer," Pete said. "How do you think I got the deal in the first place?"

Someone had gotten to him before me? "Who?"

"Sorry, but can't tell you that, either."

It had to be someone powerful and rich, someone who was also on his list, though that didn't really narrow it down.

"I know someone who teaches at Georgetown business school. I could get him to put in a good word for you."

"That's very thoughtful," Pete said, amused. "You even knew that I wanted to go to Georgetown. But I don't need help with that."

"What about an internship? I can get you one with Mackworth Systems. Or Farthing Samson."

Pete winced. "Become a corporate shill? No thanks."

Before coming, I'd made a mental list of favors I could offer Pete in exchange for this ask, but I was quickly approaching the end.

"I can manage your public image for a few weeks after you come back to school. Do damage control."

"Come on. We're both enterprising individuals. You know I don't care about that."

"What do you want, then? It seems like you have something in mind."

He hesitated. I knew it had to be a big favor if he didn't want to ask it outright.

"Just tell me."

He looked at me strangely. Did he seem nervous? "A date."

He looked at his feet when he said it, as if he didn't want to see my reaction.

"With me?"

That's when I understood why he was dressed up instead of in sweats or loungewear. Why he'd combed his hair and kept paying me strange yet somewhat thoughtful compliments. Why he'd made the cheese plate. I'd been a pariah for so long that it hadn't occurred to me that anyone orbiting the social nexus would consider me in that way.

In any other situation, I would have said no, but I really wanted to get this fix done, and it wasn't just about Amber.

"There'd have to be some ground rules," I said.

Pete looked surprised that I hadn't immediately refused him. "Of course."

"It would just be one date," I said, already wondering if I was making a mistake. "In a public place. No touching or weird physical stuff. No pictures."

"Just one. Totally hands-off. I promise it won't be creepy or weird. Just a wholesome, old-fashioned night of fun and conversation. Who knows, you might enjoy yourself."

His enthusiasm made me wonder if I was going to regret this. "Where?"

"You can pick. Unless you prefer a surprise."

"I don't like surprises," I said.

"Of course you don't. Most of the surprises you've had were bad. I get it."

It was an unexpectedly insightful observation.

"There's one more hitch," I said. "Since I normally don't include myself in the favor, and this is a pretty big ask, I need one more name crossed off your list."

Pete gave me a questioning look.

"Tiffany DeLuca." I wasn't certain she was on his list, but assumed his reaction would tell me, and it did.

He held out his hand. "Amber Garlin and Tiffany DeLuca."

I hesitated, then slipped my hand in his. For some reason, I was expecting it to feel sticky, like it was part of a prank. It was hard to imagine Pete doing anything serious. But it was just a normal hand, warm and slightly damp from nerves. I thought of what he'd said earlier about how I didn't like surprises because most of the ones I'd experienced were bad, and wondered if maybe the date wouldn't be as terrible as I thought. "It's a deal."

"So where do you want to go?" he asked.

"I have somewhere in mind."

After I left, I stood on the front stoop and texted Tiffany.

<I have a proposition for you. Can we meet?

"Done," I said when I returned to the car.

"It worked?" James asked. It wasn't lost on me how surprised he sounded.

"Don't look so shocked. Of course it worked. I'm a professional."

"What did you offer him?"

I hesitated. I didn't want to tell him. I supposed I was embarrassed. "Oh, just a minor favor."

I hoped he would let it go, but of course he didn't.

"What kind of *minor favor*?"

"Just, um, a meeting. To talk."

"A meeting? What do you mean?"

"We're just going to meet up to talk. Sometime in the future."

"Yeah, I know what a meeting is, but how is that a favor? And why are you being so cryptic all of a sudden?"

"I'm not being cryptic."

"Yes, you are. You're evading answering and you're avoiding eye contact."

"Okay, fine. It's not just a meeting. It's a date. I agreed to go on a date with him."

"A date?" James repeated. "With Pete Lasky?"

"I set a bunch of ground rules, so it's not going to be weird or anything. I mean, it'll probably be weird, but not in that way."

I tried to gauge James's reaction, but his expression was unreadable.

"You know, I thought it would be creepy, but I actually

think it might be okay. He's definitely cheesy and embarrassing, but he seems self-aware."

James looked at me like I was out of my mind. "Wait, do you like him? Is that why you were being so sheepish?"

"Of course not. I'm just doing it for work."

"Is he going to pick you up in one of his absurd neon cars?"

"Probably. I kind of hope he does. I've never been in one before."

"You're excited," James observed.

"To be in a sports car? Yes. Why, are you jealous?"

"Of Pete or the sports car?"

"Both."

"No. I'm just shocked that you said yes. So where's he taking you, to a bong shop?"

"No, I'm choosing the location. But a bong shop would be interesting."

"I can't believe you're going on a date with Pete Lasky," James said as I turned on the car, illuminating the vanity plate on one of Pete's family cars: LAST-KY.

"It's a few hours in a public place," I said, backing out of the driveway. "How bad can it be?"

Tiffany didn't want to meet at her house in case her parents overheard us, so instead she suggested a coffee shop by the waterfront. We arrived early.

"Stay in the car," I said to James as I parked.

"I know, I know," he said, and took out his phone.

The coffee shop was empty except for a few people on their laptops. I ordered a tea and chose a seat in the corner where no one could overhear us. Tiffany arrived a few minutes later. Her hair was wet and her eye makeup was slightly smudged. Crying in the shower, I guessed. She didn't look happy to see me, but that was to be expected. People thought of me the same way they did of lawyers—a necessary evil. Though I made people's problems go away, my presence only reminded them of the severity of the bind they'd found themselves in, and most wanted it all to disappear, including me.

Tiffany sat across from me, still gripping her keys as if she didn't plan on staying long. "What do you want?"

"I know you're on Pete's list," I said. "I can get you off if you tell me what you know about A Brighter Future."

"I thought that's what you were going to say."

"I'd like to help you."

"You mean you want me to help you," said Tiffany.

"It would be a symbiotic relationship."

"Why do you want to know so badly?" she asked.

"I can't share details from another case. The same way that I can't tell anyone else what you say to me in this meeting."

"So someone hired you to find out?"

"No. Not exactly. I found it on my own."

"I warned you at the party that you should leave it alone."

Her response gave me pause. Tiffany didn't seem like someone who scared easily, so if what she knew worried her, I wondered if I should be listening. But what was the worst that could happen? No one could destroy me. My life had already been destroyed. What did I have to lose?

"I can't."

Tiffany considered me. "If I tell you what I know, it can't get out that it came from me."

"It wouldn't."

"I don't know much. Dev didn't tell me a lot while he was working there."

"You know more than I do. Anything can help."

"And my name definitely won't be on Pete's list?"

"All I have to do is text him and he'll remove it."

Tiffany relaxed her grip on her keys slightly. "Okay."

Tiffany had first heard about A Brighter Future when her then-boyfriend, Dev, got a job there. His official title was Development Associate, which meant he was in charge of finding new donors and cultivating current ones. It was all very boring, at least at first.

That's when she started to notice strange things. The first was that Dev was getting paid a lot—way more than what Tiffany assumed a teenager would be getting anywhere, let alone at a nonprofit.

When she asked him about it, he clammed up, then said they had generous donors who really cared about the cause.

The second strange thing was that Tiffany didn't even understand why he was hired. Dev didn't have any experience in fundraising and had never been that great at writing, but now he was supposedly writing letters to donors all day. Dev claimed it was because he went to St. Francis and was part of the wealthy network of the school, which he was supposed to tap for money, but surely there were other people who had access to those networks who were more qualified, so why had they wanted Dev?

The third strange thing was what had sealed it for her. Tiffany was at Dev's house, using his phone while hers charged, when a series of texts came in from his work. She wasn't planning on reading them, but Dev was in the kitchen and the first text seemed so odd that she couldn't help herself.

>The Roark file is imploding.

>Did you talk to his parents yet? Are they still waffling?

>We need to get ahold of them ASAP.

>Our contact at Gtown is waiting on payment and is going to pull out if we don't send.

>They need to come up with the cash now.

Tiffany was reading them again, unsure of what to make of them, when Dev came back.

"What's the Roark file?" Tiffany asked him.

Dev's face dropped as his gaze drifted to the phone in her hand. He took it and scrolled through the messages.

"Did you read these?" he asked.

"What exactly do you do?" she asked.

"Those messages were private."

"Are you paying someone at Georgetown?"

"Of course not."

"Then what did that mean?"

"It was about one of our initiatives," Dev said. "A program we're running there."

"Don't treat me like I'm stupid. You always treat me like I'm stupid and I'm not."

"I don't think you're stupid."

"Then what's the Roark file?"

"Look, just forget about it."

"Why?"

"I'm serious. If anyone finds out about this, I could get in big trouble. So could you."

Dev looked scared enough that it chastened her. "What kind of trouble?"

"The kind of trouble that happens to you when you anger powerful people." Dev lowered his voice. "Look, I'm telling you. It was just a text from work about an initiative we're running. It was nothing. Leave it alone."

I relayed Tiffany's story to James as I drove him home.

The Roark file," James said. "Like Evan Roark?"

Evan Roark had been a year ahead of us at St. Francis.

Wealthy and generically good-looking in a Target-ad kind of way, he was otherwise completely average. I didn't know him well.

"Didn't he end up going to Georgetown?" James asked.

"He did," I said.

"So Tiffany reads texts about a family named the Roarks, who owed A Brighter Future money. And A Brighter Future was going to use that money to pay Georgetown for something?" James asked.

I nodded.

"Does that mean what I think it means?"

"Tiffany thinks that the Roarks paid A Brighter Future to get Evan into Georgetown," I said. "She thinks A Brighter Future is pretending to be a nonprofit when it's actually a front for a college admissions cheating ring."

James looked shaken by the possibility that we had uncovered something this big. "Does she have proof?"

"Outside of this, no. That's why she suggested volunteering there and looking through their files, if we can."

"This is a really serious offense," James said. "If it's true, it's not just illegal. It's national news that implicates St. Francis and all of the elite institutions that it feeds into."

"I know."

"Before we hit the ground running with this hypothesis, let's just think through any other logical explanations," he said. "Maybe these parents are donors who are funding some kind of program for underprivileged students at Georgetown."

"Why would Dev clam up like that and tell Tiffany to forget it?"

"Maybe Tiffany remembered it incorrectly," James said. "It happened a while ago. Maybe she got some of the wording wrong."

"Even if she did, she clearly remembered Dev being panicked, which seems suspicious regardless of the accuracy of the specifics. Even when I get details wrong, I always remember the feeling something gave me."

"So do I," James admitted.

"Plus, it's not like we encountered this in a vacuum," I said. "We're here because of Logan and his look-alike."

"If it is a front, and Logan was at the founder's house, then that implicates him, too," James said.

"Do you remember that article we read about the doppelganger being used historically to take the place of someone powerful or famous?" I asked. "What if Logan's doppelganger isn't a twin or a relative. What if it's someone Logan hired to take his place?"

15

The office was in a charming stone building at the edge of Old Town. Ivy climbed up the side. Nestled in its leaves was a discreet sign: A Brighter Future.

Linda, the office manager, greeted us. "You must be Hana and James," she said with a smile. She held out a warm, fleshy hand. Despite myself, I liked her. "Welcome to our little corner of the world," she said. "Come on back. Let's get you set up."

She led us down the hallway, where pictures of children in classrooms hung on the walls. A Brighter Future purportedly ran after-school programs for low-income children, offering homework and reading help. Surely they had to do some real work, though I still found myself wondering if the photos were a sham.

"We're always so glad when young people decide to give back to their communities with us," Linda said as she led me past an office that said IAN GOODJOY. The door was closed. "I hope you weren't expecting anything lavish. Most of the work we need done is administrative."

"I love administrative work," I said. "Organizing, filing. I find stuff like that soothing."

I could feel James studying me and felt slightly self-conscious. He'd never seen me at work and was clearly surprised by the sudden change in my demeanor.

"Is the director here?" James asked.

"He doesn't come in on the weekends," Linda said.

"I heard he went to St. Francis too," James said.

Linda gave us a warm smile. "We love St. Francis kids around here."

I wondered if she knew. It seemed unlikely that she didn't, but her smile was so sincere that I wanted her to be ignorant. Maybe they'd kept her in the dark; it would be to their benefit to make sure as few people as possible knew what was really going on.

"Speaking of which, we have one other student from St. Francis volunteering with us," Linda said. "I wonder if you three know each other."

My skin prickled. Another student?

"She's been with us for a few weeks," Linda said. "I hope it's okay that I have you working together."

I knew who it was before we rounded the corner and walked into the back room, before I saw her standing in front of the photocopier, the morning light streaming through the window, making her bleached hair look almost white.

Luce turned. The machine spit out copies. A brief look of surprise crossed her face. Of course, she seemed to say. It felt both shocking and inevitable, like we were being pulled together by an invisible thread.

James nudged me. *Are you okay?* he said silently. I nodded, though I wasn't so sure, and felt grateful that he was there.

"Hey," I said to Luce.

Her face was stone. "Hey."

James glanced between us. I'd never told him what had happened with Luce and me. I couldn't. "Hey," he said.

Linda tasked James with preparing the fundraising mailings and handed me a large crate of papers to file.

While Linda gave us instructions, I watched Luce from the reflection in the window in front of me. She was thumbing through photocopies. When she thought no one was watching, she slipped a copied page from the bottom and tucked it into her bag.

My theory was that Luce was a bystander, like I was. Maybe she'd stumbled across a loose thread at Logan's house that reminded her of her father and the student at her last school, of all the things she resented about St. Francis, Logan, and me. So she'd pulled that thread, slowly unraveling the mystery.

It had eventually led her here, which meant she had to already know that A Brighter Future was a front.

I considered revealing myself. It seemed like we were on the same side; we could share information. I liked the idea of talking to her again, of trusting her and her trusting me. But a little thought nagged me.

Three had hired me to follow Luce, not to team up with her. There had to be a reason for it, and until I discovered what it was, I probably shouldn't reveal my hand.

Before Linda left, she nodded to Luce. "Do you have a minute?" Linda asked her. "I have two more boxes for you in the front."

Luce forced a smile. "Sure," she said, and followed her down the hall.

I waited until they were out of sight, then darted to Luce's bag.

"What are you doing?" James whispered.

All I was certain of was that Luce had to be volunteering for the same reason we were—to find proof—and this might be the only opportunity I had to see what she'd found.

I opened her bag and took out the photocopy I'd seen her slip in earlier. I expected something obvious, something scandalizing. What I found wasn't that. It was just a letter offering employment to a tutor named Colin Graham. Strange, I thought. Why, of all the files in this place, had Luce photocopied this one?

Down the hall, I heard footsteps. Before they returned, I took a picture of the letter with my phone, then stuffed it back into her bag and hurried to the file cabinets.

I felt the focus of Luce's attention as I scanned the files, pretending to be busy. When I heard Luce resume her photocopying, I opened the file on the top of my stack.

Inside was a donor profile of an older couple, along with a record of their gifts and a few notes about their interests. Nothing remarkable, and I wondered if they were donating to the charity or to the cheating enterprise. I scanned the pages, looking to see how much they'd given. Five hundred dollars. Too small to be meaningful. I closed it and tucked it into the cabinet.

Across the room, I heard tapping. Luce had put her headphones in and was listening to music while she worked. Her sneaker counted the beats. I wondered if she still listened to the same bands she had when we were friends, or if she'd shed that version of herself.

I opened the cabinet next to me and searched until I found the name I was looking for. There, nestled in the *R*s, was a folder labeled *Roark*. I pretended to file something beside it, then slid it out.

Inside was a bunch of paperwork, most of it boring. I flipped through it until I found the donor profile. *Nathan and Gayle Roark*, it read, along with their personal information, and some notes on their interests. They had one child, Evan.

I held my breath. James and I had been right; the Roark file belonged to our classmate. I scanned the page, but found no mention of Georgetown or any services rendered. The only notable piece of information was the amount donated. Fifty thousand dollars.

The number was remarkably high. I knew enough from my mom's days in the nonprofit world to understand that it was the kind of number that got you special recognition at galas and fundraisers, maybe a glass trophy for "Trailblazing in the Community," or an initiative named after you.

I took a photo, put the file back, then searched for O'Hara. Logan's file. His was similarly uninteresting, with information about his parents, their background, their interests. No notes about doppelgangers or twins or stunt doubles. Then, on the last page, the amount they'd given. Sixty-five thousand dollars.

The number was even larger than the Roark file. Sure, Logan's parents were rich, but donating this much to a charity that most people hadn't heard of seemed strange.

My mind raced. If Logan was doing this, he couldn't be the only one. I took photos of the file before returning it, then thumbed through the folders, searching for other names from St. Francis.

Keith didn't have a file, nor did Ruth, but Marianne did. So did Cecily and Analisa. I took photos of them all and was going to keep searching when a voice interrupted me.

"What are you doing?"

I nearly jumped out of my skin.

Luce was standing behind me. Tinny music blared out of the earbuds dangling around her neck.

"Nothing."

She leaned over me and pulled a file from the cabinet. "*E* is over there," she said, eyeing the folder in my hand. It felt like a challenge.

"Thanks," I said. "I'm new at this."

"There has to be a record of it," James said when I showed him the photos I'd taken of the files. Though he tried to hide it, he was disappointed that they contained no actual proof. "Was there another cabinet, maybe? One that they kept locked?"

I furrowed my brow, then gasped. "Come to think of it, there was one that had the words *TOP SECRET* written all over it," I said. "Do you think I should have checked that one instead?"

We were sitting on a bench by the waterfront later that afternoon. James had brought two black bean buns that his mom had made, which had always been my favorite. I hadn't had them in years and couldn't bring myself to eat mine. Instead, I set it on my lap on its soft little square of steaming paper, afraid that if I bit into it, I'd be transported back to his living room, a place I wasn't ready to go yet.

James chose to ignore my sarcasm and instead continued

to scroll through the pictures on my phone. "There has to be something in these files. We're just not seeing it."

I thought of Pete Lasky and how he'd said, *Of course I keep a list. How else would I keep track of my business?* "Everyone has to have an organization system," I said. "Even people who are doing things that are illegal."

"The fact that so many parents from St. Francis have given huge amounts seems telling," James said. "The sheer volume of high donations alone is suspicious."

"Plus the fact that Luce was there," I said.

I leaned over to look at the phone with him and couldn't help but notice the shape of his neck, how smooth its contours were, like the base of an adolescent tree. What would it feel like if I put my hand on it, if I leaned closer until we were barely touching?

"Hold on," James said.

He zoomed in on one of the photos.

"What?"

He didn't respond. Instead, he scrolled to the next photo and zoomed in on that, too.

"This is strange," James murmured. "Did you notice that every donor is categorized by a tier? Bronze, Silver, Gold, and Ivy. Normal, right? Lots of nonprofits do this. Bronze is for the smaller donations, Silver is for the medium ones, and Gold is for the large donations. But what's Ivy?"

"Higher than Gold?" I offered.

"That's what you'd think, right? But it's not. Some of the people categorized as Ivy gave less money than Gold, and some gave more. So what does Ivy refer to?"

"Ivy," I whispered. "Like Ivy League colleges." I looked up at him, my heart racing. "It can't be so obvious."

"If by obvious you mean it can only be discovered by a tip-off from an anonymous client, weeks of stakeouts and painstaking research, undercover volunteer work, and taking illegal photographs of confidential files, then sure, it's obvious," James said.

James opened the photo of Logan's file. I leaned in until the warmth of his arm made my skin tremble.

There it was, on the corner of the page. *Donor Tier: Ivy.*

"The Ivy donors aren't actual donors," I murmured. "They're clients, paying to cheat their way into elite colleges."

James nodded. "We solved it. And now we have proof."

Still, something bothered me. "So Logan's parents are paying this place to get him into college. But how does it work? They just bribe officials? How does his look-alike fit in?"

That's when I remembered. I slipped my phone from his hand and thumbed through the photos until I found it. The photocopy Luce had tucked into her bag.

Colin Graham, it said. *Tutor.*

I opened a browser and typed his name into the search bar. I didn't recognize him at first. I was about to click past his photograph when I saw a glimmer of a face that I recognized.

It was a photo of a boy: symmetrical, handsome, with a bronze complexion that looked familiar. If I squinted and imagined him in dress code, he would look like Logan.

"It's him," James said.

Logan's doppelganger wasn't actually much of a doppelganger at all. It must have been the distance and the darkness, paired with their preppy outfits that had made them look identical. Sure, they looked similar, but in the few photos I'd found of him online, he looked more like a cousin than a twin. He wasn't dressed like Logan or standing with the same posture. His hair was longer, wilder, a lighter brown. His body looked less like a crew star and more like someone who spent most of his time in chem lab.

Upon further searching, this was what we learned about him: He went to a public school forty-five minutes away, where he'd won a physics prize and played midfield for the soccer team. He worked as a tutor for a company called Top Choice, where his bio listed his strengths as history, physics, calculus, and Spanish. He also offered tutoring in standardized tests, essay editing, and résumé writing. Judging from the fact that he worked while in school, I felt pretty certain that he didn't come from a rich family. We had no friends in common, and he lived far enough away that his life probably didn't intersect with mine.

"He's smart," I said. "And he needs money."

"A Brighter Future offers him a job that pays more money than he's ever seen before," James said. "But to do what exactly? To cheat for Logan?"

I studied the photo of him on the screen. It was a school athletic picture—red jersey, white background. He wasn't smiling; instead, he gazed at the camera unflinchingly as if he knew I was looking at him, as if he was daring me to come find him.

"There's one way to find out."

16

Top Choice Tutoring occupied the second floor of a modest office building in Falls Church, Virginia. I arrived early and waited in the lobby, trying to calm my nerves. A clock ticked. The receptionist murmured into the phone. A water dispenser in the corner sporadically belched.

James had wanted to go to the tutoring appointment, but I'd insisted on doing it myself. Of the two of us, I was better at getting information out of someone quickly.

While I waited, a text came in. It was from Adam.

>Remember that rumor you mentioned about Logan and Chris Pilker-Johns in the locker room? I think I know what that was about.

I was about to ask him to elaborate when a boy emerged from one of the offices down the hall.

"Elizabeth?" he asked.

Colin Graham looked less like Logan in person. Though

he had Logan's classic bone structure and bronze hair, he was nerdier, with a lopsided smile that was hard not to like.

I stood up. "That's me," I said, already starting to feel sorry for what I was about to do.

"Come on back."

He led me to a peach-colored study room, where a few tutor-client pairs were set up in cubicles. Ours had a desk that was bare other than a stack of paper and a cup of pens.

He looked like he was ready to get started, when he paused. "I'm sorry to do this, but have we met before?"

Though I was used to being recognized, in this particular setting I hadn't been expecting it and felt a jolt of panic. "I don't think so. Why?"

"It just feels like I know you from somewhere."

He was studying me in the strange way that people often did when they were scanning their brains, trying to place me. I waited to see if he would find a match.

"Maybe we've passed each other in town," I offered. "I live in Alexandria."

Colin frowned. "No, I don't think so."

"Or through mutual friends, maybe," I said, deciding to deflect by turning him on the defensive. "I go to Laurel Oak High, but also have a lot of friends at St. Francis. Do you know anyone at either of them?"

His eyebrow twitched, a subtle flash of panic. Had I not been looking for it, I might have missed it. "No. Neither."

He was a good actor. If I hadn't known he was lying, I

might have believed him. He tilted his head, and from that angle, I suddenly caught a glimpse of Logan in his face. I could see now how he was able to transform into him.

"Must just be my imagination," he said.

"Must be," I murmured.

"So what do you think you need to work on?" he asked.

"In writing or in life?" I asked in an attempt to lighten the mood.

It worked; he laughed. "In writing."

I'd signed up for essay tutoring, which his bio had listed as one of his specialties.

"Right. Well, I do this thing when I have essays on exams or standardized tests—I freeze and have a hard time figuring out where to start."

"Honestly, that's pretty common. The good news is you can practice and get better." He slid a sheet of paper to me. "Just so I can get a sense of where you're at, could you write a short answer to this prompt?"

"Sure." I pretended to read it. All the while, a lump formed in my throat. He seemed nice, which made me feel guilty. I reminded myself that he was helping Logan cheat.

I picked up a pen and began to write, though I didn't follow his instructions.

I know Logan O'Hara, I began. *And I know you know him too. Don't stand up. Don't say anything. I just want to talk to you.*

I slid the paper back to him.

His face went pale when he read it. I held my breath and waited to see if he would end the tutoring session, but he didn't move. Across the room, I could hear the muffled sound of other tutors working.

I took the paper and wrote more.

I saw you and Logan at Ian Goodjoy's mansion last month. You were dressed like him. You acted like him. I know that you were hired by A Brighter Future to work with him, and I know that they aren't just a nonprofit. I'm not the only one who knows.

He barely moved while reading. The hand gripping his pen began to falter. I could see him calculating his options, trying to figure out which he should take. He swallowed. Finally, he wrote his response.

What do you want?

What are you doing for Logan O'Hara? I wrote.

He hated me then, I could tell. But what other options did he have? He was trapped.

I'm just a tutor they hired. I don't know much. I needed money and they offered me a job.

I get it. If you help me, I'll do my best to make sure you don't get in trouble.

He hesitated. I held my breath, hoping he wouldn't walk away. Finally, he wrote a single word.

SAT

Tutoring? I wrote.

He shook his head.

He didn't have to write what he was hired to do. I understood then why he and Logan had met after hours at a different location. Why they'd been dressed the same. Why they'd acted the same. They were practicing.

Logan hadn't hired him to help him study for the SAT. He'd hired him to take the SAT as him.

My mind raced as I put the pieces together. Colin could take the SAT for him in a location far away from school, where people might not recognize him, but he'd still need to use Logan's ID, which meant he'd have to look like him. And because Logan was someone that other people recognized through crew, it would be safer if Colin acted like him, too, in case there happened to be anyone there who knew of him.

Is he your only client?

No.

Are you doing this for all of them?

No. Most are personal statements and high school essays.

I understood and I didn't. Did A Brighter Future hire tutors to help kids cheat, or did they bribe people? Or both?

What exactly does A Brighter Future do, then?

They help people get into college.

How?

All kinds of ways. It's tailored to the student.

And parents pay by donating money?

He nodded.

I should have felt triumphant. He had answered all of my questions. But a pestering feeling nagged at me. It felt too easy.

That's when he wrote another note.

What about payment?

Payment? The receptionist had already told me that I should settle with her after my tutoring session was over. He couldn't be referring to that. *What do you mean?*

They promised me double.

I didn't understand. *Who did?*

The person you work for. In exchange for information.

I don't work for anyone.

It clearly wasn't the answer he was expecting. **They said you'd be coming and that I should answer your questions to the best of my ability.**

The room seemed to warp as if everyone around us was moving in slow motion. I could hear my heart beat faster, faster. *And in exchange?* I asked.

They would pay me double what A Brighter Future is paying me.

I didn't understand. Someone had contacted Colin before I had and had told him I was coming?

How much is that? I wrote.

Ten thousand.

The number was staggering. Who would be able to do such a thing? And why? *Who do you think I work for?*

Time seemed to stretch as he wrote.

They told me to call them Three.

James was waiting for me in my car when the session was over.

"Is everything okay?" he asked as I slid into the driver's seat. He was simultaneously listening to NPR and reading a book about the Plantagenets.

"I found out what Logan is up to," I said, and told him what I'd learned, watching as James's face transformed from excited to bewildered.

"He was expecting you?" he murmured.

It felt like we were tracing a spiral round and round but never getting to the center.

"Who has access to ten thousand dollars?" James asked. "Even the richest kids at our school wouldn't be able to just withdraw that much money from their accounts and not have their parents notice."

"It's hard to believe," I said. "But it's not impossible. There are a lot of absent parents."

"But who would even think this was worth spending that much money on?"

"Someone who has skin in the game," I said.

"Maybe Three is a parent, not a kid," James said.

It was an interesting theory, but my gut reaction was that it wasn't true. "Three doesn't sound like a parent. And how would a parent know to contact me? Why would they even want to?"

James tapped his fingers on the dashboard while he thought. "Okay, so probably not a parent. Let's review what we know. First, Three is rich. Second, Three already knows what's going on and has hired you to uncover it."

"It seems that way."

"Why?"

It was the question I'd been asking myself since stepping out of the cubicle at the end of our tutoring session. "Logan and the other people using Top Choice are wealthy and powerful. Maybe Three knows what's going on but doesn't want to reveal it because then they would be subject to blowback from families who would ruin their life."

"So Three hired you to do it instead," James said.

"Maybe."

"But if Three knew what was going on this whole time, why wouldn't Three just tell you? Why hire you to uncover it?"

"Maybe they had a hunch but didn't have proof, and they hired me to do the difficult task of gathering it." It was the only reason I could think of that made sense.

"But why wouldn't Three just tell you their theory outright?"

I considered how I would have responded if an anonymous person had contacted me, telling me that Logan was cheating and I should expose it. Though intrigued, I probably would have told them that they should do their own dirty work and leave me out of it. I wasn't a private investigator, nor was I a reporter. "Because I wouldn't have taken the case."

"So who is it? This anonymous Three?"

"What if it's Luce?" I said. "She's the only one other than us who witnessed Logan and his doppelganger at the mansion—"

"That we know of," James added.

"And she had the photocopy of Colin's file in her bag, which was the only reason we found him in the first place."

"That doesn't necessarily mean she's Three," James said. "She could have found it on her own. She's been following the same trail we have. Plus, Three hired you to follow her in the first place. Why would Luce hire you to follow herself?"

He had a point.

"And she isn't rich. There's no way she could offer you five thousand dollars or Colin ten thousand."

I reluctantly agreed. "The money has to eliminate Luce. Which means that someone else knows about Logan."

I felt like I was on a circular path that kept leading me back to the beginning. I didn't understand what Luce had to do with any of this, nor did I feel like I was any closer to figuring out who Three might be. "It could be anyone."

"So what did you tell him?" James asked. "About his payment?"

I took out my phone and drafted a new message. "I told him I'd ask Three."

<I talked to Colin Graham, I wrote.

It took a few minutes for Three to respond.

>Finally. I've been wondering when you were going to figure it out.

<If you knew what was happening, then why did you hire me?

>I already told you. You'll understand when you get to the end.

<This seems awfully close to the end.

>But it isn't.

A wave of nausea passed over me as I read Three's message. What else could there possibly be?

<But I uncovered what Logan was doing. What else is there?

>Do you want to know why I call myself Three?

<Yes.

>Because you'll be fixing three problems for me.

<Three? That wasn't part of the deal. You hired me to follow Luce and help her fix what she was working on. I discovered what she was working on. She's uncovering Logan's cheating scandal.

>That's the first problem. Though you haven't fixed it yet.

<Because I'm not sure what fix I'm supposed to do.
Do you want me to make it go away, or expose it?
>I told you, you'll have all the answers you need
when you get to the end. And to do that, you need
to finish the other two fixes.
<Okay, so what are they?
>You'll find out soon.
<Who are you?
>We've already had this conversation. Please don't
be dull. The Hana I know is interesting.
<When will Colin get his money?
>The same time you get yours.
<Which is when?
>Friday night. 10 p.m. Head of the River.

"We have to tell someone."

James had been trying to convince me for the entire ride home, though I was too stunned to consider it. Three's texts and the turn of events that day had flustered me. I didn't like surprises and had designed my life to minimize the likelihood of encountering them. One of the perks of fixing was that you knew all the secrets before they spilled.

"We can't," I said. "Not yet."

"So what, we wait until Friday? That's almost a week from now. What are we supposed to do, just go to school and pretend like nothing's wrong?"

"Yes," I said.

"But we have enough information to go out with it now."

"For what?" I asked. "An article? That was never the point."

"What was the point, then?"

"I was hired to do a job, and I haven't finished the job yet. It's not over."

"Says who?" James said. "The anonymous person on your phone? How do we know they're not just messing with you?"

"They haven't been messing with me so far," I said. "Don't you want to know who it is and why they chose the Head of the River as the place to meet?"

"They chose the Head of the River because it's crew related and this entire case has revolved around Logan, the crew star," James said. "And of course I'm curious who Three is, but their identity doesn't change what we know. We have everything we need. The whole story is here."

"But it isn't."

"Does it really matter who Three is?"

"Of course it does," I said, incredulous.

"Look, the important part of the story—what it's really about—is that dozens of students at St. Francis and the surrounding schools have been hiring a fake nonprofit to cheat their way into top colleges. Is Three a fascinating supporting character? Sure, but they're not integral to the story."

"The story *you're* planning on writing," I said. "I'm

supposed to finish the job I was hired to do. And if we tell people now, I might not be able to."

"Is this about the money?" James asked.

I didn't like the way he'd asked it. "It's about finishing the job. And don't pretend like you're morally superior. You're just as interested in getting a byline as you are in exposing the truth."

"Yeah. I'm a journalist. We uncover stories and publish them. There's nothing wrong with it. It's the reason I'm here."

It's the reason he was here. So abrupt, so final. Though he hadn't meant it as an insult, his words felt like an impact to the chest. I wanted to think he was here at least partly because of me.

"I didn't mean it like that," he said, reading my thoughts.

"Like what?" I said.

"Don't do that," he said. "Don't act like you don't think about it too."

I felt a knot form in my throat. The prospect of having a conversation about the exact nature of our relationship made me feel nauseated, partly because I didn't want to admit how much I'd gotten used to being around him, but mostly because I was scared he wouldn't feel the same. I felt grateful that I was driving so I could keep my eyes on the road. "Think about what?"

"This. This thing that we're doing. Spending all this time together. Texting. Calling."

I pulled down his street and parked next to his driveway. "We're solving a case. You said it yourself. You're only here because of your article. You want it to end."

I'd been trying to put my finger on why I felt so upset, and when I realized what it was, my heart dropped. The problem was that we'd never talked about what we would do once we reached the end.

"You know everything," James said softly. "How can you not know this?"

I could feel him studying me, begging me to look at him, but I couldn't bear it.

"What happened with us?" he asked me.

It was the question I'd been dreading to hear, the one all of his other questions were leading toward. He was referring to our past life, the one where we'd been friends. It felt so distant now that I could only remember it as a dream.

"You were there," I said, trying to talk around it. "You don't remember?"

"I was, but I still don't know what happened. We were friends and then we weren't. We were talking and then we weren't."

"It was a little more complicated than that."

I didn't want to explore it anymore. It was painful enough the first time; why relive it?

I gazed up at his house. His kitchen window was lit from the inside, and through it I could see his mom chopping food and his dad setting the table. I could almost smell the scent of their house, warm and savory like simmering soup. If I shut my eyes, I might be able to convince myself that my parents were sitting at the table in the next room over, laughing while they finished their drinks. It felt so real it was painful.

"You can come in, you know," he said. "Say hi to my parents. I'm sure they'd love to see you."

"I should get home."

Anyone else might have left, but James didn't move. For some reason my heart started to race.

"They ask about you all the time," he said. "They want to know how you're doing."

"And what do you tell them?"

James searched my face as though he was looking for his answer. The windows of the car had started to fog from our breathing.

I wondered if, like me, he was reliving all the evenings we'd spent at that table.

For a moment, I thought he might kiss me. Maybe he thought it too. But instead he reached for the door. "I tell them I don't know."

17

We decided that we wouldn't tell anyone. Not yet, at least. I would work on figuring out who Three was and what the remaining two problems were in my case. Meanwhile, James would work on his article. In theory, it sounded fine. Then we went to school.

It felt uncanny. All my classmates blithely went about their day, unaware of what was going on beneath the surface. I stood on the path and watched them, unable to shake the feeling that they were actors on a set, moving on a track from one assigned spot to another. Everywhere I turned, I saw faces from the files. Cecily. Marianne. Analisa. And Logan. I almost felt bad for him, strolling from class to class, unaware that his life was about to change.

James was thinking it too. His gaze drifted to Logan in class, his focus sharpening. All the while, I thought about Three, who was sitting somewhere in the dining hall while

I ate lunch, passing me on the stairwell and handing in assignments, all right in front of me. I had no idea what the second two problems were in the case, and was confused as to why Three wanted to pay me before I'd figured out what they were. It felt like a riddle. I was sitting in class, trying to solve it, when my phone vibrated.

>**Still on for tomorrow?**

It was Pete Lasky. I'd been so distracted that I'd forgotten that it was almost Friday and that I had plans. We had a date.

<**Yes.**

"You're still going?" James asked when I told him.

It was in between fourth and fifth period, and we were standing in the rear stairway by the drinking fountains because it was one of the few spots in school that afforded privacy.

"It was part of our deal," I said. "He held up his side. I have to hold up mine. And anyway, it's a good place to do research. Maybe I can figure out what the last two fixes are."

When Pete had asked me where I wanted to go on our date, I'd asked him to take me to one of Cecily's notoriously elite parties. When I'd told James, he'd rolled his eyes, assuming that I'd wanted to feel like I had my old life back again, but that wasn't true. Logan would be there, as would Luce and every other powerful person at school. It was an opportunity.

"The date is earlier that night," I said. "I can still make it. I'll just leave early."

"How are you going to do that if Pete's driving you?"

"I was hoping you'd pick me up?"

"Who says I'm free?" James said. "Maybe I have a date too."

"You don't have a date," I said, expecting him to crack a grin. When he didn't, my face dropped. "Wait, do you?"

James never lied, so I was caught off guard when he hesitated. "Maybe. I can probably still pick you up, though."

I was too stunned to organize my thoughts. How did he even have time to set up a date? Had he been talking to someone while we'd been working on this case and I hadn't realized it?

"Who's it with?" I asked, unable to help myself.

"Samantha."

"Samantha *Ansley*?" I said in disbelief. Samantha Ansley was the cheerful daughter of a fossil fuel executive. She rode horses and had a wholesome lost-at-the-county-fair look.

James wasn't one to relish in someone else's discomfort, though he was watching me with interest. "Yeah. Why, are you surprised?"

Now that I thought about it, she had, for years, been saying that James was cute.

"I mean, yeah. I never pictured her as your type."

"What's my type?"

I begged my brain to stop panicking and racked it for an answer. "I don't know, someone smart, brooding, misanthropic."

James thought for a moment. "So, you?"

"That's not what I meant. I never said that."

"So you just accidentally described yourself?"

"I'm not brooding or misanthropic," I said.

"Sure. You just spend all of your time alone and push away the few friends you have left."

"I didn't push anyone away. They left me."

"Is that how you remember it?"

I wasn't sure how we had gotten to talking about the past again, but I didn't like it.

I hugged my books to my chest. "You know what, I'm happy for you," I said. "Enjoy your date."

"I will."

"Good," I said.

"Good," he said. "I'll see you on Friday, then, on the other side."

Pete was driving a red sports car when he pulled up to my town house the following evening.

"My lady," Pete said, opening the door for me with a goofy bow. I could tell he had tried hard to look nice.

I rolled my eyes and tried not to laugh. "Stop it."

"Ah," he said. "You prefer *sir*."

I surveyed the inside of his car, which he had cleared of

its normal detritus of wrappers and empty cans of energy drink, and smelled strongly of artificial cherry.

"Just to reiterate the ground rules, no groping or unwanted touching, okay?" I said. "This is just a casual hangout."

Pete feigned offense. "Me? I would never do such a thing to a lady. Or a sir."

"Good."

Pete looked me up and down. "You look very dashing tonight, sir."

I couldn't help but smile. "Thanks. So do you."

He grinned and stepped on the gas.

I hadn't been inside Cecily's compound since that afternoon pool party the day the news about my dad broke, and since then, it had appeared that they'd redecorated.

"Didn't they used to have a statue of a golden horse here?" I asked as we walked into the foyer, which was empty of both people and furniture. What had once looked like the Palace of Versailles was now austere and vaguely brutalist. In the distance, I could hear music, voices.

"The ugly one with the king riding it?" Pete asked.

"No, that was the one by the pool. This one was rearing up and baring its teeth."

"Oh, right. That one was ugly too. Yeah, all that stuff has been gone since last year. Her dad got remarried and his new wife switched things up. I managed to snag that painting of all those guys killing the boar."

"The one from the kitchen? Why did you even want it? It was disgusting."

Pete shrugged. "What's wrong with that?"

We walked through the dimly lit halls until the din of the party grew closer. Though Cecily and I had never been close friends, our parents once traveled in the same circles, which meant that I'd spent many evenings in the maze of rooms in the back of her house, eating canapés and ranking how cute the caterers were. We found everyone there, gathered around Cecily, who was holding up a bowl to their rapt attention. All eyes turned to us.

Cecily had started having monthly exclusive parties, which she called *salons*, not long after the Catastrophic Event. They were notorious primarily because no one knew what happened at them, only that they were a place where everyone's perfectly groomed facades could be dropped for a night. It was impossible to get in unless you had an invite, which were given only to people Cecily and her friends deemed interesting enough to merit attention. The only reason I was there was because of Pete.

I'd been slightly embarrassed to suggest to Pete that he take me to one of Cecily's parties. I'd told myself that it would be a good opportunity to see Logan and Luce in their natural habitats, but that wasn't the only reason. Over the years, I'd tried to convince myself that I didn't care about them, but deep down, I'd always wanted to go.

"Hana?" Cecily said, surprised. I understood then that

she hadn't known I was coming. She shot a questioning look at Pete, who was saying hi to Keith, either oblivious to the sudden tension in the room or purposely ignoring it.

I'd known some version of this was going to happen, but it didn't make it any easier. Across the room, Luce was sitting next to Logan and their friends. She stared at me with interest, as though she was surprised by but not displeased with my presence.

"Hey—" I began to say, when I noticed Samantha Ansley sitting on an armchair.

Wasn't she supposed to be on a date with James tonight?

I considered the possibility that he had canceled when he emerged from the hall, studying a painting on the wall with mild distaste. I didn't have time to mask my shock. He met my gaze and gave me a knowing look, clearly amused that he had caught me off guard. Then he sat next to Samantha, who whispered something in his ear.

I cleared my throat. "I'm going to get a drink," I said to Pete. "Do you want anything?"

"Mountain Dew," he said. "I don't drink."

It was unexpected, considering his line of business.

"I know. Everyone's scandalized when they find out. I don't like the taste, and even if I did, it's not good for the mind." He tapped his temple.

"Right," I said, and walked to a bar cart, which was set up with fancy glasses and bottles of mixers. Behind it stood a liquor cabinet with its doors propped open. I scanned the options, when James strode up beside me and reached for a candied nut from a bowl by the tonic. His arm grazed mine.

"Only Cecily would serve candied nuts at a high school party," James said. "Why does this party feel like an art auction?"

"What are you doing here?" I asked under my breath.

"Fieldwork. Plus, I did say I would give you a ride. Think of it as me arriving a little bit early."

I didn't want to admit it, but I was relieved that his date hadn't been real. "I can't believe you let me think you were actually going on a date with her."

"You know, she can be funny," James said.

"Great," I said, spritzing a lime into my seltzer. "I'm happy for you."

"How's your date going?" he asked.

"Fine," I said. "Good."

"Neon drink," he observed, staring at the cup of Mountain Dew. "Orange car?"

"Red one tonight."

"The scope of his interests is limitless."

As we returned to our respective dates, Cecily stood up.

"It's time for our monthly confessional," she said, and passed around a platter with pencils and little rectangles of paper that looked incredibly familiar.

"Write down the worst thing you've done in the last month," Cecily said. "Then put it in the bowl."

I couldn't believe it. It was our game.

I tapped my pencil against my jeans. James was sitting next to Samantha, considering what to write. Did he even have anything to write? He seemed like someone who rarely did anything wrong. On the couch nearby, Luce had already finished and was whispering something to Logan. Did he look distracted? Agitated? I doubted he'd written the actual worst thing he'd done in the past month. Luce couldn't have, either. Though I still hadn't figured out what she'd done to merit this investigation, it couldn't be good.

The bowl was full by the time I dropped my paper inside.

"Are you ready for some orange lies?" Pete whispered to me.

"What's an orange lie?"

"It's a little lie that you tell to distract from a truth that's much worse. Like when you're on an interview and they ask what your weaknesses are," Pete said. "You can't tell them what you're actually bad at because you'd never get the job, so you have to say something dumb like *I try too hard* or *I'm too much of a perfectionist*."

Cecily picked up the bowl and stirred with her fingers. "Drinks ready," she said. "You know the drill."

"It's a drinking game," Pete whispered to me as she chose a slip of paper. "She reads them out loud and you drink if you've ever done the same thing."

The game had evolved since the last time I'd played, and I was glad I'd written a throwaway.

An expectant hush fell over the room as she read the first confession. "*I took a few bottles of expensive wine from my parents' stash, and when they found out, I blamed it on the cleaners,*" Cecily read. "Ouch. I mean, I've definitely taken my parents' drinks. Blaming it on the help is pretty extra, though."

A look of disgust passed over James's face as Cecily scanned the room, trying to figure out who'd written it.

"If I had to put money on it, I'd guess Ruth," Pete whispered to me.

"No way," I said. "First of all, her parents wouldn't notice or care if their wine was missing. And second, she's cruel but not like that. I'd guess Marianne."

Pete studied me, clearly smitten, which made me wish I hadn't said anything.

"How about this," Cecily said. "Drink if you've taken alcohol from your parents or blamed the cleaning people for something they didn't do." She tipped her glass and took a drink. Nearly everyone else did too.

Cecily crumpled up the slip and threw it into the room. Keith caught it, which apparently meant it was his turn. He chose a slip from the bowl and smirked when he read it. "I think we all know who this one is. *I sold prescription drugs at school. I bargained with the school dean to decrease the punishment if I snitched on my classmates. I accepted bribes and favors from my classmates to take their names off my list. I also let my dog poop on a neighbor's lawn and didn't clean it up and borrowed my sister's iPad and shattered the screen accidentally."*

The room grew animated as everyone turned to Pete.

"No one else guilty of that?" he said with a smirk. "Seriously? No one can relate? Well, bottoms up."

There might have been a fallout from his confession had he included anyone in the room on his list, but he hadn't, so no one cared.

The party got louder as the game wore on. Drinks spilled. Someone cranked the music up. Everyone's attention waned as people dug through the bowl and picked confessions at random. Papers littered the ground.

I chatted with Pete, whose company I might have enjoyed had I not been so distracted by Luce and Logan, who seemed to be in the middle of a hushed disagreement unbeknownst to the revelers around them. What were they fighting about? Why did Logan keep glancing at the clock?

"So which one do you think?" Pete asked, interrupting my thoughts. He was weighing the pros and cons of fulfilling his additional community service hours at a mentoring program versus a food pantry.

"I think I'd be a good role model for little kids," he said.

I pried my gaze away from Luce and Logan for a moment.

"Yeah, sure." When I looked back, they were gone. I blinked and searched the room for them but saw no trace.

"I'll be right back," I said to Pete. "I have to use the bathroom."

I wasn't sure why I went looking for them; I only had a feeling. I pushed through the party into the hallway, which was the only direction they could have gone in without me noticing, but it was empty. I ventured down it, peeking in open doors, but the rooms they led to were all empty.

The hallway culminated in a sunroom with a door that led out back. Maybe they'd gotten into an argument and left. Or maybe they'd made up and snuck upstairs.

I was about to head back to the party when I noticed the pool through the windows. It was flanked by white lounge chairs and was lit from below, its water glimmering in the moonlight. The last time I was there was when I'd gotten the news. I could still remember how hot the ground had felt beneath my feet as I followed Cecily's housekeeper to the kitchen, where my mother's assistant, Claudia, had been waiting for me.

I slid open the glass door and stepped outside. The night was unseasonably warm, and I slipped off my shoes and was approaching the pool when I heard someone clear their throat.

Startled, I spun around.

"Sorry," a voice said. "I didn't mean to scare you."

Logan was sitting on a lounge chair, his face in his hands.

I tried to gather my composure. "I didn't realize anyone was here."

When my eyes adjusted to the darkness, I could see that he was in distress, leg tapping, hands fidgeting, expression blank as though he'd taken off a mask that he'd been wearing for a long time and didn't know what his face was supposed to look like now that it was out in the open.

Though I knew I shouldn't sympathize with him, I recognized his unabashed terror and couldn't help but feel a kind of kinship. I'd felt a version of that fear once too. "Are you okay?" I asked.

I waited for him to put his mask back on and smile, but he didn't. "Not really."

I said nothing, hoping he'd continue.

"Have you ever felt like you fucked up?" he asked me.

"Yes."

"No, I mean like, really fucked up. To the point of no return."

"Yes," I insisted. "Why do you think I got into fixing?"

He waited for me to continue.

"You know how they say that people choose careers based on what they can't get right in their own lives? Like writers write not because they know what they want to say, but because they don't know and need to spend their lives figuring it out? I fix things because I want to fix my own problems but don't know how. Maybe if I do it long enough, I will eventually."

I must have said something right, because he was listening.

"Why?" I ventured. "What did you do that's so unfixable?"

I knew he wouldn't tell me but was curious to see how he'd respond.

"Put it this way: I can't write it on one of those slips."

"That bad?"

Logan shrugged. "How did you do it?"

"Do what?"

"Face everyone. After it all went down with your dad, and everyone was talking about you. It must have been unbearable."

I didn't realize until then that none of my friends had ever acknowledged what had happened in the aftermath, and that I had needed to hear it. "I didn't have a choice. If I'd been given a way out, I would have taken it."

"Do you think it's worth it?" Logan asked. "Everything we do?"

"What do you mean?"

"Sometimes I think about animals," Logan said. "How they just sleep, eat, and roam around looking for shade and water. I think about that and then I think about all the bullshit we've created for ourselves—all the pressure and expectations. We need to go to school and get good grades and land great internships so that we can go to a good college where we then have to get good grades and land even better internships, all so we can get a good job that pays us money that we can pile up and save so that our kids can go to good schools and get good grades and land good internships. Why can't we just be like all the other animals, eating and sleeping and roaming around looking for shade and water?"

"Well, there are some upsides to being humans, like hospitals and heated water and pasta, but I get your point."

Logan let out a sad laugh. "Pasta."

I'd assumed his inner turmoil was fueled by the guilt associated with hiring someone to take the SAT for him, but my instinct told me that this seemed more acute. As far as Logan was concerned, no one knew about his doppelganger; he was getting away with it. So why was he so upset now?

"Sorry, I went off a little bit there," he said, standing up.

"It's okay," I murmured.

"Thanks for listening," he said. It was an invitation for me to leave.

"Anytime."

On the periphery of my vision, I saw him turn and stare out at the water as I retreated inside. Though it was completely reasonable for him to have second thoughts about his con, I couldn't help but wonder if there was something more that I was missing.

I was turning our conversation over in my mind when a figure filled the hallway. Keith. Something looked different about him, but I couldn't place what. Was it his clothes? He was wearing a black hoodie now, with matching black sweats. Had he been wearing all black earlier in the party?

A gym bag was slung over his shoulder. I was wondering what was inside when he noticed I was eyeing it and shifted it to his other arm. Odd, I thought.

His eyes narrowed and followed me as we passed. "Hey," he said.

The last time I'd spoken to Keith was at a chance meeting in the basement of the student center, six months after the Catastrophic Event, and as a result, he and I had a sort of kinship, too, but I haven't told you about that, have I?

My eyes traveled with him as he walked in the direction of the pool. "Hey," I said.

When he rounded the corner and was out of sight, I took out my phone and checked the time. In an hour, I was supposed to leave to meet Three at the river, where ostensibly I'd be receiving payment. That, too, was strange, considering I still hadn't figured out the other two problems I was supposed to fix.

At the end of the hall, I could see the light from the party shining through the doorway, interrupted every so often by the shadows of my classmates. I didn't want to return. Instead, I pulled out my phone and typed a text to James while I made my way to the kitchen.

<I don't know why, but I feel like something weird is going on, I wrote, and pressed send.

"What do you mean?" a voice said, startling me.

James was standing in the kitchen, drinking a soda and flipping through a cookbook.

"What are you doing here?"

"The same thing you're doing here," he said, his voice hushed. "Escaping our dates. Did you know that this house has no books other than cookbooks, and even those are for show?" James held up the book he was looking at. "It's pristine, probably has never even been opened."

"They definitely don't cook for themselves," I said.

"Wealth is wasted on the rich," James said. "Their lives are so vacant."

"Mine was better when I was rich."

"Your life isn't over yet, you know," he said.

"Easy for you to say. You don't have to live it."

"Hana Yang Lerner, always the life of the party," James said. "So what was your text about?"

"Did you tell anyone about Logan?" I asked.

"Of course not. Why?"

"I just had a bizarre encounter with him. He seemed really upset and was talking about how he envied the lives of animals and how simple they were."

"Interesting," James said. "I mean, I can understand why he'd be feeling guilty."

"It was more than that," I said. "He was acting like he'd already been caught. Like someone knew and he was about to do something terrible. It really felt like he was standing on the precipice, looking down into the abyss."

"What kind of terrible thing?" James asked.

"I don't know," I said. "And then I saw Keith going to meet him. That was weird, too. He was wearing all black and was carrying a gym bag that he moved out of view when I passed him."

"Black isn't that uncommon of a color to wear. And he's an athlete; he always has a gym bag."

"I know, but this felt different. The way he looked at me, like he was worried about people seeing him."

James considered me. "If you had a hunch, then it's worth exploring."

That's when I heard a familiar laugh in the hallway. Pete.

"Come on," James whispered, and nodded to the dining room, where a hutch of fancy china towered over a large, formal table. Of course. Without having to speak, we snuck beneath it.

It felt like we'd traveled back in time, and instead of Cecily's house, we were in a crowded hotel ballroom, taking refuge beneath the dessert table. If I reached behind me, I could almost convince myself that the creased book of minute mysteries that we used to read to each other would still be there.

From beneath the tablecloth, I could hear Pete's voice

approach. Through the chair legs I could see his shoes walk through the kitchen, pause, then backtrack.

James held a finger to his lips. Then he took out his phone and started typing. A moment later, my phone vibrated.

>Hey, he'd sent me.

I tried not to smile. <Hey, I wrote back.

It felt like we were doing something illicit, like we were kids again, surrounded by adults constantly making demands of our time, trying to zap our joy with scratchy clothes and boring fundraisers.

>Have tables gotten shorter? James wrote. This felt a lot roomier when we were eleven.

<I kind of like it cramped. Feels cozy.

>Like old times. Except now there's a real mystery.

<I miss the snacks, I wrote.

>Why do people even have dining rooms when they also have a table in the kitchen that they use on most days?

<To store their fancy plates.

>Why not just forgo the fancy plates, too? James wrote.

<If you want a big house, you have to have rooms to fill it. There are only so many living rooms a mansion can reasonably contain.

>Seems uncreative.

<Agreed. This carpet is really fancy, I wrote.

>Fancy = ugly?

<I don't think it's that bad.

>I wonder what the etymology of "Oriental Carpet" is, James wrote. Has to be racist.

<You should write an article about it.

>I'd have to ask my partner.

< . . . ?

>You didn't hear? I work on a team now. It's kind of ruined me. Hard to imagine going back to solo reporting.

<Who is this incredible partner? She must be some kind of investigative genius who's both cunning and funny, with the charm and looks to match.

>She is.

I wasn't sure what was happening and felt suddenly nervous.

<I think Pete's gone. It's probably safe to emerge, I wrote.

He typed something, then paused as if deciding whether or not to send it.

>Am I allowed to say that I don't want to?

He looked at me then, breaking the fourth wall and reminding me that he was right there beside me, his arm grazing mine. The smile had faded from his face, but he wasn't unhappy.

I swallowed, realizing then that we were alone together in a dark room beneath a table, a little place all of our own. I didn't want to leave either but was too scared to admit it.

217

I inched my hand toward his until our fingertips barely touched. Slowly, cautiously, he traced the edge of my thumb as if it was something expensive, something he wasn't supposed to touch. A prickle ran up my skin.

"Hana—" he began to say.

I laced my fingers through his as he leaned in, brushing the hair away from my eyes, when my phone alarm went off.

I jumped, shaken back into the present, and extricated my hand from his. "We have to go."

18

James and I barely looked at each other as we snuck out the side door of the party. I'd texted Pete, telling him that I wasn't feeling well and had to go home, and though I'd told far bigger lies than that before, I couldn't help but feel guilty.

I tried to shake it from my mind as I slid into the passenger seat of James's car and thought about what would have happened had my phone alarm not gone off. I'd been wanting and dreading that moment for a long time now, and felt nervous that even though it had been subverted, there still might be no going back. The problem wasn't that we might have kissed; it was what would have happened after. James was someone I couldn't keep secrets from. He was a person who found the locked doors and pried them open, and there was one door in particular that I wanted to keep shut.

James must have been thinking some variation of the same thought, because he was uncharacteristically quiet.

"So that was weird," I said, hoping that if I pretended to be unaware of the tension between us, he might play along and we could act like it hadn't happened. But he didn't.

"I don't want to play this game anymore," he said.

I swallowed. My inclination was to defuse with humor, but I knew it wouldn't work.

"What do you want, Hana?" he asked.

It took me a while to figure out how to respond. The problem was that I knew exactly what I wanted, but I couldn't have it. "I know that you're the only person I want to sit alone with in a car for hours on end. I know that I think about you when we're not together."

His face softened as I spoke. "So why do you keep pushing me away?"

I wanted to be different; I wanted to be the person he thought I was. But I wasn't. "I don't know."

He stared at the road, unable to understand.

"What do you want?" I asked.

He looked over at me, his eyes sad as though he already knew it was a foregone conclusion. "You."

The sky was clear and starless as we drove to the waterfront. Beneath it, the Potomac was black, its water flowing like ink beneath the bridge. We'd arrived early; there were no other cars in the lot. The grassy sprawl of the riverbank was empty, and below it, the docks swayed in the current. Three hadn't told me where to go, though I had a hunch.

Instead of parking in the lot, James drove by it and pulled off on the side of the road, where the car would be concealed by trees. We didn't know what we would find; it would be safer if we stayed out of sight. He was unbuckling his seat belt as if to join me when I stopped him.

"Just me," I said. "It's my client and my case."

"No way. We don't know who this person is or why they want to meet here. It could be dangerous."

I took out my phone and dialed a number. A moment later, James's phone vibrated.

"Pick up and leave the call on," I said. "That way you'll know what's happening. If I need help, I'll say . . ." I thought for a moment. "Ruby."

"Ruby as in your dog?" James asked. "I love Ruby, but how are you going to sneak that into conversation without it being obvious that you're signaling?"

He had a fair point. "Fine, I'll say, *It's getting late.*"

"Too easy to get lost in conversation and too common. You could say it accidentally."

"Do you have any ideas, then?"

James considered it. "How about you clear your throat, then say, *Sorry, I think there's something in the air?*"

It was a good suggestion, and despite the awkwardness between us, I was grateful to have him there. "Okay."

I slipped on the hood of my coat and crept past the

picnic tables, down the hill to the water. The boathouse stood by the docks, its lights off, its doors locked. There, I waited in the shadows, where I could see Coin Rock jutting out of the side of the hill, its brass marker catching the light from the streetlamps above. That, I was almost certain, was where we would meet.

I waited. The phone in my pocket felt somehow heavier with the call on. Though James's end was quiet, I could almost hear the *shh* of his breathing. It was a comfort knowing that he was with me.

Then, the sound of tires on pavement. A car pulled into the lot and idled by the curb. Its headlights were off, which felt like a sign. I squinted at it, then took out my phone.

"Can you see who it is?" I whispered to James.

A car door slammed.

"One driver," James said. "Tall. Broad shoulders. Wearing a hood, so it's hard to see his face."

"Do you recognize the car?"

"Blue SUV. Audi."

There was a handful of kids at school who drove Audis, but only one person drove a blue SUV. "It can't be. That doesn't make any sense."

"Why, who is it?"

"Logan," I whispered.

I couldn't make out his face as he scanned the park, but I recognized the shape of his shoulders, the slant of his posture as he trudged down the hill.

If Logan was Three, that meant he had hired me to investigate himself, which I could hardly believe he'd do. I had to be missing something. I waited to see what he would do.

He crept to Coin Rock, scanned the riverbank to see if anyone was watching, then placed a duffel bag on the grass beside it. Quickly, he pulled out a phone and sent a text. Then he hastened up the hill to the parking lot and drove away.

Who had he texted? And what was in the bag?

"Is he gone?" I whispered into my phone.

"Yeah," James said.

"He left a bag," I said. "Should I get it?"

"I don't know."

That's when my phone vibrated. It was a text from Three.

>Logan should have left a bag on Coin Rock. Do you see it?

So Three wasn't Logan. Was Logan working for Three? That didn't make sense either.

<Yes, I wrote back.

>Good. Pick it up and open it.

The docks bobbed in the water as I snuck up to Coin Rock. If Three was somewhere on the riverbank watching me, I couldn't see them. The duffel bag that Logan had left behind was surprisingly heavy when I picked it up. My phone vibrated again.

>Inside, there should be three bags. Do you notice a theme? Tell me the colors.

I unzipped it to find three smaller nylon bags of varying sizes.

<One is blue. One is red. One is black.

>Good. The blue one is for you.

The blue bag was the smallest of the three. I opened it to find rolls of money held neatly together in rubber bands. My payment. Judging from the feel of the other two bags, they were also filled with cash.

<I don't understand, I wrote. Why is Logan paying me?

>He isn't, at least not that he's aware of. He's paying me.

My mind raced. Why would Logan be paying Three?

<Does he know who you are? I asked.

>He knows me as Three, just like you do. Only you each owe me a different set of three. For you, it's three problems. For him, it's three bags.

My mind raced. If Logan owed Three money, he couldn't have been hired, which left only one explanation for why he was dropping duffels of money on the banks of the Potomac: Three had discovered his con and had black-mailed him.

<Who are the others for? I asked.

>You'll see soon enough.

<Why are you paying me when I haven't finished

the job yet? I've only uncovered one of the three problems you said I had to fix.

>But you are fixing the second problem. Right now.

"What?" I whispered.

That was when I heard a phone vibrate in the distance. I spun around and peered into the darkness, where I saw the dim glow of a screen in a pocket. "James?" I whispered, hoping it was him.

The screen moved toward me. I tried to make out who it was, but I couldn't find their face. Were they wearing all black?

James's voice sounded through my phone. "Is everything okay?"

My mouth went dry. It wasn't him. I gripped the bag and backed away. The screen had disappeared so that all I could see in the night was the outline of its owner as he stalked toward me.

I was too scared to move quickly and stumbled as I turned to run up the hill. Then, remembering my phone, I cleared my throat. "Sorry," I said, hoping James would hear me. "I think there's something in—"

Then a voice called my name. "Hana?"

I stopped. I knew that voice. It was deep and surprisingly textured, perfect for delivering soliloquies.

"Keith?" I whispered. "What are you doing here?"

He pulled off his balaclava and ran a hand through his

hair. Keith had always looked older than he was, but in the past two years his features had gotten more pronounced, like he was an exaggeration of his ninth-grade self.

"It's you?" he asked in disbelief. "You're Three?"

"What? No," I said. "How do you know about Three?"

I distinctly remembered searching and not finding a folder for Keith at A Brighter Future, which I assumed meant that he wasn't implicated in the cheating scandal. Before James's voice could sound from my phone, I slipped my phone in my pocket and turned the volume of the speaker down so that Keith wouldn't know someone else was listening.

"I'm not answering any questions until you tell me why you're here," he said, his eyes darting around the park.

"Three hired me for a case," I said. "They told me to come here tonight to collect my payment. I've never met them, nor do I know who they are. Now, why are you here?"

Keith didn't answer immediately. "As a favor to Logan. Three was blackmailing him. He asked me to come here and watch the money drop and tell him who picked it up, because he assumed it would be Three."

His gaze drifted to the duffel in my hand. The unspoken part was that once he told Logan who had blackmailed him, he and his family would ruin them.

I tightened my grip on the bag and inched away. "And what are you going to tell him?"

Keith clenched his jaw the way he had during Macbeth's monologue, when his character was trying to decide whether or not he should kill the king. I saw then why Keith was a good actor; he was torn between selves, between conflicting loyalties. "I'm not sure."

"Do you know what he's done?" I asked. "To justify the blackmailing?"

"A little," Keith admitted.

"And you're still protecting him?"

Keith's face looked pained. "He knows about me. And he's protected me."

"So have I," I said.

Keith faltered, pulled between two choices.

I backed away from him. "I'm not Three," I said. "I'm asking you not to tell him that you saw me."

The phone in his hand lit up with a call. It had to be Logan. I wondered if he would pick it up, if he would tell Logan that he found me.

"Please," I whispered.

He let it ring.

"How do I know you're not lying?" he asked.

"You just have to trust me," I said. "Like you did before."

19

"Don't worry. No one's talking about you."

That's what Marianne told me just after the Cata-strophic Event, when I'd confided in her that I was scared of what people would say about me at school.

"You're not your dad," she said. "Everyone knows that."

I wanted to believe her and was grateful for her kind-ness. She'd been one of the first people to call me after the news had broken and had checked on me after my falling-out with Luce, after my fight with James. Though Marianne and I had been friends for years, we didn't actu-ally have a lot in common, and I'd always felt that we were still skimming the surface. So I'd never expected her to be the one who was there for me in a time of need, to be so generous or considerate, and I felt bad for all the times I thought poorly of her.

I repeated Marianne's words as a mantra as I walked

through the hall after third period, where every few steps I thought I heard my name. It was a month after the Catastrophic Event, and my family was still in the thick of our legal spiral, our faces still a regular fixture on the evening news. The only way I could get through the day was to remind myself of what Marianne had said. No one was talking about me. I was just stressed and paranoid.

It was free period, and though Marianne, Ruth, and Cecily had invited me to go to the student center with them, I'd declined for the library instead. After the upheaval of the past month, I'd fallen behind and needed to catch up on my assignments. I was already outside when I realized I'd forgotten one of my books in the classroom and hurried upstairs. That's when I heard voices beneath the stairwell.

"I heard they were being forced out of their house," Cecily whispered. "Apparently the victim is suing them."

I froze. Was she talking about me?

"They have to sell all their things," Ruth said. "Their furniture. Their appliances. I heard her mom even has to sell her clothes."

"Can she even sell them?" Marianne said. "I know everyone says she has good taste, but I always thought she was trying too hard."

I felt like I'd been punched in the stomach. Marianne was talking about me too?

"I know," said Ruth. "Wearing all those Asian outfits

because she knew she would get photographed in them. Those silk dresses she wore looked so tacky. Way too shiny."

"Ugh, the reds and golds," Marianne said. "She looked like an airline attendant."

"And no one could say that she didn't look good because that would be offensive," Ruth said. "You could only say that she looked *amazing* or *daring* and was *paying homage to her cultural heritage.*"

Was this what they really thought about me? About us?

"Everyone always talked about Hana like she was this golden child, but was she ever really that special?" Cecily continued.

"I always found her a little boring," Ruth said.

"She has that smug smile," Cecily said. "Like she thinks she's so perfect."

"She's not perfect anymore," Ruth said.

"Honestly, she's kind of pathetic now," Marianne said. "All she does is complain and worry that everyone's going to hate her. It's getting old. I mean, come on, of course people aren't going to want to be seen with you now that your father's guilty of nearly killing someone. But I can't tell her that, so I just have to nod and reassure her that everything is going to be okay. Honestly, the most surprising part is that she seems to buy it."

"She's desperate," Cecily said. "And in denial."

"I still can't believe you're spending so much time listening to her," Ruth said. "It's charity work, really."

"I know," Marianne said. "I should log the hours and turn them in for my community service requirement."

They all laughed. Their voices were hollow, terrible. Witches under the moonlight.

I wanted to disappear, to press myself into the wall. I wanted to hurl my bag at them, to make them know what pain really felt like. Instead, I backed away and escaped outside.

The day was cold and drizzling, the trees naked, the sky gray. I hurried down the walkway to Woodward Hall. It was a quiet building; no one hung out there except to go to the college counseling office on the first floor. I wasn't going there. I walked past it to a door by the back stairwell and opened it.

The room smelled of dusty sheets and yellowed piles of paper. It used to be a music room, where orchestra instruction and after-hours lessons were held—a perfect application because the walls were thick and it had no windows, which meant that sound didn't travel.

After the orchestra moved to a renovated space in the theater, the room fell into disuse and was now mostly used for storage. I'd always known about it but had never spent time there until recently, when I'd stumbled upon it while looking for a place to eat lunch without the stares and whispers from the dining hall.

Now I retreated to the stool and table that I'd set up by an old piano, while Marianne's voice played in my head on repeat.

Then the door opened. Startled, I hid behind a bookshelf. I assumed whoever it was had followed me there. But why? The only reason I could guess was to harass me, to see me at my worst. But no one had been following me. I'd checked.

I waited until I heard voices.

"Did you tell her?" a boy said. It sounded like Keith.

"Of course not," another boy said. This one sounded like Adam Goldman.

Strange. I bent down to inspect their shoes to make sure I was right, and sure enough, there they were—Keith's sneakers and Adam's loafers.

Though Keith had starred in *Macbeth* the previous spring, which Adam had done the marketing for, to the best of my knowledge, they weren't friends.

"Then how does she know?" Keith asked, his voice panicked.

"She must have seen us."

Seen them do what?

"Where?"

"At the movie theater, apparently."

Keith started to pace. "We should have been more careful," he said. "I knew we shouldn't have met outside. We should have met in a house."

"Whose, yours?" Adam asked.

"No, of course not."

"Mine?"

"Yours is better than mine," Keith said.

"My parents don't know either, and though they've probably guessed by now, I doubt they would appreciate finding us on the couch in the living room."

I had a pretty good idea of what I was hearing but almost couldn't believe it. All the girls at school thought of Keith as a heartthrob, and as far as I knew, he'd always said he was interested in girls. Though, had he? Or had he just let everyone believe it? Now that I thought of it, he'd never dated anyone, and not due to a lack of external interest.

Was it possible that he was dating Adam? Adam and I had never been close. In fact, all of my friends, now former friends, despised him. I thought back to the last party I'd been to at Logan's house. How Keith hadn't joined in when everyone was hating on Adam. How the handwriting on the confession I'd chosen from the bowl had looked like Keith's. *I haven't been honest about who I am.* Maybe this was what he had meant.

"We should have gone to a movie theater farther away," Keith now said.

"Next time we will."

"I don't care about next time," Keith said. "I care about this time. We can't let her tell anyone. No one knows about me. My parents would flip if they found out. And my older brother."

"I know," Adam said softly.

"Do you, though?"

233

"Of course I do," Adam said. "Why are you acting like this is my fault? It's not like I caused this or forced you to do anything."

There was a long silence. "I know," Keith said. "I'm sorry. I just don't know what I'll do if anyone finds out."

"Is it that bad?" Adam said, his voice cracking. "To be seen with me?"

Keith hesitated. "You know it's not about you."

"Isn't it, though?" Adam asked. "If it was someone else, someone with more social capital, would you be less ashamed?"

"I'm not ashamed," Keith insisted.

"You're a good actor," Adam murmured.

"I'm not acting."

Another long pause. "Maybe we can figure this out," Adam said. "Clarissa is someone who's on the periphery of the popular group. What if you tell her that if she tells anyone, you'll make sure she's never invited to another crew party again?"

There was only one Clarissa at school, which meant they had to be talking about Clarissa Page.

Clarissa was one year older than us and was the human embodiment of a car rear-ending a minivan that spun out and crashed into a bus, which skidded diagonally, knocking out a row of cars before blocking the road and hitting a fire hydrant that then flooded the street. She wore heavy mascara that always seemed to be smudged from crying and looked perpetually like she was wearing an outfit that she'd accidentally fallen asleep in on the bathroom floor.

The problem with Adam's plan was that it wouldn't work.

Though I didn't know Clarissa well, I'd encountered her once in the bathroom. She'd been crying over a breakup and had asked me if I had a lighter. When I'd said no, she'd asked me how I'd managed to be so perfect. I wasn't perfect, I'd told her, and she'd laughed. But you are, she'd said.

I cleared my throat. Keith and Adam spun around, and though I couldn't see their faces, I could feel their panic rippling through the room.

"Who's there?" Keith demanded.

I emerged from my hiding spot and gave them an apologetic look as they took me in.

"Hana?" Keith said.

"You've been here this whole time?" Adam said. "Just listening to us?"

"Now another person knows," Keith said, his voice frantic. "Soon it'll be the whole school."

"I won't tell anyone," I said.

I met Keith's gaze, but he quickly looked away. He was embarrassed, I realized.

"And I don't think your plan with Clarissa will work," I added.

"I didn't ask your opinion," Adam said.

"I know," I said. "But it seemed like enough was at stake that I should at least tell you."

"Why should we care what you think?" Adam asked. "It's not like your life choices have done a lot of good for you, considering you're here."

It was a cruel thing to say. If they didn't want to hear what I had to offer, then fine. I didn't care. I picked up my things and was about to leave when Keith stopped me.

"Why don't you think it'll work?" he asked.

"Because Clarissa has the power right now. If you threaten her, she'll just tell everyone about you. You'll be ousted from your throne and won't be able to get her disinvited from parties because you won't have any social clout. Plus, people usually don't respond well to threats."

It was something I'd learned from watching my dad. He'd always said that the best way to negotiate is to make sure everyone feels like they've won. Making people happy, doing people favors—that was how to get people on your side.

"She might be right," Keith said to Adam.

"Okay, Hana," Adam said. "Newly minted social outcast and general creeper and eavesdropper. What's your idea, then?"

I considered what my dad would do if he was faced with this problem. He'd tell me that the first thing I had to do was figure out what Clarissa really wanted. Not a fleeting or superficial want but a deep want. One that kept her up at night, that she fantasized about while she was in class. If I could solve that problem for her, then I would have her on my side. Then I could ask her to do whatever I wanted, and she would happily oblige. No threats. No blackmail. Everyone wins.

Though I wasn't familiar with the peaks and valleys of Clarissa's emotional landscape, I was aware of one thing that she wanted desperately.

"She wants to be allowed back into Blue Label."

"Blue Label as in the coffee shop?" Keith asked.

I nodded.

Blue Label was a boutique coffee shop that all of the upperclassmen hung out at. It wasn't just a high-end place to get a snack while studying—it was a place to be seen, a place where alliances were forged, where gossip was traded, where power congregated. There was a handful of locations in the DC area, though the one St. Francis kids always went to was in Alexandria.

A year before, Clarissa had showed up at Blue Label after getting dumped by her boyfriend and had locked herself in the bathroom. She'd stayed there for over an hour while an increasingly long line of exasperated customers waited outside, followed by two baristas banging on the door, then the manager, who called the police, who eventually had to break the door to open it. Inside, they found her sitting on the floor blasting music from her headphones, surrounded by shredded paper and a dozen small candles, which had filled the room with haze. Beside her, the toilet was clogged with crumpled pages from her journal.

They'd escorted her out and brought her to the hospital, where she was deemed okay to go home. Blue Label didn't ban her then, though everyone looked at her funny when she returned. It wasn't until a few visits later, when a barista caught her stealing an insulated mug and a bag of coffee beans from a display shelf, that they told her she couldn't come back to that shop or any of their other locations nationwide.

That was a week before I'd run into her crying in the stall, when she'd asked me for a lighter and had demanded to know how I managed to be so perfect.

Since then she'd tried to go back to Blue Label dozens of times, at first casually and later showing up in sunglasses and heavy hats in attempted disguises. They never let her in. It had become an ongoing joke at school, with Clarissa at its center. A laughingstock.

"How are we supposed to do that?" Keith said.

"I can do it," I said.

"How?"

"A woman from corporate at Blue Label used to go to fundraisers for my dad. They were family friends of ours. I could ask her daughter if her mom could make a phone call."

"Are they *still* friends with your dad, though?" Adam asked.

"I mean, no, not publicly, but this wouldn't be public. Plus, this girl owes me one. I got her a date with this guy that she always liked, and now they're together. She hasn't forgotten."

Keith glanced at Adam. They were considering it.

"And you won't tell anyone?" Keith asked.

"You have my word."

"And you're sure it'll work?" Keith asked.

"Well, no," I said. "But I think it's worth trying."

Adam sighed, irritated that he had to accept my assistance.

"Why are you offering to help?" Keith asked.

I didn't know why. Maybe it was because I felt guilty for eavesdropping on a conversation that wasn't meant for me. Maybe it was because I wanted to feel necessary again or that I wanted a taste of what my old life felt like. Maybe it was because I knew what it meant to have your life ruined, and I wanted to save them from it if I could. All were a little true, though the real reason I'd offered to help was because it felt good to be distracted, to be immersed in someone else's problems for a change. It felt like I had peeled off the weight of my skin and stepped into someone else's life, leaving mine behind, if just for a moment.

"What do you want in return?" Adam asked.

It hadn't occurred to me to ask for anything. The only thing I wanted was to get my old life back, and no one could give me that. I shrugged. "Nothing."

That was my first fix. How I earned Adam's trust, how we eventually became friends.

"You should really charge for this," Adam told me after I'd finished the job.

It was an interesting idea. Although I didn't want to admit it, I needed money. My whole family did. "Maybe I will."

Though Adam and I grew to be behind-closed-doors friends, I didn't speak to Keith until later that year, when we'd bumped into each other by the vending machines in the basement of the student center on an odd day when no one else was there.

"Hey," Keith said.

We hadn't spoken since my fix and had acted like we were no longer friends. By then, I'd had a few more clients and was slowly honing my craft, realizing that it was something I was actually good at.

"I always meant to say something but could never find the right time or figure out the right way to say it," he said.

"What are you talking about?" I asked.

"I've just always felt bad about what happened. For the way everything played out with you at school. The way we treated you. I just wanted to say that I'm sorry."

I hadn't been expecting an apology and felt my breath catch in my throat. Why was it that the smallest act of kindness in the face of cruelty felt just as painful as the original offense?

"I want you to know that I've always appreciated that you never told anyone about me."

"It's not mine to tell," I said.

If my father were there, he would have patted me on the shoulder and told me that I'd done good a job. Everyone felt like they'd won. Except, maybe, me.

20

I didn't realize how shaken I felt after my encounter with Keith at the riverfront until I slid into the passenger seat and realized that my hands were trembling.

"Are you okay?" James asked.

"I think so."

I was glad to be with him in the familiar comfort of his car.

"So Three blackmailed Logan for money and hired you to unknowingly pick it up," James said, piecing together the bits of conversation he'd overheard through the phone. "And Logan, in an attempt to figure out who his blackmailer was, asked Keith to hide nearby and watch the money drop so he could tell Logan who came to pick it up, expecting it would be Three. Only it was you instead."

I nodded.

"So we still don't know who Three is."

I shook my head. "We do have this, though," I said, and passed him the duffel. "Courtesy of Logan."

His face went slack as he opened each bag. "There's got to be at least twenty thousand dollars in here."

"I know."

"Remember how we thought that Three had to be rich to offer you five thousand dollars for this case?" James asked.

"It's not true," I realized, now that we knew that Logan was the one who was paying me.

"It doesn't really narrow down the possibilities," James said. "Three still could be rich and just not be using their own money."

I rubbed my face. My mind felt tangled. I wanted to find the loose end and pull, but it was lost. As if on cue, a text came in. It was from Three.

>875 Coventry St.

The address didn't sound familiar. I assumed we were supposed to go there but I didn't know why. Who lived at 875 Coventry?

<Is that where you are? I asked.

>Don't be naive. Put the red bag beneath the bush by the mailbox, flash your lights twice, then text me that it's done.

James put the address into his phone and showed it to me. It was forty minutes away, in a town neither of us frequented.

<Who lives there? I asked.

>You've met him before.

Him?

I thought back to what Three had said when we'd texted after my tutoring session.

When will Colin get his money? I'd asked.

The same time you get yours, Three had written back.

"It's Colin's house," I whispered. "Three got me to pick up the money so that if anyone was caught, it would be me, and now Three wants me to distribute it. Distributing the money is the second fix."

I'd expected James to share in the excitement of my discovery, but instead he looked chastened. "We shouldn't do it."

"What?"

"We shouldn't go."

"We have to go," I said. How could we not?

"Taking blackmail money and distributing it?" James said. "That doesn't sound legal. We could be aiding and abetting a crime. And even if we weren't, it's risky, which is exactly why Three wants *you* to do it."

I knew he was right but didn't want to turn back now. We were so close to figuring it all out; we were standing in front of the curtain, ready to pull it open. "But we're doing it to reveal a larger crime."

"Still," James said. "We could have revealed it before. We didn't have to come here tonight."

"No one has to know you were involved in this part. It can just be me."

"It's not just about me," James said softly. "I don't want you to get in trouble, either."

Though I appreciated his concern, I was willing to take the risk. What did I have to lose? My life had already been destroyed.

"If you don't want to come, you can drop me off at home and I'll go there on my own. No hard feelings."

James sat for a moment, deep in thought. Then he put the car in reverse, and to my surprise, he turned on the directions.

"I can't let you do it on your own," he said, pulling down the street. "We're partners, right?"

I didn't smile, but I wanted to. I supposed he was right.

We tried listening to music on the radio, then from my phone, but both felt jarring, like a ball shattering the window of a library, so instead, we rode in silence, listening to the sound of tires on pavement.

"What if Keith tells Logan that he saw you?" James asked.

"He won't."

"How are you so sure?"

James didn't know about my first fix, about my history with Keith and Adam.

"I helped him once," I said. I wanted to tell James how but couldn't; it was a secret that wasn't mine to share. "Nothing like this. It was about something personal."

James looked like he wanted to ask more, but didn't. That's when I had the twinge of a thought, the kind that's so nascent, it feels like particles barely cohering.

Thinking about Adam and Keith reminded me of the last text Adam had sent, the one I'd never followed up on.

Remember that rumor you mentioned about Logan and Chris Pilker-Johns in the locker room? I think I know what that was about.

I thought back to what had gotten James started on this case in the first place—the tip that Logan had been threatening Chris Pilker-Johns in the locker room. It was one of the many unsolved questions in the case, but one that had been nagging at me.

"What did Logan say to Chris Pilker-Johns in the locker room?" I asked James.

"'I'll ruin you'?" James said.

"No. After Chris apologized."

"Logan said, 'Tell that to him,'" James said.

"Him," I repeated. "Logan told Chris to apologize to *him*."

"Okay," James said, clearly confused as to why I was bringing it up now. "What does this have to do with Keith?"

I considered all the disparate pieces of information that I'd been collecting, the odd details and bits of conversation that I hadn't been able to fit into the reconstructed narrative of this case.

What Keith had just said of Logan. *He's protected me.*

How when James had questioned Chris about the incident in the locker room, he'd insisted it hadn't been about Logan, but that it instead had to do with one of Logan's friends.

I pulled out my phone and texted Adam.

<What did you want to tell me about Chris Pilker-Johns?

A few minutes later, Adam responded.

>It was about me and K.

K for Keith.

>He saw us and told one of the other recruits on the team.

I let out a breath. This was why Keith was keeping watch for Logan on the riverbank. He was repaying a favor.

>Logan found out and threatened them so that they would keep it a secret.

I stared at my phone, understanding now why Logan had threatened Chris. He'd been protecting his friend.

The address that Three had instructed us to go to in order to complete the second fix was a humble ranch house with vinyl siding and an old Toyota parked in the driveway. Logan's doppelganger, Colin, lived at 875 Coventry Street. A single light was on in a downstairs room. The window blinds were dented and bent at the bottom, revealing a small sliver of the house, through which I could see a brown carpet, the bottom of a recliner, and the base of a lamp.

We pulled up to the mailbox. The red bag was heavier than mine, though not as heavy as I'd expected, considering how much was inside.

I reread Three's instructions.

>Put the red bag beneath the bush by the mailbox, flash your lights twice, then text me that it's done.

"So this is what ten thousand dollars in cash feels like," I said, remembering that Colin had told me exactly how much money Three had promised him in exchange for revealing what Logan had hired him to do.

I was completing the second fix of Three's problems, which was to pick up the money and give Colin his share. Before stepping out of the car, I unzipped the bag and looked inside. I couldn't help myself; I'd never seen this much money before.

James wasn't as curious. He stared at it with apprehension. "Are you sure you want to do this?"

I wasn't. All I knew was that I wanted to know where this path led.

Following Three's directions, I tucked the bag under the bush by the mailbox and returned to the car. James flashed his high beams twice. A moment later, the light in the window of the house turned off.

James pulled down the street and idled under the cover of an elm tree while I texted Three.

<It's done.

>Good.

>And now for your third problem.

I held my breath, knowing it had to do with the final black bag of cash.

>55 Settlement Circle.

Settlement Circle. I felt all the color leave my face. I knew that street.

<Is this a joke? I asked.

>No. Why? Do you find it funny?

I must have gone pale, because James gave me a questioning look. "Are you okay?"

If my parents had been there, they would have told me to lie and say I was fine, but I couldn't. I wasn't.

>I'd give you instructions, but I think you already know where to leave the bag.

James was already googling the house, zooming in on the street view. He had always been good at research; it would only take a few minutes before he found out who it belonged to. "Why is Three asking you to go here?" he asked.

I didn't respond. Nausea rippled through my body, making me feel light-headed.

"Hana?" James asked. "What's going on?"

What was I supposed to say? I couldn't tell him.

>I assume you know what it is now. This third and final fix.

I swallowed, wishing I could rewind time to the party earlier that night so I could tell James that I was going to meet Three on the riverbank on my own. Or maybe I would go back even farther and tell James that I didn't want to partner with him on the case, that he should figure out his article on his own. But why stop there? I could keep going and reject the case when Three had first tried to hire me, or go even farther back and erase the last two years of my life, undo the Catastrophic Event, move back into my childhood home with my family, and live happily ever after.

"What is Three talking about?" James asked. His voice became deliberate as he slowly realized that I had been keeping something from him.

My head was spinning. I felt dizzy. James peered over my shoulder at my phone.

>Are you up for it? Three asked. **Or are you going to run again?**

"Run?" James said.

I understood then who Three was. There was only one person who knew this place. Only one person who knew what had really happened here.

"Hana, what does Three mean?" His tone was different then. Instead of confused, it was pleading, as if he was asking me to reassure him that what he thought was going on wasn't true.

I couldn't bear to look at him, to see the way his face changed as he put the final pieces together. I wanted to tell him I was sorry but didn't know where to begin.

"What's the third fix?" James asked.

I thought back to what Three had texted me weeks before.

You. You're the case you haven't been able to fix. But don't worry. We'll fix that, too, by the end.

I swallowed. I wasn't going to 55 Settlement Circle. Not that night, not ever. "It has to do with something I've done."

21

You don't have to feel sorry for me. I feel sorry enough already. What you have to understand is that I was trapped in a room where the walls were closing in on me.

Smile. Square your shoulders. Look cheerful. Always wear the right clothes. Nothing too revealing, nothing too tight. Represent the family. Look friendly, relatable.

That was my life. Never be sad, never be angry. The only acceptable emotion is happiness, but not too much. Be gracious. Be grateful. Always say the right thing.

Ace your exams. Rewrite your papers until they're perfect. Memorize your conjugations, your historical dates, your order of operations. Make sure you're at the top of the class. Don't be a disgrace.

Practice the piano. Cultivate interesting hobbies. Stay up on current events so you know what's going on. Read books so you sound impressive. Make connections with important people and call on them to help you get elite summer internships. Write thank-you notes, write cover letters. Volunteer in your free time. Build your résumé. Tour the Ivies. Rank them by choice. Start your applications.

Never drink in public. Never do drugs. Manage your weight. Carefully curate what you post online because everyone is looking. If something goes wrong, keep it a secret. If you need to seek help, make sure no one finds out. You're happy. You're a model citizen. If you pretend your life is perfect, it will be.

I felt like a lever was pressing down on me. I couldn't breathe; I couldn't think.

"How do you do it?" Luce asked me once. It was the third week of tenth grade, just before the Catastrophic Event.

We were sitting on my bed, Luce leaning against the pillows next to Ruby, whose head she stroked mindlessly with one hand.

"Do what?"

"Smile so much when you're clearly miserable."

"I'm not miserable."

Luce let out a laugh. "Okay."

"I'm not," I insisted.

"You know you don't have to live like this," Luce said. "Trying to do everything right all the time. Trying to be the person your parents or the media or your dad's constituency want you to be."

"What am I supposed to do then, just stop trying?"

"Maybe, yeah."

I assumed she was joking, but she wasn't.

"It's an impossible task, trying to be perfect constantly," she said. "Don't you ever just want to be yourself?"

"I am being myself. This is who I am." I hadn't intended to sound so defensive.

"Is it, though?"

Though her voice was gentle, I couldn't help but feel like she was no different than everyone else, telling me who I should be and what I should do.

"Who am I, then?" I said. "You seem to think that you know the right answer. Why don't you share it with me?"

Luce stiffened. "I'm not claiming I know the answer. It's just hard to watch you do things that make you unhappy. It doesn't have to be that way."

"What makes you think I'm unhappy?"

"Um, the fact that you're about to have a panic attack about an internship application?"

"I'm not about to have a panic attack."

"You just told me that when you thought about all the things you had to do, you felt like it was hard to breathe."

"Well, it's a stressful situation. It's really competitive, and if I don't get it, then I won't have anything to list on my college applications this year."

Luce studied me as though I were proving her point. "You're living in a golden cage and you don't even see it."

"Of course I see it," I said. On the bed, Ruby jolted awake. "You don't know what it's like. No one's watching you the way they watch me. No one cares about you the way they care about me."

It was a mean thing to say, but I only realized it after the words had left my mouth.

"Right," Luce said.

The playlist we were listening to had started from the beginning again and the repetition of the same songs made the night go suddenly stale.

"It's getting late," she said, her voice stiff. "I should probably go."

Without speaking, Luce closed her book and stuffed it in her bag. I didn't get up as she stood to leave. I couldn't even meet her eye.

"You don't have to be perfect to be happy. In fact, it's the opposite," she said as she opened the door.

I wanted to have the last word but couldn't muster anything smart to say, so I had to sit there with a dumb look on my face as she shut the door.

People often think anger is reserved for those we hate, but I knew from Luce that the most infuriating people were the ones who saw you as you really were.

I couldn't sleep after she left that night. Instead, I stayed up late thinking of all the possible responses I could have said while she was walking out the door. Some were witty, most were mean, but the one I kept coming back to was a question that I refused to speak out loud, even to myself.

We didn't talk the next day or the day after that. I walked through school trying to convince myself that she was wrong. I wasn't miserable or caged. I was ambitious and enjoyed striving for excellence. It was part of my personality. That's what I'd always believed, at least, though now Luce's voice intruded on my thoughts. "Is it your personality, or have you tied achieving to your self-worth and can't imagine another way?" her imaginary voice asked. "Are you happy being perfect, or are you just good at it and get rewarded by others for following their rules?"

I tried to push her out of my mind, but she wouldn't go away.

"Why are you forcing a smile when you don't want to?" her voice said. "Are you worried that people won't like you?

"Why are you a school ambassador when you'd rather be in the art history club? Is it because someone told you it would look better on college applications?

"Why do you hang out with people whose company you don't enjoy? Is it because they're rich and powerful and you think you need them?"

That evening, before my mother went out to a fundraiser, she knocked on my door. She was wearing an elegant jade dress and makeup intended for photographers.

"I just wanted to check in to see how those thank-you cards were going," she said.

"They're fine," I said.

She peered over my shoulder to the stack of cards on my desk. I was supposed to be writing them to people who had interviewed me. She and my dad wanted me to get a part-time internship during the school year at one of the lobbying groups in DC. It would look good on my résumé and applications.

"Have you even started them?" she asked.

"I'm drafting what I'm going to say."

"Thank-you cards only work if you send them soon."

"I know," I said. "Don't worry. I'll do them."

My mother inspected me, taking in my messy hair, my tank top, and the note I'd written on the back of my hand of a song lyric I liked, which read, *Find your way, who are you today?* It was a habit I'd borrowed from Luce. My mother eyed it, then rubbed it with her thumb as if trying to wipe it off.

"You shouldn't write on yourself," she said. "It's not good for your skin."

Was that even true? I wasn't sure.

"Make sure you wash it off before the brunch tomorrow," she said. "And try to go to bed early. You don't want to have circles under your eyes."

It was a normal interaction, no different from hundreds of others we'd had over the years, but that night it felt different. What if I didn't care about circles under my eyes? What if I didn't want to write thank-you notes or spend my time at an internship that I wasn't actually interested in? I touched the smudged words on the back of my hand, upset that I couldn't even draw on my hand without someone trying to wipe it off.

I knocked on my brother's door. The shades were down, and his room was dark except for the glow from his video game, which gave the room an eerie green tinge. "Hold on, guys," he said into his headset, then turned to me. "Yeah?"

"Do you think we live in a golden cage?"

"What do you mean?"

"You and me. Do you think we're obsessed with pleasing other people?"

"You, definitely. Me, not so much."

His matter-of-factness surprised me.

"Is that it?" he asked, clearly uninterested in exploring the topic further.

"Yeah."

He turned back to his game, and I paced around my room, taking out my phone, then putting it away until I pressed the call button before I could change my mind again.

Luce picked up on the third ring. "Are you calling to apologize?"

"Only if you apologize first."

"That's not how it works. But fine. I'm sorry for revealing the innermost yearnings of your soul so that you can free yourself from the tyranny of being born into public life before you rot from the inside. Your turn."

"I'm sorry I said that no one cares about you. It was cruel."

"Now you're supposed to say that it isn't true and that people do care about me."

"It isn't true and people do care about you," I said. I tried to make it sound convincing but wasn't sure that I was successful.

"You know, for someone who's good at lying, you really did a crap job with that one."

"I mean, is it true?" I asked. "I care about you deeply and so does your family, but the general public? They don't exactly know who you are."

Though she didn't let on, I knew Luce well enough to know she was grinning.

"So now that I've liberated you from the lie you were living, what are you going to do?"

It was the question I'd kept coming back to after she'd left my room that night. *So what would you have me do?*

I didn't have an answer. All I knew was that I wanted to do something that I wasn't allowed to do, something that would make the ink scrawled across my hand seem so minute that it could barely be considered a transgression. Something that made me feel free.

"Are you busy tonight?" I asked.

"Other than this English paper, no."

"I'll be there in half an hour. You'll know because I'll flash my lights twice."

"What do you mean?"

"Just be ready to go."

My mom was out at a fundraiser and my dad was in for the night. Though he was purportedly catching up on reading and watching the news, I could hear him snoring through his office door.

I slipped on one of his baseball hats from the hall coatrack. He wore them to outdoor events when he wanted to look casual and approachable, a man of the people.

My father's Land Rover was in the garage. He rarely drove it; back then, we had drivers who shuttled us around in more practical cars. I grabbed the keys from the bowl by the door and climbed inside.

Why did I do it? I could have called a car, but that was exactly the point—I didn't want to. I was tired of being monitored. I couldn't go anywhere without someone noting where I was or what I was doing or wearing or saying. For once, I wanted a night without anyone watching.

It took me a few minutes to get my bearings. The blinkers, the headlights, the seat adjusted for my height. Carefully, I backed out of the garage. Though at the time I was in tenth grade and had practiced driving with my parents, I didn't have my license yet.

Using my phone to navigate, I drove to Luce's house.

Though I'd been driven around Alexandria for most of my life, I'd never done it on my own and felt disoriented trying to navigate the turns and lane changes. It felt terrifying and exhilarating to be hurtling through the night, the fog parting around the front of the car, the pavement appearing before me like a carpet unrolling into the unknown.

"I thought you were your dad," Luce whispered as she climbed into the car. "What are you doing?"

For the first time in a while, Luce looked genuinely surprised. Maybe even a little scared.

"Something out of character."

I was scared too. It was a new sensation to not know what was going to happen, to not have the next ten steps already prepped and scheduled.

"You don't even have your permit yet. Do you know what could happen if you get caught?"

I had an idea of what would happen, but I didn't want to think about it, because if I did, I might chicken out and turn back. So instead I tried to steady my voice. "Yeah. We just can't get caught."

The plan I had was simple. With a few jolting turns, I pulled out of Luce's driveway and followed my phone's navigation beneath the streetlights of the quiet suburban streets.

"Are you sure you know how to do this?" Luce said, gripping the handle on the door.

"Not really," I said, trying to calm my nerves as much as hers.

The Old Mill Country Club was dark when we drove past it, parking instead in the back by the edge of the golf course, which, at night, looked like the ocean—a vast expanse of darkness as far as the eye could see. It was a relief to be off the road, to slow to a stop and put the car in park. I'd done it; I'd gotten us here. My insides vibrated with adrenaline as I cut the lights and opened the door.

"What are we doing here?" Luce asked as she followed me to the chain-link fence.

I climbed over it less gracefully than I'd thought I would, then dropped into the soft, manicured grass on the other side. I didn't know exactly what people did when they snuck out of the house. Partied and drank, of course, or made out in cars. Those options all sounded fine, if not a bit clichéd, but they all presented the risk of being seen and photographed or gossiped about at school.

I ran across the fairway, through the domes of mist created by the sprinklers. Luce ran behind me, laughing and squinting as the spray clung to our eyelashes.

I knew my way around Old Mill well; my parents had been members for years. I led Luce past the parked golf carts and the shuttered restaurant to the pool, which was so still it looked like glass.

I didn't have to tell Luce what to do. Using a rattan chair from the lounge nearby, we climbed over the iron pool fence and dropped to the other side. There, we shed our clothes. I stood at the end of the diving board as Luce jumped in, her body long and fragmented as she swam underwater. Holding my breath, I dove in.

The water was cold and felt like a slap to the chest. I surfaced and gasped, feeling as if I had been woken from a dream. What had I done? What was I doing?

"I've always wondered what this place was like," Luce said, catching her breath.

I gazed around at the empty lounge chairs and wondered if the country club had security cameras. They had to, I rationalized, though I doubted anyone watched the footage unless something was found amiss.

"Are you okay?" Luce asked.

"Yeah," I murmured. The water lapped against my lips.

"Are you having regrets?"

"Is that what this feeling is?"

Luce laughed. "Welcome to life with the rest of us. You do dumb things and make mistakes and have to live with them."

I pried my gaze away from the outside walls of the clubhouse, vowing not to worry about the security cameras, and let myself drift on my back. The sky was black and starless, the way it always was from the ambient light from DC. A distant plane flew overhead, its white light mimicking a shooting star. It was hard to believe that it was filled with people, so small and high they couldn't see us. For a moment, I was no one, just a speck on Earth, moving around with other specks, laughing, crying, grieving, maneuvering, chasing things we wanted. What did any of it matter?

I felt less anxious on the drive home. Luce did too. She'd relaxed her grip on the door handle and was fiddling with the radio, lamenting how all the popular music today sounded like it was made via focus group.

"None of it has any life, you know?" she said.

"You sound like my dad," I said. "According to him, everything was higher quality when he was growing up."

"Speaking of your dad, why are you wearing that hat?"

"To hide my face. In case anyone sees us."

"Look around," she said, gesturing to the neighborhood we were passing through. Houses lined either side of the street, their windows dark. Up ahead stood a small park shaded with trees. "We're on an empty road, late at night, in a car. Who's going to see us?"

That's when I saw the figure in the road. Before I could swerve out of the way or understand what was happening, our car hit a hard bump on the ground, and we spun out of control.

I slammed on the brakes. Through the beam of our headlights, I saw a flash of a person in front of us, one arm raised to her face as if bracing for impact. Then darkness. A grotesque thud on the front of the car. A sickening crunch as we skidded through the grass. Then stillness.

"What was that?" Luce said.

My heart was racing. I took inventory of my body.

Nothing was bleeding. I could move my legs. Everything seemed intact. "I don't know," I said, my hands trembling. "Are you okay?"

Luce's face was drained of color. She didn't answer my question. Instead she pressed her face to the window. "What do we do?"

We had ended up on the other side of the sidewalk on a patch of grass. I had no idea how we'd gotten there. Had I not noticed that there was a curve in the road? Had I hit the curb and spun out of control? Had the person illuminated by my headlights actually been standing on the sidewalk?

I felt suddenly sick. I could still feel the thud against the car, heavy like a bag of potatoes; I could feel its shape deform beneath my tires, once, twice, as we passed over it. No, it couldn't have been. It was a statue. Not a person. No one was out this late walking. They would have cried out. They would have moved out of the way.

"It was just a statue," I said, feeling a knot rise in my throat. If I said it forcefully enough, it had to be true.

"It looked like a person."

"Statues look like people," I insisted.

"Why would there be a statue here?"

"There are statues everywhere," I said, desperate for her to agree with me. "It's a park."

"How are you so sure?" Luce's voice quivered, betraying her panic.

"Because it has to be."

"We should check."

"We can't." I don't know why I said it, but I knew with every fiber of my being that I could not step outside of the car.

"We can't just leave her there."

"There is no her," I said. "There never was a her."

I must have been shouting, because Luce shrank back into her seat.

"What if she needs help?" Luce asked, her voice small.

I knew then that I had to make a decision. I pressed on the gas and winced at the crunch of glass beneath the tires. "It wasn't a person," I said. I realized then that I was crying.

22

We were never there. That's what we decided. No one had seen us. We wouldn't tell anyone what had happened. We would forget about it and return to normal life. We vowed to never speak about it again.

After I dropped her off and made it home, I cut the lights, pulled the car into the garage, and crept into my room. I didn't know what I would say to my parents once they found out. Maybe it would take them a few days to notice the dent in the car and the smashed headlight, since they rarely drove anymore. In the meantime, I would think of an explanation. Maybe I could convince them that someone had broken into our garage and taken it for a joyride. Or I could err closer to the truth and admit that I'd taken the car to practice driving and had swerved out of the way of a deer and hit a tree.

I climbed into bed, grateful to be home, enveloped in

the comfort of familiar things. I stared at the ceiling and tried to wish the night away. From the safety of my bedroom, the events of the night had already started to feel like a bad dream. Maybe they were. It was a statue, I told myself. If I repeated it enough, it might come true.

Luce wasn't in school the next day or the day after that. That's all I remember. I walked the halls of St. Francis in a fog, unable to focus on the present. My friends talked around me. They might have asked if I was okay, if I was listening to them. I must have answered, though I couldn't remember what I said. All I could think of was the figure in the street and the flash of her face in our headlights before we'd spun out of control. Had she looked at me? Had I seen her eyes?

Three days after the crash, I came home from school to find the television on. That in itself wasn't notable; it was always on, even if no one was watching it. My mother was on a call. Genie was cleaning the stove. The reporter was saying something about smoke from wildfires in the West. Without warning, I felt like I was going to be sick and leaned over the sink and gagged, but all that came out was acid.

"Are you okay, Miss Hana?" Genie said.

I couldn't bring myself to answer and hurried upstairs, passing Zack on the way. "What's wrong with you?" he asked.

"Nothing," I managed to say, and slammed the door.

That night, my parents noticed the car. It started with them arguing. They rarely fought, so it was surprising to hear, and I turned off the music in my headphones and listened to their muffled voices through the door.

"What aren't you telling me?" my mother asked.

"Nothing. I have no idea what happened."

"But it's your car."

"I'm telling you, I haven't driven it in over a week," my father said.

"Was it someone on your staff?"

"I doubt it. They have their own cars."

"If it wasn't you, then who did it?"

A long silence ensued. Then came the knock on my door.

I'd been mulling over what I was going to say for days. Lying normally came easily to me, but when confronted with their questions, it felt suddenly difficult.

I admitted that I'd taken the car. I told them that Luce had called me. Her dog was vomiting and needed to go to the emergency vet, but her parents weren't home or answering the phone. She didn't want to call a car service because she didn't think anyone would take a sick dog in the back seat. If it hadn't been an emergency, I wouldn't have done it. On the way over, I'd hit a deer in the road. I was okay but shaken. I'd driven back home and had meant to tell them but was too scared to admit that I'd taken the car without permission. I knew it was rash and stupid, I told them. I wouldn't do it again. I was sorry, so sorry.

I watched their faces soften. We hugged. They made me promise I would never do anything like that again but told me it was okay. They'd get it fixed and it would be in the past. They were glad I was okay, and they were proud of me; I'd taken the car because I was trying to help, and it was always good to try to help others. I felt even worse then.

They didn't fix the car immediately. It sat in the garage, its presence a constant reminder of what I'd done. I could feel it beneath me while I lay in bed, a rot at the base of the house. I worried that the longer it sat there, the more likely it was to spread.

The ensuing days were unbearable. I couldn't eat. I couldn't sleep. When I closed my eyes, all I could picture was the flash of my headlights and the eyes caught in their glare. On top of that was the lie that I'd told my parents. It was too big to forget about. I couldn't risk letting myself slip, so I had to keep it at the forefront of my mind, which meant thinking about it constantly, turning it over until it was smooth, until it felt real.

My mother watched me with concern. I looked tired, she remarked. Was everything okay?

I wanted to tell her, but every time I peered off the cliff, I imagined how her face would drop and she'd back away from me in horror, how my father's jaw would go slack and he'd look at me as though I were a monster, and I walked myself back from the edge. I could never tell them.

"Did you see the news?" Luce whispered into the phone.

It was the middle of the night, and I'd been waiting for her to call me for days. She hadn't been picking up or responding to my texts. She'd hadn't been at school. Had I been in a better mental space, I might have wondered if she was okay, but I was so busy trying to rid myself of the thoughts that tormented me day and night that I didn't have the bandwidth to consider her.

My grip loosened on the phone. A looming feeling of dread pulled at my stomach. I didn't want to hear about the news. "No," I managed to say.

"A woman was found."

I felt suddenly light-headed, as though I had left my body.

"She's alive," Luce said, reading my thoughts. "She's been in the hospital in critical condition. They're not sure if she's going to make it."

I was going to be sick.

"Do you think . . . ?" Luce let her voice trail off.

I grabbed a cup from my nightstand and heaved into it, but nothing came out. It couldn't be. I wanted Luce to change the subject.

Luce lowered her voice. "They found her near where we were that night. They're looking for the driver."

It had to be a coincidence. Luce hadn't said she was found at the spot where we'd spun out. It had to be another car, a similar spot.

"Her name was Mary Cannon Davis."

Was.

I wanted to unhear the name. It was just another person on the news, another tragedy that didn't have anything to do with me. Instead, it burrowed into my brain. Mary Cannon Davis.

"Is," I corrected.

"Is," Luce repeated.

"I can't sleep," I said.

"Neither can I."

"Have you told anyone about what happened?" I almost didn't ask for fear of what she might say.

"No. Have you?"

I released the breath I was holding. "No."

"She has two kids," Luce said. Her voice wavered.

I didn't want her to tell me that. I didn't want to know. The information made my eyes blur, made my face sting. I touched my cheeks. They felt wet. Why? Why was I crying over someone who had nothing to do with me? I had to pull it together.

"I just want it to go away. Do you think it will go away?"

Luce didn't respond for a long time. Finally, she spoke. "I don't know."

After we hung up, I wrapped a sweater around me and

crept downstairs. The door to the garage seemed to pulse. I lingered in front of it, wanting to retreat back to my room, before turning the knob.

At first glance the car looked pristine. It was magic; a weight lifted. I allowed myself to consider the possibility that my parents had fixed it, or that maybe nothing had happened in the first place. It was just a nightmare, a punishment for wanting to momentarily veer from the rules.

Then I walked around the front of the car. The smooth curve of the bumper was suddenly interrupted by a concavity that spread like a wound to the passenger side. The headlight was smashed, a bit of plastic dangling from the socket. A vestigial piece of glass lay cracked on the polished concrete. My heart was a fist, clenching, clenching. The paint had been scraped off, and the metal beneath was dappled with a strange dark residue. I bent down. I didn't dare touch it, didn't dare look too closely. It was black, I told myself. Not red. That had to mean something. Then I saw it. Wedged into a gash in the metal. A single brown hair.

I couldn't touch it, but I had no choice. I pulled it off and stuffed it in the kitchen trash before hurrying back to my room.

The next day, I saw the police car pass in front of our house. I wanted to believe that it was nothing. Just the neighborhood security patrol cruising by. But then there was another, followed by another, and our neighbor Susan, peering out the window, her face pinched with concern. I ventured downstairs. A knock on the door, a ring of the bell. Genie's vacuuming sucking the air from the house.

It couldn't be for me, I told myself. No one other than Luce had been there that night. No one had seen us. It had to be for something else. A routine check—police did that, right?

So I snuck out the back and went to Cecily's pool party, where I tried to recreate the feeling I'd had at the country club pool, where the world shrank away and nothing mattered. If I wasn't at home, I could pretend like everything was normal. It was just a day where I went to a friend's house.

My mother's assistant, Claudia, picked me up and rode with me through the throngs of reporters pressing against the gate of our house. I'd assumed that they were there for me, that everyone knew and would escort me to the police station in my swimsuit, wet hair dripping as they thrust me into a yellow-tinged interrogation room. So when I asked Claudia what had happened, I was bewildered when she'd said, "It's your dad."

I didn't piece together what had happened until I was inside. My mother was pacing in the kitchen, talking into one phone while the other rang and rang. Ruby barked at my feet. The television blared. I approached it. Over the din of the room, I saw my father being escorted down the steps of the Senate building. I saw the grainy nighttime footage of his car drive off the road and make impact with the pale husk of a figure, flimsy as a ragdoll as it was flung off the side of the car and rolled onto the sidewalk.

I had to steady myself against the counter. I barely registered the car spinning out or pausing or speeding away. All I could see was the husk lying on the sidewalk, tremoring once, twice, then going still.

I couldn't look away. It was a statue, I'd told myself. But statues didn't move. Statues didn't tremble.

"Longtime senator of Virginia, Skip Lerner, has been accused of driving the car that was involved in a collision with a pedestrian, then fleeing the scene," the reporter said.

They thought it was him, but it was me. In my father's car. Wearing my father's hat. Ruining my father's life.

All evening, I listened to my mother talk on the phone with the lawyers, insisting that it was a mistake. I tried to interrupt her and tell her the truth, but she waved me away, barley registering my presence.

That night, while lying in bed, I saw a pair of headlights stretch over the window. It was a trick of my imagination, I thought. I was dreaming.

Then the downstairs door opening. My father's footsteps on the stairs. My mother shuffling up from the couch, her voice frantic as she spoke to him. Was he home? Was it over?

I waited until I heard a soft knock on my door.

"Hana, are you up?" he asked.

I considered pretending I was asleep but knew I couldn't. Not that night. "Yeah."

He was still in his work clothes from earlier that day as he slipped into my room, though they were slightly worse for wear. He was trying to look calm, but I saw a crack in the facade. I tried to pinpoint exactly what frightened me about his expression. Then I realized. He was scared.

He sat on the side of my bed. My mother stood in the doorway, watching. He put his hand on mine. "It wasn't a deer, was it?"

My mouth had gone dry. My tongue felt like wool. I wanted to take the whole night back, to rewind time, to make it all go away. We were good liars, so good that lies seemed to morph into the truth. So why wasn't that happening now?

"No," I whispered.

My father sank as if deflating. In the doorway, my mother made the strangest sound, like a child crying out in the dark.

"Why did you leave?" my father asked.

"I don't know." It was an honest answer.

"Oh, Hana," he said, his voice strange, weak. Was he crying?

I was sorry. I was sorry. I was so very, very sorry.

I didn't ask him to do it. On the contrary, I begged him not to, but the lie was already in motion. They believed that he was the one who was driving, and he wasn't going to dispute it. It was a mistake, and he would comply and hope that the courts would be merciful.

I had my entire future ahead of me, he said.

It would be fine, he said.

They'd go easy, he said.

All the while, my mother barely spoke. At night, I heard them fighting.

The rims of her eyes were red. She stopped dressing in favor of robes. She stayed up late, her feet padding against the floor as she circled her room. She wouldn't talk to me, wouldn't make eye contact. When she looked at me, all she seemed to see was what I'd done.

We didn't tell Zack. We didn't tell anyone. No one could know.

23

"Are you out of your fucking mind?"

Luce's voice was shrill and tinny in my earbuds. I winced.

We only talked on the phone now. No texts, nothing in writing. I could picture her pacing in her room, music blaring to drown out our conversation.

I was hunched over the bathroom counter in front of the mirror, trying to apply enough concealer under my eyes to make it look like I hadn't been crying. I was already running late.

"Don't shout at me," I said. My hands were shaking.

Luce ignored me. "We have to tell someone. You can't let this happen."

"It's already done," I said. "He already told them."

The makeup wasn't working. I threw the sponge in frustration and opened a bottle of foundation, but it slipped through my fingers and splattered all over the dresser. "Fuck!" I shouted. "Fuck."

It had gotten on my dress. My lucky dress, the only one I wanted to be seen in when walking up to a podium in front of dozens of reporters and having my image broadcasted into every screen in the country. What would I wear now?

"What if they find out?" Luce asked.

"I don't know," I said, trying to blot out the stain with a damp facecloth. Didn't she understand that I'd already cycled through all of these thoughts?

"*I don't know?* That's it?"

I couldn't focus under the constant assault of her questions. I rubbed the washcloth against my dress and tried to calm my breathing.

"You're just going to stand there behind him while he takes the blame?" Luce continued. "And what, we'll just never talk about it again?"

I threw the washcloth on the counter. "What do you want me to say?" I asked in a shrill whisper. "That I'm sorry? That I was wrong? That I shouldn't have driven away? That I shouldn't have taken the car in the first place? Of course I wish I could take it all back. And yes, the right thing to do would be to tell them I did it. But then we'd all be screwed. Me, my dad, and you. Confessing isn't going to undo what we did."

"What *we* did?" Luce said. "You were the one who was driving."

"You could have opened the door and gone outside," I fired back. "You had a phone; you could have called the cops. But you didn't. You just sat there and asked me if we should. You didn't want to check on her, you just didn't want to be the person to decide. So I did it for us."

"That's different—" Luce began to say, but I cut her off.

"If you hadn't pushed me to break the rules and go out, I never would have done it."

"Pushed you? I wasn't pushing you. Your parents pushed you. You pushed yourself. All I suggested was that you live your life on your own terms. I didn't tell you to sneak out of the house in your dad's car before you had a license."

"Do you think I don't feel bad enough already? That I haven't been tormented by these thoughts since I dropped you off? I was fine before you started to mock me about living in a golden cage. I was doing all right. If you hadn't kept pressuring me, I would have stayed home and spent the night stressing over my cover letters."

"This isn't my fault," Luce said.

"You're right. It's mine. Absolve yourself. Blame me. I don't care."

"Fuck you," she said, the last words she ever said to me on the phone.

Then the line went dead.

By the time we made it to the press conference, the

stain was barely visible. Still, it bothered me. I felt its presence as we walked out into the glare of the press conference, while my father announced his resignation, while the moth fluttered against the back wall. Though it was hard to make out, if you looked closely, you might see its outline—a soiled mark on my dress that I had rubbed out, hoping no one would one notice. My secret.

That night, after the press conference, I was blasting music in my headphones, trying to drown out my thoughts, when my phone rang.

"Hana," James said, surprised. "You picked up."

Up until then, I'd been ignoring his calls. Not because I didn't want to talk to him—I wished I could—but because I didn't know what to say.

"Are you okay?" he asked. "I've been trying to call you."

"I'm sitting on my bed, staring at the wall. So I guess you could interpret that as either okay or not okay."

I meant it as a joke, but he didn't laugh. "I'm serious. Are you all right? I called when I saw the news, but you didn't answer. And you haven't been at school."

The sincerity with which he said it made me feel even worse. I swallowed, wishing I could fold myself up into nothing. Not wishing I was dead, but not wishing I was alive, either. After hours of sitting in a dark room, emptying my brain with music, I'd been able to hold everything that had happened back from the forefront of my mind, but the mere mention of the press conference made my thoughts swell. I could feel them pressing at the gates, threatening to burst through.

"My mom said she's been trying to reach your mom, but she isn't calling her back."

My mother must have been avoiding her. Of all of us, she was the worst at lying, so she tried to avoid it as much as possible. In this scenario, that meant not answering when her best friend called to ask her how she was doing. "It's been really busy over here," I said. "Lawyers. PR teams."

"What happened?" James said.

"If you saw the news, then you know what happened."

"But is it true?"

I wanted to tell him. I did. But I couldn't. "It is."

There was a long pause in which I realized that James really did think that it had all been a big misunderstanding. "But how?" he asked.

"What do you mean?"

"It just doesn't seem like something your dad would do."

James could tell that something was wrong. Of course he could. He knew my parents better than anyone else at school.

"My mom's calling me," I said, lying. "I have to go. Can we talk about it some other time?"

"Sure. Are you coming to school tomorrow?"

Since my dad's arrest, it had been an unspoken assumption that neither Zack nor I would go to school. We didn't want to, and no one mentioned it when drop-off came and went and we were still home. Who could go to school at a time like this? But we did have to return eventually.

"Yeah."

James must have sensed my apprehension. "It'll be fine," he said. He never lied, so I knew he believed it.

I could have laughed. Of course it wasn't going to be fine.

I did see him at school the next day, but there was little time to talk. The buzz around my father's case made it so that I was never alone. My old friends wanted to know what had happened, and everywhere I went, people looked at me and whispered, hoping for a front-row seat to the unfolding drama that had become my life. All the while, I had my eye trained on Luce, who seemed to flit in and out of every room I was in like a ghost, reminding me of the truth.

In the following days, the scrutiny only got worse. I found myself avoiding the dining hall and other public places so I wouldn't have to hear the whispers or withstand their collective focus. James often found me in the library or on the bench on the far side of the quad, eating my lunch in solitude or trying to quiet my mind with music and my assignments, but even James only wanted to talk about the incident, though the tenor of his interest was different.

"I still don't understand how it happened," he kept saying. "Why did he veer off the road?"

"I don't know. It was dark. He wasn't paying attention."

"The news is accusing him of having a drinking problem," James said. "But I've never seen your dad drink. I remember him always ordering a Coke."

If I hadn't been so distraught, I might have appreciated the reminder of my dad the way he was at his happiest: jeans and a button-down shirt, holding a cold Coke while he chatted with constituents. Like he was in a commercial for it. And James was right—my father rarely drank alcohol. Even when he was given a beer at a fundraiser or political event, he never finished it.

"People on TV say all kinds of things that aren't right," I said.

"But why was he swerving like that?"

"He said he thought he saw something in the road."

James shook his head. "It just doesn't make sense. I've driven with your dad hundreds of times. It doesn't seem like him."

I knew James didn't mean to make me upset, but his questions only put me more on edge.

"People get into car accidents all the time," I said, finding myself in the strange position of having to convince James that my father did, in fact, do something terrible.

"And then he hit a woman on the sidewalk and just drove off? Your dad would never do that."

I'd stopped eating; I'd lost my appetite. He was right. My dad wouldn't have done it. I had to change the subject;

I had to get him to stop talking about it, but I felt too sick to think.

"You know, I never told you this because it wasn't really worth mentioning," James continued, "but once, at one of those fundraisers we were at, I saw him in a rare moment by himself. He had just finished talking to someone and was on his way to the bar when he noticed that a little vase of carnations had been knocked off one of the tables. The flowers and water had spilled across the floor. He could have left it there and let the caterers deal with it—everyone else was walking over them like they didn't exist—but your dad picked them up, rearranged them in their vase, and wiped the water from the floor. It wasn't anything monumental. It's not like he deserved a prize for it, but most people don't do stuff like that, especially when no one is paying attention. But your dad did."

The story, though small, overwhelmed me. Part of me wanted to time travel back to that moment so I could see it happen. The other part wished I could unhear it. If my father was a person who cleaned up messes when no one was looking, then I was now the opposite—the person who made the mess, the person whose problem he had to clean up in secret. How could I live with myself?

"So how could someone like that hit a person with his car and drive away?"

It was a good question, good enough to make me antsy. "I don't know," I said, wanting to change the subject. But to what? The rest of the world had become inconsequential. This was all there was now.

"And he left the car in the garage and no one noticed it until the police found the video?"

"Yes," I said. "He wasn't paying attention to the road. In a moment of panic, he drove away and left the car in the garage. We don't drive it that often, so we didn't notice. We've already gone over all of this. You saw the press conference. You watched the news. That's it. That's the story. Is it really that hard to believe?"

My tone must have been more forceful than I'd intended, because James stiffened. "Sorry," he said. "I just want to get the details straight."

"Look, I told you everything I know and I don't really get why you're asking me all these questions."

"Because it doesn't add up. I just—I can't imagine your dad doing it. He wouldn't. I talked to my parents. They can't believe it either."

"What do you want me to say? That you're right and it's not true and it's all a big conspiracy or cover-up?" I swallowed, having said the truth out loud.

"Well, no, but don't you agree that some of it just doesn't add up? Aren't you curious?"

"I can't be curious," I said. "This isn't some story that I can look at from afar. This is my life. Can I believe it? No. And yet there it is, playing on loop on every channel, on every website, on every social media post. They have him on video doing it. So can you please stop asking me?"

"Okay," he said. "Okay."

But he didn't. He couldn't help himself. All of our conversations somehow returned to my father, to that night, to his unanswered questions. He was watching me, turning the facts in his head like he was winding a screw deeper, closer to the truth. At home, I heard my mother having near-identical arguments with James's mom. Too many questions with insufficient answers.

"You know, I looked up where he said he was that night and it doesn't make sense," James said. "To get to your house from the park he said he drove to, he wouldn't even have to go on that road. So why was he there?"

I felt my throat tighten. "Can you stop being a reporter? Just for once? Why do you keep making me relive it?"

"I'm not trying to make you relive it. I'm just asking a question."

"Why, so you can write an article about it?"

"Of course not. Why would you think that?"

"I don't know. Why are you so fixated on this?"

"Why are you not?" James asked.

"Because there isn't anything more to know," I said. "There's no trick. There's no twist. It's just a sad story."

"What's going on?" James asked, staring at me like I was a stranger. "Why are you acting like we're on opposite sides?"

I swallowed. "I'm not. I'm just asking you to stop."

"Stop what? Calling you to see how you're doing even though you never answer anymore or call me back? Asking you about the major event that's affecting every part of your life? Do you really just want me to pretend like it's not happening and ask you about what TV shows you're watching?"

"I want you to stop pretending like you're a reporter, because you're not. You're an impostor. You're just someone who asks too many questions. I didn't ask you to solve this for me. It can't be solved."

"An impostor?" James said. "What?"

I had to do it. I had to push him away.

"Where is this coming from?" he asked. "Why is this suddenly about me?"

He was getting too close to figuring out what had really happened.

"It's just—it's too much. On top of everything, I can't do this."

"Do what?" James said.

The truth was pressing against my ribs, threatening to burst out. I wanted to tell him. I wanted to tell him so badly. The prospect of us being friends suddenly seemed impossible with this rot inside me. How could we go on while I kept this secret from him? How could I keep it hidden?

I stuffed my things in my bag, unable to make eye

contact for fear of him seeing the truth. "I can't talk about it anymore. I just—I need to be by myself for a while."

"Hana, I'm on your side. Don't you see that?"

I turned so I wouldn't have to see the expression on his face. "I have to go," I said. "I'm sorry."

"It was you?" James asked.

We were back in the present, sitting in the car down the street from Colin's house after just finishing the money drop. Three's texts lingered unanswered on my phone. The engine was off, and my skin prickled in the cold. I hugged my chest, wishing I could seek refuge from myself.

"You were the one in the car that night?" James continued. "You were the one who ran?"

"I panicked. I thought I had hit a statue. I didn't know."

"You just left her there? You could have at least checked. Why didn't you check?"

"You don't think I've asked myself that a thousand times? It was a mistake. I never meant to hurt anyone."

"You let me think that I had done something wrong," he said.

"You were asking too many questions." I was pleading with him then, begging him to understand.

"So you just ended our friendship?"

"I couldn't lie to you."

"You did lie to me," James said.

"What was I supposed to do?" I asked.

"I don't know," he said in disbelief. "The right thing?"

He always made it seem like the right thing was obvious. He sank back into his seat, stunned.

"I'm not like you," I said, my voice wavering. "I'm not good inside. I don't always know what the right thing is."

I took a chance and reached out and touched his hand, but he pulled it away as if I'd shocked him.

"What about your dad?" he asked.

No.

His eyes searched mine, demanding an answer. "Your dad," he repeated.

My lip quivered. It was the last lie I hadn't faced, the one I still couldn't bring myself to look at. "Please don't ask me about him," I whispered.

James ignored me. "He's just been in prison this whole time?"

I was begging him.

"All this time, he's been wasting away for something you did?"

You must be wondering what he's talking about.

"He hasn't been wasting away," I said. "It's not like that—"

He looked at me the way I always feared he would, as though I was bad inside. "How do you know?" James asked.

My throat felt like cotton. I couldn't speak, couldn't think. I'd spent so long telling myself a lie that I almost believed it.

"See?" he said. "You don't."

He turned on the car.

"What are you doing?" I asked.

"Driving you home."

The ride was a blur. All I remember was the radio, which he cranked so we wouldn't have to talk. He didn't look at me when he pulled up to my town house. I opened the door, wondering if this was the last time we'd speak.

"James, please," I said.

"Please what?"

I didn't know what I wanted from him. Forgiveness, I guess, but why should he give me that?

"I'm sorry," I whispered.

"Don't forget your money," he said.

I didn't care about the money. Still, I took the duffel from the floor and watched as he backed up and disappeared into the night.

I stood in the driveway, stunned. The wind made the trees around me sway, and I wondered how I was still standing when things as old as oaks could be moved by nothing but air.

You must be confused. I'm sorry. I haven't been honest with you.

24

"Still hungry?" my father said. He'd found me in the kitchen, making a cheese plate out of odds and ends in the fridge.

It was fall of sophomore year and my father had just negotiated his plea bargain and was out on bail, waiting to see if the judge would accept it and what the sentence would be.

"I'm pretending we're at a fancy function," I said.

He threw a napkin over his arm and pretended he was a caterer. "Would you like a refill?" he asked, gesturing to my glass of seltzer.

I wanted to roll my eyes but couldn't help but laugh.

In the bedroom above us, I heard feet pacing. "How's Mom?" I asked.

The smile faded from his face. "She's okay. Surviving."

"No date night anymore, I guess," I said. I was partially humoring him, partially humoring me. For the longest time, he and my mother had gone out twice a month under the pretense of a date night, but I knew that they had actually been going to couples' therapy to cope with the pressure of public life. They hadn't been able to go since the news broke, though.

"Not until things die down," my dad said, snagging a slice of manchego from my plate.

"Hey," I protested. "I wanted that."

My father grinned. For a moment I could almost forget that in a few days we'd be called back to court to hear his sentence. That this might be the last late-night snack he'd have for a while.

I slid the plate to him. I wasn't hungry anymore. "You have it."

He must have understood what I was thinking, because a shadow fell over his face. "I already ate," he said, sliding it back.

"Dad, what's going to happen?" I asked.

"That's the beauty about life. You just don't know until you get there."

He was such a die-hard optimist that it was hard to tell when he was charming you and when he was telling the truth.

I swallowed. "Am I a bad person?"

"Would I have done all of this for a bad person?"

I shrugged. I truly didn't know.

"You made a mistake," he said. "An accident and a bad decision. But those things don't define who you are."

I frowned. Of course they defined who I was. They were now the only meaningful facts about me.

"This idea of a person, of who you *are*—it can't be reduced to a single bad deed or good deed."

"But I did a terrible thing."

"You did," he murmured. "And you've been given a second chance. So now it's your job to figure out how to put more good into the world."

It felt like an impossible task. How could I put good into the world when I was capable of inflicting so much pain? I felt irredeemable.

"How am I supposed to just go on and pretend like everything is normal?"

"You won't have to," he said. "Nothing will be normal after this."

Through the ceiling, I could hear the muffled sound of my mother running the bath. "I should go see what's happening up there," he said, patting the table. Before he left, he turned to me. "Someone's calling you."

While I looked at my phone, which was dark, he snagged the last olive from my plate.

"Hey," I said as he backed down the hallway.

"Kids these days. You're way too easy to trick."

Then he tossed the olive into the air and caught it in his mouth—his classic party trick—and disappeared upstairs.

Does it sound familiar?

* * *

We spent the next week at home. My father barely left the house; none of us did. What was the point? The property was surrounded by reporters. Instead, we settled into a wrinkle in time that kept us suspended in a state of limbo. With the curtains closed and the screens off, day and night bled into each other, and time seemed to slow.

I wish I could say that we spent those last days together, but we were too unmoored to interact. None of us could sleep or had any appetite to eat, and thus were each on our own trajectory, napping and waking and attempting to scrounge something from the fridge, then scraping the food into the trash and starting over again.

My mother was the angriest. She stewed in it, barely speaking, refusing to look at me. To distract herself, she embarked upon a deep purge of the house. During the day, I avoided her wrath by hiding in my room when I heard her footfalls. At night, I listened as she stuffed old clothes and shoes in bags. Zack shut himself in his room and lost himself in video games, emerging only when he had to use the bathroom or get another Gatorade. My father spent a lot of time in the backyard, walking around the garden, admiring the flowers, which he had never done before, or sitting under the pergola in silence for what I considered to be a concerning amount of time. I found myself blaring music in my headphones to drown out the noise of my brain. Without them, all I could hear was the phantom sound of sirens in the distance, the *click click click* of cameras taking our photos as we left the press conference, and the newscaster's voice as he said my victim's name.

The night before the sentence was delivered, my father suggested we get takeout. None of us knew what would happen the following day, and we hadn't had a proper meal together all week.

He suggested Vicenzi's, an Italian restaurant that he and my mother occasionally went to for a quiet night out. He ordered the veal, like he always did; she ordered the eggplant. Zack and I got pasta. When it arrived, the food was cold, so my mother put it in the oven to warm. That's when the phone rang, when she got distracted by talking to their lawyer and the food burned.

"Open the window," my mother shouted to my brother.

My father stood beneath the smoke detector, fanning it with a baking sheet, while my mother opened the foil containers and inspected the contents. Her face grew slack. Then we all watched in silence as she dumped them into the trash.

"Hey, it's okay," my father said to her. "We'll have something from the freezer."

"It's not okay," my mother said. "None of it is okay."

Through the open window, I thought I could hear the sound of the reporters in the distance share a joke, then laugh.

That night I couldn't sleep, so I went downstairs and turned on a nature documentary.

"What is it tonight?" my father said. "Ah, the Serengeti."

He eyed my warm milk and graham crackers. It was a trick he'd taught me.

"Can I join you?" he asked.

"Sure," I said, and scooted over on the couch. "You can't sleep either?"

He let out a sad laugh. "No. How could I?"

His answer was so stripped of charm or optimism that it surprised me.

"I'm scared about tomorrow," I admitted.

"Me too."

"What if you don't come back?"

"I'll come back. If not tomorrow, then soon after." Though I knew he wanted to believe it, he didn't sound like he'd convinced himself yet.

"You know what I'll miss the most about our old life?" I said. "It's stupid, but I'll miss waking up and seeing the particular pattern of sun stretching across the ceiling and feeling excited about the day, like I have this whole unknown future ahead of me and it's only going to be good."

"Things will still be good," my dad said.

"It doesn't feel that way."

"No. It doesn't." He stared at the screen. "I'll tell you

what I won't miss. I won't miss commuting to work. Or the nonstop phone calls and emails. Or the endless onslaught of fundraisers."

"So many fundraisers," I said.

"Everything is a fundraiser," he said with a laugh. His smile quickly faded. "I will miss the people. The way it feels to shake a stranger's hand and connect with them in a way that makes their face light up.

"I'll miss going for walks in our neighborhood, and having Melinda and Dave and James over for dinner. I'll miss your mother and the way she always harasses me about leaving the cabinet doors open and spending too much time on my phone. I'll miss turning into our driveway after a long day at work and seeing the house lit up from the inside. The way it feels to see you and Zack for the first time all day. Even if you mostly ignore me." He swallowed. "I'll miss you. I'll miss seeing you every day."

"Dad," I whispered. "I'm sorry."

He wrapped his hand around mine. "It's okay."

The next day he was sentenced to three years in prison. A shock. The lawyers had promised us leniency. He had cooperated. It was his first offense. He was a beloved senator. In the courtroom, my mother sat paralyzed as the officers escorted him away. She refused to look at me on the way home, or maybe she just couldn't. You did this, she seemed to say to me, and she wasn't wrong.

Do you understand? I couldn't help it. I had to write

him back in. It was the only way I could have him here. It was the only way I could fix it.

The light was on in my mother's bedroom when I went inside. I was back in the present, the terrible present, where James had just discovered my secret and had sped into the night, probably to never speak to me again.

I crept up the stairs to my mother's door, where I hesitated. I rarely went into her bedroom. It felt like a mausoleum—the curtains drawn, the furniture dusty and unused, the air still and thick with the savory smell of sheets that were due for laundering. My father had never seen her bedroom, nor mine. He'd never stepped foot in our town house. Maybe that was why I hated it so much.

I knocked.

"Yes?" my mother said.

She was sitting in the armchair by her bed, still fully dressed in casual work clothes, and I wondered if she'd met with a new client that day.

A stack of official-looking papers stood on the side table next to her. They were flagged with yellow stickers that said *Sign here*.

In my desperation to see only what I wanted to, I told myself that they had to be contracts for a new job. Except my mother didn't seem excited. She looked like she was grieving.

An awful feeling tickled the bottom of my spine.

"What are those?" I asked.

"Hana—" she began, then stopped as she searched for the right words. Did she look nervous? "I've been meaning to tell you."

The curtains trembled. "Tell me what?"

"I've been meeting with a lawyer."

"About what?" I felt a vibration beneath my feet.

"They're divorce papers."

The lamp above the bed rattled in its socket. A crack formed in the ceiling.

"Your father and I are getting divorced."

The room around me was collapsing.

"The lawyers are serving him the papers tomorrow."

I backed away as the ceiling caved in on the bed in a cloud of dust.

"Hana?" my mother said.

I blinked and the room was back to its original state—clean, undamaged. I steadied myself against the nightstand.

"Hana, are you all right?"

I wasn't. I hadn't been for a long time. I looked up at my mother, who had protected me as best she could from the worst consequences of my actions for the last two years. Whose life had been dismantled by the things I'd done and the lies I'd told. Did she resent me? If she did, I couldn't blame her.

She must have sensed what I was going to say, because her expression sharpened.

"James knows."

25

"Did you talk to him?" my mother demanded.

It was Saturday morning. I opened my eyes and winced into the light. From the blur of sleep, my mother slowly took shape. She was standing in the doorway of my room, her expression sharp, her forehead creased.

When I looked at her, all I could think of was my dad. I knew people always said that kids felt responsible for their parents' divorce and that it wasn't true, but this time it was. It was all my fault. I had torn them apart.

"Not yet," I said. I'd spent the night feeling like I'd been stripped of my clothes and left in the elements. James knew my secret, and the only thing that made me feel better was curling up beneath the covers with the hope that if I stayed concealed long enough, everyone would forget I existed. Then, maybe, my problems would go away.

My mother must have noted the time—eleven thirty—

but if she disapproved of me spending the day in bed, she didn't say anything.

"Do you think he's told anyone?" she asked.

"Maybe. James always tries to do the right thing."

The color drained from my mother's face. "You have to talk to him. Tell him what it could do to us."

Though I, too, was scared that he would reveal my secret, I was mostly tired. Tired of talking to people, trying to get them to do what I wanted. "I'll try," I said, and rolled over and stared at the wall.

She waited in the doorway. I could feel her exasperation radiating toward me as she tried to figure out what she could say that would impart how urgent her request was.

What I didn't tell her was that although I'd expected to be frightened, what I hadn't thought I'd feel was relief, to have someone else know, to not have to keep it inside anymore. I was tired of pretending.

When I heard the door shut, I exhaled. Slowly, I mustered up the courage to take out my phone. Three had texted me in the middle of the night, and the mere sight of the notification had sent me into a spiral. I hadn't been able to bring myself to look at it until now.

>So you're not up for the job, Three had written.

Taking a breath, I wrote back. <I know who you are.

There was only one person who could have led me to 55 Settlement Circle. Only one person who knew that I had run.

Luce.

It took a few minutes for her to reply. **>I didn't hire you to figure out who I was.**

I thought back to when she'd told me about why she'd transferred schools. *I would have ruined him,* she'd said of the boy who had gotten her father fired. It was what she'd hired me to do, just for a different boy.

<You wanted me to do your dirty work so you wouldn't get caught doing it.

>That is what hiring usually means, no? Getting someone to do work you don't want to do?

<You didn't tell me it would be this kind of work.

>Oh, come on. You knew it was a risk. It's not like you work in retail.

<How did you find out about Logan? I asked. It was a question I'd been turning in my mind since discovering Three was Luce.

There was a long pause. I wondered if she wasn't going to answer, when a message came in.

>I don't know what you mean.

Either she didn't want to tell me, or she didn't want to put it in writing. I guessed the latter and let my finger hover over her phone number before closing my eyes and pressing call. Miraculously, she picked up.

"Hi," Luce said. The sound of her voice through the phone was so familiar that it felt like I was listening to an echo of myself.

303

"Hi," I said.

"This doesn't change anything," she said. "We're still not speaking."

"I know. I just need to know how you found out."

She hesitated, as if deciding whether or not she should tell me, then spoke. "He had been acting strange for a few months."

She was talking about Logan.

"My first thought was that he was cheating on me, so I looked at his phone and saw texts from an unlabeled number, telling him to meet at an address in McLean at night. I went there, expecting to see him meet with a girl, but instead it was a man. I watched them shake hands and go inside. Logan looked nervous."

I could picture Luce sitting in her car at night, both relieved and bewildered at what she was seeing.

"I was able to figure out from the tax records that the house was owned by Marion Goodjoy," she continued. "I looked her up and saw a photo of her with the man I saw Logan with. Her grandnephew, Ian Goodjoy. I researched him and discovered that he ran an education nonprofit called A Brighter Future, which seemed innocent enough, though Logan was getting more and more secretive, so I knew something was off. I kept watching him."

I could hear music playing softly in the background and could picture Luce lying on her floral quilt while the faces in the posters above her bed smiled at her, illuminated by the dim lamp on her nightstand.

"I eventually found a slip of paper on Logan's desk," she said, lowering her voice. "On it he had written the address of the mansion, *$65,000*, and the name *Colin Graham*. The address, combined with the amount of money caught my attention, and I started to wonder. I looked up Colin Graham and saw that he was a tutor nearby who worked on college essays and standardized testing. It got me thinking.

"I knew Logan was stressed that he might not get into the colleges he wanted. Though he tried to keep it a secret from me and everyone else at school, I knew his grades had been slipping after seeing a few of his exams in his bag. I also knew that he bombed the SAT, even though he told everyone he got a high score, after I overheard him and his dad talking about how he had to retake it."

"So he doesn't confide in anyone," I murmured.

"Maybe Keith, but definitely not me," Luce said. "The only thing he told me was that he was worried that he wouldn't be recruited for crew, which was what he was banking on. I guess the scouts didn't show as much interest in him as he thought they would, or maybe they required higher grades and scores to be considered. All I know is that he was freaking out about it. At first, I thought he was sneaking around because he was taking an SAT class and didn't want anyone to know. But what SAT class costs sixty-five thousand dollars? And on top of that, he wasn't studying, nor did he seem worried about retaking it.

"By that point, I knew something was going on and that it had to do with cheating. The more certain I became, the harder it was to look at him. There I was, working so hard to get by at school, while he sat comfortably next to me, knowing that everything was going to be taken care of. I grew to hate him. He reminded me of the boy at my old school who got my father fired. Except this time, I could do something about it."

It was exhilarating to hear that my hunch about Luce and her vendetta had been right. I wanted to tell her that I'd guessed as much, but caught myself. Like she'd said— none of this changed anything. We weren't friends and weren't speaking.

"I knew that if I went public with what I had, it would somehow get back to him that it was me, and he'd ruin me and my family, the same way that that boy had ruined us at my old school," Luce continued. "And anyway, I didn't have any hard evidence and I wasn't sure if I would be able to find it on my own without Logan noticing that I was looking into it. So I decided to hire you."

It was strange hearing her mention me. When we were friends, I'd always wondered what she really thought about me, and now that I was about to find out, I wanted to retract my wish.

"It was a perfect solution," Luce said, her voice hardening.

"By that point I had already planned on blackmailing him. I wanted to make him feel scared and vulnerable the way the rest of us feel when we don't have money to insulate us from our mistakes. I would text him from an anonymous number and tell him that I knew what he was doing and demand that he pay me, no parents involved or I would go public. I wasn't sure what I would do with the money, only that it had to be a lot. I could use you to pick it up and drop it off wherever I liked. Having you digging around would also take the focus off me if he started to suspect anything."

My mouth felt dry. I couldn't help but resent the detached way she was talking about me, like I was just a chess piece to be moved around the board when it suited her needs.

As if reading my mind, she said, "It isn't any different than what you do, is it?"

Despite myself, I had to admit that she was right.

"I didn't want you or anyone else to know it was me who was hiring you," she continued. "Not at first, at least, not until you got far enough that you couldn't quit. And I knew that if the job was to look into Logan, you'd guess it was me immediately. So I hired you to look into me instead."

"So you led me to the mansion?" I asked.

"It was sort of a happy coincidence. I saw you staking out my house but wasn't sure how to clue you in to what was going on. And then, like a gift, I saw texts on Logan's phone telling him to go back to the mansion one evening, so I led you there. That's when we saw him meet with Colin."

"So you knew I was there that night," I said.

"I knew," Luce said. "I thought then that you would take off running, but for some reason you stopped making headway. I started to get worried that you were getting bored of the case or just weren't up for it. It was getting closer to the SAT exam date, and I couldn't wait any longer, so I decided to pick up the case again. I volunteered at A Brighter Future in secret, hoping to find proof. I found Colin's file and copied it so that I could confront him with it and get him to go on record about what was really going on at A Brighter Future, when you and James showed up.

"The rest you know. You went to meet Colin, like I knew you would. By then I'd already messaged him and bought him to our side. He told you what he was doing for Logan. You thought you had solved the case and were done. But you weren't."

"So you wanted to punish me," I murmured. "For what I did."

"It wasn't a punishment," Luce said. "The problem was that I didn't want Logan's money. The idea of spending it felt dirty to me. He didn't deserve it, but I didn't either, and honestly, neither do you. Not after what you and I did that night in the car. So I broke the news to you. You weren't done, you had only finished one of three fixes: the first, to follow me and uncover the cheating scandal; the second, to collect and distribute the money to Colin; and the third, to drop off my portion, and yours, to 55 Settlement Circle. Our victim."

I was frozen in place, unable to think, unable to speak. *Our victim*. A horrible phrase that I'd been running from for the past two years.

"You've finished two, but the third still remains," Luce said.

"I can't," I said.

"You've always wanted to fix yourself. This is your chance. It's not about the money. It's about facing it. It's the only way we can make it right."

But she was wrong. There was nothing we could do that would make it right.

"I'll return the money," I said.

"To me? That money isn't mine and I don't want it."

"Then who am I supposed to give it to?" I asked.

"That's your burden now."

The remaining bags of money were slumped beneath my desk. I could see their contents deforming the bags from my bed. They should have been easy to keep; it was just money, after all, and yet I couldn't bear the thought of it, couldn't even stand looking at them. I tried to figure out why they made me so uncomfortable, when I realized what the feeling was. Guilt.

"I don't want it," I said.

"That's the beauty of this case," Luce said. "You can quit before the third fix, but you can't, really, can you?"

I didn't want her to be right and spent the day trying to find a way to rid myself of the case. I could drop the bags of money at Luce's house, but that would only get them out of sight. It didn't solve the root problem of what I'd done, and that no matter how hard I tried to look away, it would still be there.

Though I told my mother I would talk to James, all I could manage to do was open his text window and stare at the cursor. What was I supposed to say? I couldn't badger him into keeping my secret, nor could I convince him to forgive me. I had no defense for what I'd done, so what else was left?

I found myself on my phone's browser, typing the words that had been haunting me for the past two years. *Mary Cannon Davis.*

She lived on 55 Settlement Circle, just a few houses down the road from where the crash occurred. I hadn't intended to look her up, but there she was, her face staring back at me from my screen. I'd never googled her; I hadn't been able to bear it. Still, I knew her face from the newspapers, the internet. The sight of it transported me back in time and made my heart flutter with a familiar mixture of panic and guilt.

Mary, a name that was now inextricable from mine. She looked a little older than my dad, with graying brown hair and a thin smile. I studied her face and imagined what James would say if we'd lived in a parallel universe where I hadn't hit her with my dad's car, where instead we encountered her at a fundraiser while we played our guessing game beneath the table, prompting James to nod at her and ask me who I thought she was.

"Therapist," James might say. "She looks trustworthy but also a little troubled, like someone from an arthritis commercial who spends her time knitting sweaters and reading biographies."

"No way," I might say. "Definitely a museum curator. See how her glasses match her scarf?"

In truth, I wasn't quite sure what she did. Government, budgeting—something indistinct enough that I had never been able to retain it, which I honestly preferred; it allowed me to not have to picture her life and all the ways I'd ruined it. All I knew about her was that she was married and had two adult children and that her prognosis at the time of the plea bargain was unclear—she would be able to walk again, but not the way she once had.

I allowed myself, for the first time, to consider her. Why had she decided to take a walk by the park that night? Had she been antsy, unable to sleep? Had she been upset and seeking a momentary escape from her house, just like I had? Or did she simply want to breathe in the night air and admire the moon?

That night, before I went to sleep, I texted James.

<Hey, are you up?

I didn't expect a response, so I wasn't surprised when I was met with silence. I typed to him anyway.

<I guess not.

<I know you don't want to hear from me. You probably hate me. I would too.

<The only excuse I have for what I did is that I was scared.

<I don't even really know why I'm sending this to you. Probably because you're the only person who always seems to know what the right thing to do is.

<So I guess I'm wondering what I should do.

<What would you do? If you were me?

<I guess you never would be me, since being me requires a whole series of bad decisions that you wouldn't have made.

<But imagine you did and you found yourself where I am now. I made a really big mistake and ran away from it because I was too cowardly to take responsibility. Then my dad took the blame so it wouldn't ruin my life. Only it still did ruin it, just not in the way any of us expected.

<If I tell people now, it'll have all been for nothing. My dad, the lie. We would have to relive it all over again, only worse. What would happen to him? What would happen to me?

<But if I don't tell people, I'll have to live with the lie

312

for the rest of my life, which means I have to keep
pretending, and I don't know if I can anymore.
<I guess what I'm saying is that I'm scared.
<I wish I had told you when it had happened.
<I wish it had never happened at all.

I knew James had published his story when I saw the
reporters swarming the gates of the school. The *Kestrel* was
published online and on paper, and though it was just a high
school publication, enough students had already read the
story and posted about it that word had quickly spread to
local news channels and journalists. It was a crisp Monday
morning, three weeks after the money drop, the kind of day
that was too perfect to be true, that was primed for a rock to
shatter it. I felt my throat constrict—a familiar feeling from
a familiar scene. I didn't want to drive through the cameras
and sank low in my seat. James had never responded to my
texts, and we hadn't spoken since the night at Coin Rock.
I had no idea what he'd put in his article or what he'd said
about me. I considered going home, but it was too late—
there was already a line of cars behind me; turning around
would only draw more attention.

I didn't expect the reporters to barely notice me, to let
me pass without any fanfare and instead direct their focus
to a car pulling into the parking lot from the west-side
entrance. They crowded it, pushing their microphones into
the unsuspecting face of the boy stepping out. Logan.

I watched the realization creep over his face. The shock, then terror as reporters pummeled him with questions. I knew how he felt. The shame that reverberates in your stomach, that makes you feel nauseated, that makes you want to disappear.

When I walked into Hadsley Hall, the building was buzzing with the news. It wasn't clear that classes were even going to be held that day. Copies of the *Kestrel* were scattered around the halls and stairwells, and teachers were being called to the dean's office for a meeting. In the classrooms, in the hallways, everyone was whispering names, mostly Logan's, but also others. I listened for mine and felt relieved when I didn't hear it.

I picked up a copy of the school paper. James's headline was in bold on the front:

UNDERGROUND CHEATING RING UNCOVERED IN COLLEGE ADMISSIONS SCANDAL

My hand trembled. I was scared to read it for fear of what it might say, but no one seemed to be paying any attention to me, which I took as a good sign.

I read the first few lines.

AN IN-DEPTH INVESTIGATION REVEALED THAT
dozens of students and alumni at St. Francis have been

donating to the alleged nonprofit A Brighter Future to cheat their way into elite colleges. A Brighter Future, which is run by St. Francis alumnus Ian Goodjoy, and which claims to be a charity supporting the academic endeavors of underprivileged children, hides its payments in the form of donations, and in exchange offers a range of illegal services, including essay and homework completion, standardized-test body doubles, bribery of admissions officials, and potentially a lot more. The case was discovered through high-profile student and crew star Logan O'Hara, who employed A Brighter Future to hire a look-alike to take the SAT for him.

It felt surreal to read everything that James and I had uncovered in one place, as if an author were narrating my life as I was living it. I scanned the rest of the article, bracing myself for my name, but it never came. Miraculously, he had left me out. I was both relieved and confused—surely it couldn't be that easy. I turned the page and checked the other articles. Maybe he'd written about my lie in a different piece, since it wasn't directly related to the cheating scandal, but nothing in the edition mentioned my name. I leaned against the wall, overwhelmed with disbelief. James was keeping my secret.

I took out my phone and wrote him a text.

<I read the article. It's incredible.

I paused, then added, <You didn't include me.

I wasn't sure if he would write back, but in a few minutes, he did.

>I wanted to.

Though I hadn't expected a warm or friendly response, I wasn't prepared for his bluntness. I typed a message, then deleted it, then typed it again.

<Are you going to?

>If you're asking if I'm going to rat you out, the answer is no.

I let out a breath.

<Thank you.

>Don't thank me. I'm not doing it because I want to or because it's the right thing to do.

<Then why are you doing it?

>Because it won't fix anything, it'll only make everything worse.

I should have felt relieved, but I only felt miserable.

<I've wanted to fix it. I've been trying to.

>Have you been trying to? Or have you just been telling yourself that?

I felt my face turn red. I glanced around me, embarrassed, even though James was nowhere to be seen and no one was paying me any attention.

<I have been trying, I insisted.

I imagined what he would say in response and came up with a bunch of things I'd done that would prove him wrong. Then I waited for him to write back. But minutes passed; the bell rang. People walked by on their phones, talking about Logan, about the *Kestrel*, about James. All the while, my phone remained silent. He wasn't going to write back.

I stared at our text exchange, bewildered and angry. But most of all, I felt ashamed. For the first time, James thought that I wasn't worth arguing with. All this time, I'd told myself that I was a good liar. That I could convince anyone of anything. Maybe I was right, but what was the point of any of it if I was also lying to myself?

26

I remembered the way. Left, then right. Right again. I drove with the radio off, listening to the sound of my blinker.

The church that I arrived at looked the same as it had the previous month. It was the one I'd seen Luce go into the night after Tiffany's party, the one with the little yellow window by the side door, glowing as if all roads had always led there.

The truth was, I hadn't discovered the church that night. Though I hadn't been intending to go there, I hadn't stumbled upon it either. I'd known about it for some time after lurking in message groups and reading about it online.

I pulled into the parking lot and scanned the cars until I found Luce's station wagon. She was there. I turned off the engine and walked toward the door.

The basement of the church was just as I'd pictured it—linoleum floors and walls decorated with children's artwork. A paper sign pointed down the hall. I followed it to a classroom where a handful of people were already sitting, their chairs arranged in a circle.

I lingered by the door, fighting the urge to leave, when I saw Luce sitting by the window. A flash of surprise passed over her face when she saw me.

"Welcome," a woman said to me with a sad smile. "Feel free to sit anywhere."

I sat by the door and felt my face grow hot. Should I leave? Would anyone recognize me?

I had almost convinced myself to go when the woman stood up. "Okay, let's get started. For any newcomers, my name is Beth, and I'm leading the meeting today.

"Seven years ago, I was driving drunk and hit a car. The driver was a young woman coming home from work. They rushed us both to the hospital. Only one of us came out, and I've had to live with the fact that it shouldn't have been me ever since.

"This is a meeting for people who have caused accidental collisions. Everything that's said here stays within these walls. It's a nonjudgmental place where we can talk about the journey we face as people who have inflicted pain on others, while we search to forgive ourselves for what we've done."

A few people murmured in agreement. While another member introduced himself and began to speak, I found Luce. Her face had softened and her expression looked melancholy, as though she'd finally allowed herself to take off her mask.

When there was a lull in conversation, she spoke.

"My name is Luce," she said, lingering on me briefly before looking away. Was she embarrassed? "Two years ago, I was part of a hit-and-run that severely injured someone. I still have nightmares about it. I can't sleep; I can't help but feel like I'm cursed. Like I'm tainted and can never be good again.

"Sometimes I drive to the victim's house and park outside," Luce continued, staring at her feet. "I don't even know what I'm doing there. I fantasize about telling her that it was me and begging for her forgiveness, but what would that even do? It wouldn't take back what we did.

"On the outside, my life looks better than it's ever been, but in reality, I'm filled with guilt and anger. I go to a fancy school and have always hated my rich and privileged classmates who do terrible things all the time without consequence or guilt. They glide above it all, carefree, stepping on everyone else so that they can get ahead. What I hate most is that I'm one of them now. I did this awful thing and got away with it. I'm no different than they are."

I tried to meet her gaze, but she refused. Other people introduced themselves and talked about their lives, but all I could think about was Luce and how sorry I was for what I'd done. When there was a pause, I cleared my throat.

"My name is Hana," I said, trying to steady my voice. "Two years ago, I hit someone and drove away because I was terrified. I didn't want to see what I'd done. I wanted it to go away. It was just one bad mistake and it didn't seem fair. People make mistakes all the time. How come the mistake that I made led to this?"

Across the room, Luce was still as stone, her gaze trained on her shoes as though she didn't care that I was speaking. I couldn't read her expression. The only tell was the way she rotated the ring in her ear—a sign that she was listening. My confession was for her.

"It's hard to describe how it felt to drive away," I said. "Sometimes I wake up in the middle of the night and feel like I'm still in that car, my heart beating out of my chest, my face cold with sweat, my skin feeling like it's going to crawl off my body. I think I've been driving away this whole time, too scared to look back. I'd like to figure out how to stop.

"One of the worst parts was that there was someone else in the car with me, a friend whose life I ruined along with mine, who's had to live with the consequences of this secret for the last two years. We're not talking now, but if we were, I would tell her that it wasn't her fault, and that I'm sorry."

I silently pleaded with Luce to look at me, to show me that she heard. She hesitated, then swallowed. When she finally met my gaze, she was crying.

As the meeting came to a close, I took out my phone and texted Luce.

<It's my turn to offer you a set of three, I wrote. **So here it is: Tomorrow. Settlement. 8 p.m.**

I watched Luce as she read it.

>Okay, she wrote, then tilted her head at me in acknowledgment before slinging her bag over her shoulder and walking past me out the door.

The next day, the national news descended upon St. Francis, flooding the parking lot with reporters and camera crews. Everyone was talking about James's article. Logan wasn't at school, nor were any of the people who were implicated in the cheating scandal. I kept my head down and pretended it was all new. It was a particular kind of pain to hear James's name whispered in the hallways and classrooms and not be able to talk to him, to ask him how he was doing or hear how it felt to be interviewed by national reporters whom he'd always idolized.

That day, before going home, I texted him one last time.

<I'm finishing the job, I wrote to him.

<I'm not doing it because you think I should, or because anyone does. I'm doing it because it's right.

<I don't expect a standing ovation or even forgiveness, and I don't know what's going to happen after. Probably nothing good.

<I just want you to know that I couldn't have gotten here without you. So thanks.

I didn't expect him to write back, so when he did, I felt my heart seize.

>When?

<Tonight, I wrote. **8 p.m.**

I didn't go home after school. Instead, I drove three towns over to a nonprofit I'd seen everyone talking about online in response to James's article. *If you're looking to donate to an actual nonprofit that helps underprivileged kids, donate to this one*, a local journalist had written.

Rise Up Literacy was in a small concrete building close to the highway. Paintings drawn by kids decorated the front door. I didn't announce myself. Instead, I tucked the third, black bag of money, along with the one intended for me, inside the double doors, with an unsigned note saying that it was a donation. Luce had been right: the cash didn't belong to either of us, and though she'd intended for me to give it to our victim, it didn't sit right with me to try to exchange money for forgiveness. I knew from my research that of the many problems Mary Cannon Davis had, money was not one, and it only seemed right to distribute Logan's payment to students who actually needed help.

That night, I could barely eat dinner. I was too nervous. My mother eyed me, clearly concerned but unable to speak her mind while Zack was at the table. He still didn't know about our secret.

"Did you hear about the O'Haras?" my mother asked.

"Yeah," I said. "Wild, right?"

"Shocking, really," she said.

"I heard he hired a stunt double," Zack said as he helped himself to another slice of pizza.

"It wasn't a stunt double," I said. "It was just a tutor who looked slightly like him."

Zack gave me a strange look. "How do you know?"

"One of the reporters on campus mentioned it," I said quickly.

"Huh," Zack said.

"I heard James wrote the article," my mother said, then gave me a pointed look. "Have you talked to him?"

"I did," I said.

My mother gripped the serving spoon for the salad. "And?"

I tried to think of a way to answer without revealing my secret to Zack. "He said not to worry. He did write the article about Logan but wasn't planning on writing any more."

My mother locked eyes with me, silently asking if my coded message meant what she thought it did. "Good," she said, and returned to her dinner.

I'd fretted over the decision to tell her what I was planning to do but had ultimately decided against it. I already knew how she would react—she would tell me that she forbade it and that I was ruining my future, which, to her credit, maybe I was. What she didn't understand was that the future was impossible to envision when you were trapped in the cage of the past.

Zack looked between us, confused. "What are you talking about?"

"Nothing," my mother and I said at the same time.

Zack raised an eyebrow, and for a moment, I thought he was going to pursue it, but instead he shrugged. "Whatever."

That night, when I walked out to my car, James was waiting for me.

I blinked, unsure if it was an apparition, but he was still there, sitting in his car, listening to the radio as if he was picking me up to go to another stakeout.

When he saw me, he nodded to the passenger seat. I hesitated before opening the door. If I closed my eyes, I could almost believe that in some twist of luck we had traveled back in time three weeks to when he didn't yet know.

"What are you doing here?" I asked.

"Picking you up."

"Why?"

"You said you were going to finish the job. We're partners, remember?"

I hadn't been prepared for how it would feel for him to show up at my door. For him to forgive me. Was he forgiving me? I could barely allow myself to consider it.

"I thought you hated me."

"I don't hate you."

A lump rose in my throat. "Why not?"

James's face dropped, as though my question was more telling about how I felt about myself than about how others felt about me. "People are more than their mistakes."

"Even Logan?" I asked.

"Even Logan," he murmured. He looked at his lap. "You know, once, I thought you hated me."

"I didn't," I insisted. "I was scared you'd find out. I was scared of what you'd think of me."

"I told you two years ago," he said. "I'm on your side."

Of course I remembered. "I didn't believe you."

"You still don't believe me," he observed.

"No," I admitted.

"That's okay," James said. "I'll show you."

As he backed out of the driveway, he reached over and slipped his hand in mine.

I wish I could tell you that there's another twist. That I wasn't actually responsible for the wreckage. That's how stories are supposed to end—everyone happy, everyone redeemed.

How do you fix something that's unfixable? You can't change the things that you've done. The only fix is to face them.

The house at 55 Settlement Circle looked different from the street-view photos online. The owners had installed a metal ramp going up to the front door. For a wheelchair, I realized.

Luce was already parked out front when we arrived. I peered up at the house. An autumnal wreath hung on the front door and the windows emitted a buttery-yellow light. A shadow moved behind the blinds of the living room.

"Is this a mistake?" I asked James.

"I can't decide that for you," he said. "I'm not the one who has to live it."

I swallowed. "What if she hates me?"

"Then she hates you."

I supposed I could live with that.

"What if she calls the police?"

"Then we deal with it."

We. As in James and me.

He must have known what I was thinking, because he tightened his grip on my hand. "Go," he said. "I'll drive you home when you're done."

I slipped my hand from his and opened the door.

Luce met me at the front walk and glanced back at the car. "So you and James?" she asked.

"Yeah."

She raised an eyebrow, which she used to do when she wanted be to clear that she'd been right. "I always knew it would happen. It was only a matter of time."

It felt easy being around her, like waking up on the first warm day of spring.

"Are we really doing this?" I asked.

"I guess we are."

We walked up the front steps. Before we reached the door, I stopped her. "Hey," I said. I'd been trying to think of what I could say that would express all of the conflicting emotions I'd felt the past two years, but nothing I'd come up with could do it justice. So instead I opted for the simplest version. "I'm sorry."

"I am too," Luce said.

I gave her the beginning of a smile, then took a breath and rang the doorbell.

CODA

"Are you sure it's here?" Luce asked.

"Nothing is sure," I said, like the wise almost high school graduate that I was. "But it probably is."

It was six months after I'd solved Three's case, and Luce and I were walking up the spiral staircase of a mansion owned by a Helen and William Kline, corporate strategist and investment banker. The din of a fundraiser filled the house behind us.

I didn't know the Klines, and outside of the fact that they frequented the Old Mill Country Club, where my parents had once been members, I didn't have any connection to them. I was only there because their son, Nate, had something that I wanted.

"I guess that's him," Luce said, nodding to a school portrait of a teenage boy hanging in the hallway. He had a scatter of freckles across his face and was grinning at the camera in a smug, self-satisfied way.

I knew from my research that he went to one of St. Francis's rival schools. I knew he wasn't in the house that day because he played lacrosse and his team had a game. And I knew I didn't like him.

We were there on a job.

Apparently, some of the teenage boys at the country club who caddied in the summer as a way to network with older members had found a bunch of discarded security videos on thumb drives in the back office, including one of me and Luce from two and half years before, when we'd hopped the fence and gone skinny-dipping in the pool. Nate Kline was one of those boys.

He'd taken the thumb drive home and had been planning on hosting a watch party with his friends. Supposedly, the video was grainy enough that it wasn't clear who we were, though rumors had been circulating, first at his school and then at St. Francis, that a boy had a video of two girls getting naked at the country club pool at night and was going to unveil it the following weekend. Everyone was trying to guess who was in it. We needed to get it back, which was why we were sneaking up to his room on a Saturday afternoon.

I'd gotten us invited to the fundraiser through a classmate named Carly Vargas, whose mom had been invited, and who had agreed to attend and bring me and Luce along.

In return, she asked for nothing at all. As it turned out, Carly knew Nate from camp and had always hated the way he leered at her and talked about girls when he thought no one was listening.

His room looked exactly as I'd pictured it would. Preppy and bland, with a pile of laundry on the foot of his bed.

"If you were a teenage boy with no respect for the dignity of others, where would you keep a thumb drive?" I asked.

"Boys like Nate think they're entitled to videos like this," Luce said. "I bet it's not even hidden. I bet it's in his desk drawer."

She was right. There, among his pens and highlighters, was a thumb drive. Luce slipped her laptop out of her bag, plugged the thumb drive in, and opened its file.

"This is it," she murmured.

My eyes darted between her and the door as she watched it. I'd already decided that I didn't want to see it. I didn't need to relive the hour before the Catastrophic Event, which would forever be overshadowed by what was about to follow.

Luce closed her computer and tucked it into her bag along with the thumb drive. Then she grabbed Nate's laptop from his desk and took it, too. "Just in case," she said.

"How did it feel?" I asked Luce on the way home. She was driving.

"I was nervous at first, but I liked it," Luce said. "It was like jumping into a cold lake. What about you?"

"It felt good," I said, my voice quiet. "It felt like I was doing what I was meant to do."

It was Luce's first fix and my first since Three's case.

After our visit to 55 Settlement Circle, I stopped fixing. It didn't feel right the way I had been doing it. Doing favors to hide the secrets of the rich and powerful, to further insulate them from the consequences of their actions, was something that the old me did, and the old me was someone I was trying to grow out of.

"It was you?"

That's what Mary Cannon Davis had said when I told her why I was there.

She'd recognized me, of course, the moment her husband had answered the door. We were inextricably connected, though not in the way that she'd thought.

I'd told her I was sorry. That it was a mistake, I'd panicked out of fear, I'd made so many bad decisions that I wished I could take back.

I'd assumed I was going to prison. It was a dumb thought; I knew how the legal system worked and that my father and I wouldn't immediately switch places the moment I confessed, and yet I still assumed everything after would happen quickly. My life was over.

She'd sat in a stunned silence for a while. And then something unexpected had happened. "It took courage for you to come here tonight."

She'd reached out a hand and put it on mine. "Thank you for telling me," she'd said. "It's going to be okay."

And it was okay, or at least better than it was before. Though she didn't go to the police, telling her had changed things. It felt like I'd been given permission to forgive myself. The only condition was that I try to be better than I was before.

"Do you want to come over and work on the website?" Luce asked as we drove back from the Klines' house.

In the months that had elapsed after Three's case, Luce and I had begun the long and cautious exercise of trying to trust each other again. She'd broken up with Logan, who was on academic probation from school and was under investigation, along with his family, by the FBI, and though Three and the case had played an instrumental part in our second attempt at friendship, we had an unspoken agreement to leave it all in the past.

Instead, we were in the process of making a website for anonymous tips. It had been Luce's idea that I get back into fixing. I was good at it, she'd argued. I didn't have to go back to fixing the way that I used to. This time, I could use my powers for good and work on fixes that helped people who needed it. And if I was open to it, I had an ex-ex-best friend who was interested in being my partner.

"I can't right now," I said. "I have to go home. Today's the day."

"Oh my god," Luce said. "I was so caught up in the fix. I can't believe I forgot. Are you nervous?"

"I feel like I'm going to puke."

"If you are, tell me so I can pull over."

She dropped me off at home, where Zack was sitting at the kitchen table with two bags of groceries, bobbing his head to the music in his earbuds while my mom anxiously cleaned the kitchen. "Are you ready?" she asked.

We climbed into her car and drove fifteen minutes away to an apartment building near an office park. My mother was holding a vase of flowers, which she picked at nervously while we rode the elevator up.

The apartment was small but sunny and still smelled of fresh paint. Though it looked nothing like our first house, something about the décor made it feel familiar, like it was a refracted version of the past.

"You did a good job," I said to my mom while she busied herself arranging the flowers and unpacking the groceries.

An hour passed. Then Zack, who had been keeping watch at the window, held up his hand. "He's here."

The stretch of time between my father stepping out of the car and turning the key to the apartment felt like an eternity. Zack and I stood in front of the door, unsure of what we would see when it opened.

My dad paused in the hallway when he saw us. His hair was longer, his face was thinner, his eyes looked somehow more deeply set, as though he had aged much more than two and a half years. He'd been released early on parole, and though it was supposedly a joyous occasion, his expression had a quiet desperation that looked unfamiliar to me. But when he walked toward me and wrapped me and Zack in his arms, I recognized him.

"Hana Bear," he whispered in my ear.

I pressed my face into his shoulder. "Dad."

"So this is home?" he said, stepping back to take in his apartment.

"It has three bedrooms," Zack said. "One for each of us."

My dad's smile faltered slightly at the word *three*, as it so clearly left out my mom, but he quickly recovered. "I love it."

"Mom decorated it," I said. "She tried to make it have the spirit of our house."

My mother was standing behind us in the kitchen, uncharacteristically quiet.

My father met her gaze. "Thank you."

She nodded. "You're welcome."

"So how's school?" he asked Zack, putting his bags down. While Zack filled him in on the programming club, the door buzzed.

My dad gave us a bewildered look. "Who's that?"

It made me sad how the sound had shocked him, bringing back some bad memory of reporters or police officers or maybe something worse. I'd felt thrust back into the past by the sound, too, even though I knew it wasn't any of those things because I'd arranged this guest.

I opened the door to find James standing in the hallway with his parents and two bags of takeout.

He ran a hand through his hair, brushing it away from his eyes. "Hey," he said to me, his face warm like the sun.

Behind him, his parents beamed. "Hana," his mother said. "So good to see you."

"Is everything okay?" James whispered to me as our parents approached each other, nervous but hopeful that this time it might be different.

"I think so," I said. In the kitchen, my mother laughed while she and James's mom unpacked the takeout and set the table.

As we sat down to eat, I handed my dad an envelope.

"What is this?" he asked.

The letter inside was printed on University of Virginia letterhead. An acceptance.

He read it with a mixture of pride and confusion. "This is wonderful, Hana. Congratulations. But I thought you wanted to go to Yale?"

"That was the old me," I said. "We lost a lot of time together. So I wanted to stay close."

My father rubbed his face and looked at his feet. It was what he did when he couldn't control his emotions.

I waited until he gathered himself. When he finally faced me, his expression was pained. The table went quiet.

My father looked like he was about to speak but was suddenly distracted by something on the table.

"I think someone's calling you," he said.

I turned to my phone, and when I did, he stole an olive off my plate and tossed it into his mouth.

"Still gullible," he said with a grin.

"Hey!" I protested. I knew then that everything was going to be okay.

Beneath the table, James's hand reached out for mine. I grabbed it and held on tight.

ACKNOWLEDGMENTS

This book wouldn't have been possible without the editorial guidance of Katherine Tegen and Sara Schonfeld. Thank you for teaching me how to write a mystery and for helping me become a better writer.

I am eternally grateful to Ted Malawer, part agent, part plot wizard, part therapist. This year and this book were especially hard, and I couldn't have gotten through either without your support.

I feel so lucky to have such an incredible team behind me at Katherine Tegen Books, including but not limited to: Lisa Calcasola, Aubrey Churchward, Marinda Valenti, Laura Harshberger, Mark Rifkin, Lisa Lester Kelly, Sean Cavanagh, Vincent Cusenza, and Vanessa Nuttry. I am in awe of Yuta Onoda and his beautiful cover artwork, and of Molly Fehr and Amy Ryan for their artistic direction.

Thank you to Nana Howton, for sharing your Virginia knowledge, and for always opening your home to me.

I can't thank Sara Davis and Stephanie Arndt enough for reading early pages of this book. Our little workshop has transformed the way I write, and I can't imagine working on another novel without it.

Thank you to Lindsay Sproul, for always knowing when I needed to be checked in on; Rebecca Song, for answering all of my law questions; and Katherine Soverel, for tolerating it in our group chat.

Yvonne Miaoulis, I truly did not know how much I needed another Yvonne in my life until I met you. Thank you for going on this Yvonne journey with me.

Thank you to Becca Sansom, for always being my hype girl; Anna Kurien and Jacob Thomas, for celebrating with me and consoling me and watching my kids when I was on deadline; Emily Straffin, for answering random book-related questions at any hour, on any day; and Lauren Saphire, whose friendship continues to expand the meaning of the word.

Writing a book is rarely done alone, and I couldn't do this job without the support of my family: Paul Col and Nananda Col, who always have time to help me solve a plot problem, and Chee-Wai Woon, who provided invaluable childcare for the year that it took me to plan and write this book. I couldn't have finished it without you.

And finally, Ayla and Judah, who can't read this yet but

who keep me grounded by always reminding me that what really matters is whether or not they have a snack, and Akiva Freidlin, for always helping me with plot, for cheering me on, and for keeping the house running and the cats fed and the kids alive. I'm grateful to have you on my side.